CAVEAT

George Osol

ISBN 978-0-9976458-0-4

191 Bank St.
Burlington VT 05401

DEDICATION

To Geoff and Tanya for their patience and love,
and to my friends for their support and interest.

You know who you are.

"Here is your cross, your nails and your hill;

Here is your love that lists when it will."

Leonard Cohen

CHAPTERS

1. AN INTIMATE VIOLATION

"Everything okay boss?" asked the bartender. He was a skinny, overgrown kid with a tangle of red hair perched on a bony, freckled face.

"All good," said Michael Boylen, although the tension in his voice suggested otherwise. "A pint of Guinness and a shot of Powers. Thanks."

The kid nodded at the big green Rolling Rock clock on the wall. "If you're hungry, we serve till nine. 'Bout another hour or so, boss."

"I'm not your boss," growled Boylen, "and I'm not hungry. Just bring me the drink."

The bartender backed away. As he was pulling the pint, he noticed the man's bloodied knuckles. It crossed his mind that he might have a problem on his hands, but the guy was sitting quietly now, staring at the TV screen above the bar.

He set up the drinks and watched as Boylen downed the whiskey and chased it with the entire pint.

"Again."

The bartender's eyes widened, but he picked up both glasses without a word and set to work.

As the alcohol began to uncoil his nerves, Michael continued to sit motionless, chin propped in the palm of his left hand and eyes on the TV. The only sign of tension was the steady drumbeat of his fingers on the polished wooden surface of the bar. He appeared to be watching the Nets game, but if you had asked him what the score was, he wouldn't have had a clue.

He ordered a third round as his mind mulled over the situation with Katherine. *How could she?* thought Michael for the umpteenth time. *How could she?* The mantra kept pinging his mind as his thoughts circled their troubled orbit. Earlier tonight, his wife of eighteen years had decided to push him away, seemingly without reason. Yet, he thought, of course there is a reason. There has to be.

From his experience with friends and coworkers, the process of marital disengagement most often began with one person's discontent, which would fester but lie dormant until an opportunity that created an out came along. Unhappiness opened the door to infidelity and, if the affair had legs, it would catalyze the separation.

So what was it with Katherine? Was she lying? Was there someone else after all? And why had she chosen to hit him with this tonight, the night before he was leaving home for a month or more?

And then there was the pregnancy piece. Michael's expression morphed into bitterness.

We've been trying to get pregnant for three years at least, he thought, maybe more? It seemed like forever. The ovulation detection kits, the doctor's visits, the fertility counseling, the adoption brochures. God knows they'd been through it all, and Katherine would be turning forty this summer. What kind of woman would give up her own child at that age, and do it without telling her husband? Michael's head pulsed with the contradictions and inconsistencies. *What didn't he get?*

He sat for some time thinking, drinking, trying to fit the jumbled pieces together. At least the initial fury was subsiding. If not his mind, then at least his heart had quieted, and the vise that had gripped his chest earlier, when he'd stormed out of the house, had eased.

Something between them had indeed changed over the past year, he decided and, for whatever reason, he'd chosen to ignore it. Katherine had become increasingly distant, more reluctant to have sex. The excuses—"I'm too tired," "I don't feel well," even the classic "I have a headache"—were more frequent.

He'd attributed it to time, or to their failure to conceive and all that came with the effort—the lack of spontaneity, the recurrent sense of mutual failure manifest most pointedly in the 'I started my period' phone call. Admittedly, their sex hadn't been as exciting as it once had been, but that was a fact of time, of life. There were other rewards to marriage - comfort, trust, stability.

Or so he'd thought.

He signaled for a final round, then changed his mind and asked for the check instead. It was after eleven and he was wiped. He didn't need a DUI on top of everything else.

Michael drained the last of the stout, paid the bill, and pulled on his jacket. Walking across the parking lot in the cold November air, he remembered a quote from some long-forgotten English class: *in every relationship there is one who loves, and one who allows themselves to be loved.* Maugham?

In a very simple way, it captured the essence of balance or, more accurately, imbalance in a relationship between two people. It really never is equal, is it?

When it came to him and Katherine, it was probably he who had loved and she who had allowed herself to be loved. During their worst fights it was she, not he, that would threaten to leave. For Michael, that type of threat belied the "for better, for worse" nature of the wedding vow, the mutual commitment. Even though it could cross his mind, it would remain unsaid as a matter of principle, of respect. With her more volatile temperament, Katherine didn't abide by the same restraint. He might crouch, he might growl, but it was she who would pounce.

He fired up the car and let the engine idle for a few minutes while the defroster took effect. The windshield was speckled with frost and, even in the ever-present light of New Jersey suburbia, the stars twinkled overhead, each pinpoint magnified by the etchings on the glass.

Despite the alcohol, Michael's mind was lucid, and a strange sense of calm settled onto him. Tonight was a total mess, he thought—an emotional sucker punch—but at least he hadn't done anything regrettable other than bloodying his hand on the sheetrock of the garage. He would go home and sleep in his own bed. He would sleep with his wife—she was still his wife—and talk things out in the morning. One didn't throw away eighteen years of marriage without giving it an honest go. Hopefully, the morning would bring its own clarity and equipoise.

One thing was clear, though: their relationship was likely forever altered. The irrevocable power of words, thought Michael. *How could she?*

Upstairs, Katherine was lying on her side in the familiar posture of sleep. Michael climbed under the sheets but didn't touch or wake her. Instead, he lay on his back for some time thinking about her, about them, and about the fact that, by this time tomorrow, he would be six miles high and a thousand miles away.

2. LANGOUSTE

They stepped onto the patio, snorkels and fins in hand. The flat stones underfoot were streaked with dew, and the trail of footprints in their wake was unmistakably that of a woman and a man.

The gravel path beyond the patio led to a staircase, and Michael paused while Katherine began her descent, excited at the prospect of a pre-breakfast swim. It would energize them, and the first cup of coffee would taste all the better afterward.

The crescent bay below was a mottle of blue and green, with a break in the coral halfway through the white arc of reef. It was the one place they could swim through to the open sea without worry.

Birdsongs, and the chirr of insects in the tropical underbrush contrasted with the muted rumble of waves breaking beyond the reef. Katherine and Michael made their way down the stone staircase to the water's edge and sat down on the packed sand that was still cool from the night before.

After donning their gear, they walked backwards into the water holding hands, fins slapping at the water, until Katherine broke free and dove in. Michael followed. Enjoying the coolness of the sea, tasting its saltiness around the mouthpiece of the snorkel, he kept his eyes on

Katherine's pale form ahead. She was treadmilling, propelled easily by the lime green fins, and he followed in her wake.

As they swam further out, the sun's rays cleared the hilltops and the water lightened. The ribbons of sand below alternated with clumps of dark sea grass. Michael glanced up to get a bearing and saw that Katherine was just entering the deeper blue of the cut.

He rolled over and glanced landward.

Except for the occasional east-facing slope, the foothills were still in shadow. Their hotel—tan, with a rippled red roof of Spanish tile—squatted atop the nearest hill, and the stone steps they had walked down formed a gentle curve against the hillside. He rolled back onto his belly and flattened himself, kicking more forcefully to pass cleanly through the break in the reef.

As he entered the cut, he felt a new energy in the water. The swell lifted him up and down, and the surf on the outer edge of reef had become louder. Then he was through, and the wall of coral dropped away sharply to the sandy bottom some fifteen or twenty feet below.

The waves were trying to push him back into the reef, but Michael resisted, knowing that its white and smooth appearance was deceiving, and would cut mercilessly. Even a few drops of blood in the water were a beacon for the unwanted. Hadn't he read somewhere that sharks could sense a drop of blood from half a mile away? Bobbing in the swell beyond the reef, he flipped up his mask and looked around for Katherine.

Although there might be some large fish about this early in the day, Michael wasn't worried. He'd spoken with the manager the night before, who'd told him to stay away from the nest of hammerheads a quarter of a mile to the south but that, otherwise, there was nothing of concern.

Katherine burst through the water to his left and waved at him furiously. "Michael! Michael! Down here! Hurry!"

Michael slipped the mask back onto his face and swam toward her. He was a good swimmer—less graceful than Katherine, but comfortable in the water and fit from his daily workouts. He drew a deep breath through the snorkel and dove down, not sure what to expect.

At first, it was only greenish water, slightly murky from the sand kicked up by the surf, but then he saw the lobster trap made of wood and chicken wire. The buoy must have broken off, for he would have noticed one on the surface; yes—there was the strand of yellow nylon rope, its tattered end lying on the sandy bottom.

Two *langoustes* were crowded into one corner of the trap. At the opposite end was a small octopus. Its tentacles held a third *langouste* whose dark, mottled claws were arched backwards, snapping wildly, while its thin black antennae waved aimlessly in the water.

The octopus slid two of its tentacles up the lobster's arms, spreading the claws apart while another tentacle wrapped around the base of the whipping tail, immobilizing it. The tentacles were dark and iridescent, and he glimpsed the parallel rows of suction cups on their undersides.

Slowly, unhurriedly, the octopus turned the *langouste* so it faced him and slid the helpless creature into its mouth. With one crunch of its powerful jaws, the lobster was beheaded. Michael saw the green cloud of roe and innards spilling out of the body, but he was now out of breath. He swam up and burst through the gleaming surface of the sea, and looked around for Katherine. She was nowhere to be seen.

Captivated, he took a few deep breaths and dove down again. The octopus had already bitten off the *langouste's* tail, and now it gutted the dismembered body in one swift motion of its beak-like jaws before releasing the two halves of the shell. Inside the trap, the remains of what seconds before had been a living creature floated away, the dark green carapace tumbling slowly through the water.

Out of breath again, Michael shot up to the surface and pulled the mask up on his forehead. Treading water, he turned in a circle, searching for Katherine. The sea heaved around him, its azure surface sparkling in the morning sun.

Where was she?

He looked toward the reef, thinking she might have started to head back in, but the cut was empty. The wind was picking up, and the outer edge of the reef was churning with sea foam.

Michael turned two full circles before he spotted her, some forty or fifty feet away, floating face down in the water. She wasn't moving, and her snorkel stuck forward at an odd angle, almost parallel to the surface.

"Katherine!" yelled Michael, unsure of what was wrong. She didn't respond and he began to swim toward her. But now the current was sucking him back into the reef and, despite his best efforts, he was barely gaining. Another glance only worried him more, for he realized she was being pulled out to sea by some unseen current.

Michael shouted "Katherine!" He yelled again, louder this time, as he slapped the surface, trying to get her attention.

Suddenly, Katherine's body turned and her head rose out of the water. She pulled off her mask and snorkel, and flung them away in a careless motion. What in hell? She looked distant, a touch grotesque even, with strings of fair hair hanging over her face, eyes smeared with black mascara. She gave him an odd, hollow look—half smile, half grimace—before rolling and diving down into the sea. For a moment, her bright green flippers poised above the water like a fish tail, then disappeared.

Had she gone mad? Surprised and fearing the worst, Michael continued trying to swim in her direction. On the edge of panic, he kicked frantically but his legs were hardly moving and the water felt as thick as honey as he churned full force to no avail. Glancing back in desperation to see what was wrong, he felt the fear rise in his throat as he saw a dark brown tentacle the width of a man's forearm coil itself around his ankle. Slowly, deliberately, it crept up his leg even as it began to pull him down toward the hulking shape below.

3. MORNING AFTER

Michael awoke and lay on his back for a few minutes, disoriented by the nightmare. His sense of relief evaporated as he realized where he was and remembered last night, which now seemed as unreal as the dream.

Katherine was already up.

Logy with the accidie of a hangover, Michael swung his feet to the floor and sat on the bed for a few minutes, getting his bearings. His right hand ached when he tried to make a fist, and his whole body felt stiff from last night's alcohol. His mouth felt like it was stuffed with wet cardboard, and the morning light was much too bright.

She was at the kitchen table reading the paper.

"Morning," said Katherine without looking up.

"Hey," said Michael, but didn't kiss her as he normally would have. He stood for a minute looking at her before pouring a cup of coffee and sitting down across from her.

They sat quietly for a few minutes. Outside, a neighbor's dog began to bark.

"You ok?" said Katherine finally.

Michael nodded.

"Where'd you go?"

"Town," he said. "Gleason's."

"That's what I guessed."

She gave him a wistful look. "I'm sorry Michael. I should have been more gracious last night, but it's been building up inside me for so long. I had to do it. I had to put it on the table. Can you understand that?"

On the table, he thought. *There's a lawyer for you.*

"I just don't get what's going on," he said, voice gravelly with hangover. "Life isn't perfect, but I thought we were basically doing okay."

"That's the problem," said Katherine. Her voice turned brusque. "We're *not* doing ok. At least I'm not."

"I get that," said Michael. "What I don't understand is why you feel the way you do. Is something else going on?"

Katherine squinted up at him. "Like what?"

"I don't know," he said. "Something…" he searched for the right word. "…organic? Have you thought about having a work-up, getting checked out?"

She took a sip of coffee and looked away before answering.

"I did, as…" Katherine hesitated. "…as part of the procedure. I told the doctor that I feel tired all the time, down. Kind of numb. They took blood tests and such."

"I see," said Michael, though he hardly did.

He looked across the kitchen table at his wife. Eyes downcast and shoulders slumped, Katherine looked frail and dejected. He put his hand on hers and gave it a squeeze. She didn't pull away, but didn't respond either.

Katherine sighed. "I wish you weren't leaving tonight," she said, "and that this didn't happen when it did. I should have brought it up weeks ago. And," she added, "I didn't mean it to be so harsh."

"I thought the same thing at first," he said. "But maybe my leaving is not a bad thing after all. A little distance might help us - help you - get some perspective."

"Always the optimist," said Katherine.

Michael smiled. "I try."

He made some eggs while Katherine put on another pot of coffee.

Over breakfast, Katherine mentioned looking into therapy, which offered some hope. At least she was willing to try. All in all, decided Michael, this morning was very different from last night. Less confrontational, more mutual, less angry.

Later, as he started packing, he realized that there were two things his mind kept returning to over and over.

The first was that business about her still loving him, but not being 'in love' anymore. She'd said it last night and, as trite as it was, he realized that what hurt was the intimation of finality. Could one fall back in love after falling out? It didn't seem likely.

The second was her choosing to have an abortion without involving him. He was all for choice, for a woman's rights, but this was his child too after all, wasn't it? By all but the most compassionate measure, it was a deal breaker, but he *was* compassionate—he prided himself on that—and he wasn't ready to break the deal. At least not yet.

Michael glanced at his watch. Almost noon. He had arranged to meet Chris for lunch and considered cancelling—it would be easier, and he could use the extra time—but decided against it. The easy wasn't always the right. It would have to be quick, but it might help to see his best friend, and to get out of the house for an hour or two.

He could certainly use the distraction, and they didn't have to leave for the airport until five.

4. PREDATOR OR PREY?

"Excited about France?" asked Chris. "Aren't you heading out tonight?"

They were sitting in an outdoor patio at The Inn, a small restaurant in Wayne.

"I *was* excited," said Michael ruefully. "And yes, overnight flight on Air France. Nine thirty."

"From Newark?"

"JFK."

"Need a ride?"

Michael shook his head. "No, Katherine is bringing me." He paused. "I think."

Chris cocked an eyebrow. "You *were* excited? You *think*? Wassup man?"

Michael took a sip of water.

"I don't know," he said. "Things have been a little weird lately. Guess Katherine decided she isn't happy with our relationship any more. She tells me last night, so we had a domestic. I ended up taking off and getting loaded at Gleason's."

"Whoa," said Chris. "How long has this been going on?"

"A while. Trying to figure it out myself. Plus, she hasn't been feeling well." Michael paused, not sure what to say, as things weren't all that clear in his own mind.

"She getting checked out?" asked Chris.

"Yeah, she is. We'll see what happens."

"How long will you be away?"

"A month, maybe more."

Michael had come with the intention of sharing his situation with Chris, but now it didn't seem like the right time. It was too heavy a subject.

He shifted the conversation onto a different track. "How are you and Annie doing? Any plans for Christmas?"

The waiter brought their sandwiches, and their talk wound its way from the personal to the political, and then the whimsical, with Chris relating a play he had seen in the city the previous weekend, where the performers had all reversed gender.

"It was in-sane!" he said, breaking the word into two syllables. It was his favorite expression, and Michael had kidded him about it in the past. "Totally messed up the stereotypes, if you get my drift."

Michael grinned. "There you go with the in-sane again. Gender-bender, eh? What was the premise?"

Chris shrugged. "Honestly? Haven't got a clue. I don't get art sometimes. You think I'm simple-minded?"

They continued to talk as they ate. Michael was enjoying being with his friend - it was comforting in a simple kind of way. Half-paying attention (he could almost predict what Chris would say, as he knew him so well), he took in the scene around them.

The tiled patio was trellised with ivy, each table adorned with a green and white umbrella. It was busy, and everyone seemed to be enjoying the unexpected late-autumn warmth.

Four women came in and sat down at an adjacent table. Both men noticed them and cast some subtle (or, if you would have asked the women, probably not-so-subtle) glances in their direction.

Chris caught Michael's eye and leaned forward. "You know," he said quietly, "when it comes to women, I sometimes feel like a predator."

"What do you mean?" said Michael, surprised at his friend's choice of word. Chris could have meant something else, for he wasn't particularly careful about language; Mr. Tambourine Man once became Mr. Tangerine Man.

"Come on," said Chris with a wink. "Of all people, you should know. That lust, man. It's wicked!"

"No question we're hard wired that way," said Michael. "But, 'predatory' implies some kind of harm. Makes me think of stalking, while what you're talking about is quite harmless. Nothing wrong with being attracted to women, you know. God gave us eyes for a reason."

"You are *so* cerebral sometimes," said Chris with just a hint of annoyance before recanting. "But maybe you're right. Predatory does sound a little creepy. So what's a better word—obsessed?"

"No," said Michael. "That's also too strong. Isn't it just natural desire? It's when it turns to craving or, as you put it, obsession, that things go off track." He thought for a second. "I truly love women, although, at times, I do resent the power of beauty. It's so…" He fished around for the right word. "…compelling."

Chris nodded. "Sure is. There is an impelling quality to it, isn't there?"

Michael suppressed a smile as Chris continued. "We want them so much and, because of that, it's not entirely benign. It's like we're one step away from predatory, and a small step at that."

Michael held up his hand. "Wait," he said. "I think I've got it. Desire is too weak, craving too strong. How about yearning—desire with a little pepper on it?"

"I guess," said Chris, although he sounded unconvinced. "It's so very biological, so…"

Here it comes, thought Michael, and, sure enough, Chris didn't disappoint.

"In-sane."

Michael laughed. "Yep, *in-sane* it is," he said. "It's also wonderful. Appreciative, reverent even, but I get what you mean. But getting back to the predator thing—from what I've seen, we're more often the prey than the predator. It's the illusion of control rather than…"

Chris cut in. "Zactly! We're kind of pathetic. We want it too much, and that plays against us. I mean, I have a hard time relaxing at the beach! It's funny how a woman might pull down the hem of her skirt to reveal less leg in the office, yet go to the beach and parade around in a bikini and not bat an eyelash!"

"Sure," said Michael. "Circumstance breeds its own reality. But, as I already said, it does keep the world turning after all. Without attraction, life would be pretty dull. What you say reminds me of an old song - *Standing on the Corner*. Remember it? Very un-PC these days, but it's from a simpler time."

"I'm sure I've heard it, but I don't remember the words," said Chris. "How does it go?"

Michael glanced at the women. They were busy chatting. He leaned in so only Chris could hear.

"Like this." He quietly sang: "*Standing on the corner, watching all the girls go by; standing on the corner, giving all the girls the eye.*" Michael gave Chris a conspiratorial glance. "But the next part is what I was thinking of, the part that relates to what you're saying: *Brother you can't go to jail for what you're thinking, or for that 'ooh' look in your eye...*"

Chris laughed. "Ha! They do say jail, don't they? Perfect!"

"Sure is," said Michael. "And that was at least fifty years ago! Some things just don't change."

5. EN ROUTE

"Ominous," said Katherine, nodding at the grey bank of clouds hanging over the city. "Hope you get off all right."

"Me too," said Michael.

They were driving across the George Washington Bridge, and he stole a quick glance past his wife's profile to the jumble of skyscrapers that was midtown Manhattan. Below, the Hudson River was a dark green sheet of angry-looking water. He slapped the blinker arm and did a quick lane change onto the exit ramp that wound down to the Major Deegan.

The East Side of Manhattan was shrouded in a dull, late-afternoon light. The mass of buildings in the distance, crowned by the spire of the Empire State Building, was shadowy and grim. Soon the lights would start coming on. Just as Michael glanced at Katherine, a flash of lightning lit up the sky and, seconds later, the low rumble of thunder rolled over them.

It was an odd day for the end of November—nearly seventy and humid, although the storm portended a change in weather. The snout of a cold front pushing through, he thought. Would it mess up his departure?

Until last night, Michael had been thrilled at the prospect of being in Paris. He knew the city well from previous travels, and this time the company had complied with his request to rent a small apartment instead of the usual hotel. Today was November 28th and the rental started on December 1st, Tuesday, so he would have to hotel it for a few days, but that would give him something to look forward to. The hotel and the apartment were both in the Marais district, a residential part of the old city: the Hotel St. Gabriel and then apartment 3C in #19 on a small street nearby called Rue Beautreillis.

Michael had envisioned having the evenings to himself and the sweet anonymity of strolling across the Seine to have a bite in one of any number of small restaurants on the Ile St. Louis or over on the Left Bank. A free man in Paris, like the song, although his sense of adventure was now dampened by marital uncertainty, and the idea of being unfettered took on a different shade of meaning.

Still, he imagined the old city festooned with Christmas lights and holiday decorations—seductive, festive, and yet a touch melancholy as well. Paris was complex that way.

Katherine talked about flying out for the holidays, but the subject hadn't come up in the last week or two, and now was not the time to bring it up.

A flash of brake lights snapped Michael out of his musings. He did a quick lane change in anticipation of the Van Wyck expressway on-ramp a half mile ahead. The traffic was now thick but erratic. Just as he sped up, a forest of taillights lit up ahead, and he had to brake once more. Typical New York, thought Michael.

They were only a few miles from JFK, and the dashboard clock said 5:52. He had plenty of time and was more concerned about Katherine's trip home. Heading back through New York on a Saturday night with the stormy weather slowing things further could make for a nasty commute. Born in Iowa, Katherine still wasn't used to the ways of the city. With her Scandinavian roots and Midwestern ethics, she never quite assimilated to the relentless pace of the New York metro area, even though her family moved East when she was only twelve.

When they first met in high school, she was the perfect girl-next-door. Blue-eyed with straight, fine blonde hair, Katherine had an athlete's build—long legged and flat chested. Beauty had brushed up against her but fell a step short of full embrace. Her face was a bit narrow, and her nose—aquiline, with its slight bump—further accentuated the thinness of her face. High-strung and not reflexively sensual as some women are, she kissed with more energy than passion. Michael sometimes wished Katherine was a bit more languorous, a little slower that way. But she was feisty and smart and down-to-earth. Nothing if not practical: he remembered her teaching him to French kiss by passing a piece of gum back and forth from her mouth to his.

With time, Katherine's face had since lost some of the softness of youth, and she was even thinner than she had been in college. Self-control had always been a fundamental part of her psyche and, as she aged, there seemed to be an ever growing need for restraint and caution, tendencies that came to be expressed in her appearance. As someone once said, by the time someone turns forty, they have the face they deserve.

Michael took his wife's hand and gave it a squeeze. She squeezed back briefly, but kept looking straight ahead.

Rain began to patter the roof of the car, and they rode the last few miles to the airport in silence, each lost in their own thoughts.

6. DANNY'S STORY

Sitting in the Brooklyn Beer Garden bar in Terminal One, Michael glanced at his iPhone. No messages.

The rest of the drive to JFK had been quiet. When they pulled up to the terminal he tried to kiss Katherine on the lips, but she managed to turn her cheek and gave him a hug instead.

"You'd better go," she said hurriedly. "Those security lines are unpredictable."

Hoping for a tender moment, Michael wondered why the extra minute would matter, but left the thought unspoken.

"You take care of yourself," said Katherine as they parted. "Maybe see you around Christmas."

Thinking ahead, thought Michael, but also keeping her options open. So very Katherine.

"Sure," he said. "That would be great."

Katherine nodded and looked him in the eyes before glancing away. Were her eyes glistening, or was it just a reflection of the wet pavement?

He stood for a few seconds, looking at her as the taxis and cars swarmed around them.. The scene was noisy with the swish of tires on wet pavement, the blaring of horns and announcements from the airport PA system. A jet engine began to whine in the distance, and the air smelled of exhaust and jet fuel. Not a place to linger.

Michael reached down for his baggage and set it on the curb before turning back to her.

"Listen, I'm worried about you, Katherine," he said. "I'm worried about you, and I'm worried about us. Let's Skype when I get to Paris, but do think about this, about all the…"

"I know," she said curtly. "I will. You know I will."

It was now an hour and a half later, and he wondered whether Katherine was home yet. He considered calling but decided against it. There was nothing more to say and he, too, needed some separation, some distance.

Michael took a sip of his beer and sat back on the high stool. The bar was crowded, but he had been lucky to secure a small table near the concourse, where he could people-watch to pass the time. The stormy weather had backed things up and his departure was now delayed until 10:30 p.m. He had a solid hour to kill and nothing to do but be.

"Hey Tex, mind if I join you? Nowhere to sit in this damned place!"

A tall black man stood opposite him across the table, holding an orange duffel bag in one hand and a small leather saxophone case in the other. Michael took it in at a glance—an alto.

"Sure," he said. "Let me move my bag."

"Thanks, brother. Appreciate it. I only have my horn and this little satchel. Okay if I leave them here by the chair while I grab a draft?"

Michael stood at just over six feet, and this man had at least three or four inches on him. Lean, and in his late sixties or early seventies, his black hair was tightly curled and streaked with grey, and his brown eyes were a bit faded with age. But his voice was strong—a deep baritone, loud and clear despite the background noise. He could have been an actor or a professional announcer the way he naturally dominated the scene. Michael's first impressions were of masculinity and integrity, and he liked him instantly.

The man put out a hand. "Nice to meet you. My name is Danny. Since you're so kind, let me get you a beer. What are you drinking?"

Michael's pint was down to a sip, and he nodded appreciatively. "Sure, that would be great. Pennant Ale. I'm Michael."

"Good choice Michael," said Danny as they shook hands. He smiled. "Hang in there, I'll be right back."

Michael drained his glass, happy for the unexpected company and the chance to focus on something other than his own woes.

Danny came back with two pints, set them down on the table, and slid one over to Michael. Michael picked it up, and they clinked glasses.

"Where you headed?" asked Michael.

"St. George's, Grenada," said Danny. "I teach at the medical school down there and play some gigs in town at night." He gestured at his sax case. "Been doing this shit for years. Getting a little tired of it. Grenada's a fine place, but going down four times a year, well…" his voice trailed off. "Even paradise begins to fade if you have to visit it too often."

Danny laughed a big hearty laugh. "Listen to me! Seriously, man, what the hell am I doing complaining about going to a tropical island in late November, leaving this bullshit behind!" He took a sip of beer. "What about you? Where you off to?"

"Paris."

"Ah, sweet!" said Danny. He held up the pint in a mock toast. "City of lights. City of love. City of art. I love that town! I've only been three or four times, but it's funny…" He hesitated, and Michael could see he was remembering something. "Every time I go, something crazy happens. Something weird," he added with a shake of his head. "Just my karma I guess."

"Weird? Like what?" asked Michael, intrigued.

"Oh, you know" said Danny dismissively. "Come to think of it, maybe it's not all that interesting. I don't want to bore you."

"No, no," said Michael. "I'm interested." He could see that Danny had a large personality and was a natural storyteller.

"Well," said Danny, "for example, last April, I was there for a science conference. We were staying at the Lutetia. Know it?"

"Can't say I do."

"My favorite hotel. Left Bank. Headquarters for Hitler's SS during the war. I'll tell you, those bastards had good taste! I had to take the subway to get back and forth from the conference, and one morning this guy sits down opposite me on the train. Nicely dressed, Middle Eastern by the looks of him. Takes out a paper and starts to read it. It's Arabic or something. At the next station, a girl gets on, comes over, and sits down next to him, and they start talking, almost like it's prearranged. Pretty chick with nice dark eyes. For some reason, I remember thinking Lebanese. I don't know about you, but I think they're among the most beautiful women in the world with those white teeth and dark eyes.

"Anyway, they start talking as if they know each other. Both get off at the same station. A few days go by, and I'm sitting at some street-side bar, when who waltzes in but this same couple! They plant themselves right next to me - you know how it is in Paris, with the tables and chairs set right on the sidewalk? I introduce myself and say, 'You may not remember me, but I saw you two on the subway a few days ago.'

" 'You mean the Metro?' says the guy without missing a beat.

" 'All right,' I say, 'have it your way—the Metro. I'm from New York and we call it the subway, but no matter. Where you all from?'

" 'We live in Paris,' says the girl, dodging my question." Danny took a sip of his beer before continuing. "They speak good English. And I do mean English, not American.

"We start talking, and they say they're both in finance, whatever that means. Tameem and Talia. I remembered their names because they sounded like a comedy team! Very pleasant. I offer to buy them a beer or a wine, but they decline. 'We're *mussulmans*,' they say. 'We don't drink alcohol, but thank you very much anyway.'

"My beer and their coffees come, and we get to talking about this and that and, eventually, about food. Now I love a good couscous and mention ordering it, as it's on the menu. 'Oh no, no,' they say in unison. 'Not here, no. It's terrible here! If you want good couscous, you should go to our favorite place—it's only a few Metro stops away.' Well, I'm hungry and I don't feel like traveling, but now I can't order the damned couscous without being," Danny's eyes crinkled, "you know, disrespectful. So I get a ham and cheese sandwich instead and, while we're making small talk, the dude writes down the name of this place on a napkin and gives it to me. 'Best couscous in Paris,' he says. 'Just as good as Morocco. Trust me. Well worth the ride.'

"My next night was free, so I decided to give this place a shake. Science conferences are pretty social. You're on all day, talking to people, so I enjoy escaping off by myself, especially at night, to get some feed, maybe hear some music.

"It's a cold April night out, pourin', nasty. But I've a target in mind, so I show the concierge the napkin, and he directs me—take this train to here, then transfer to there. You get the picture. Four subway rides away, but I figure, what the hell, the best couscous in Paris is worth the effort!

"As I'm talking to the concierge, though, I get the feeling he's a little bothered. He says, 'May I ask, *monsieur*, what you are looking for?' I get the impression he's giving me a signal that this may not be a good area. I call him on it, and he gives me a wishy-washy something or other. 'No, not too bad, but not too good either.' You know how the French love their *comme ci, comme ça*. He suggests that there's nice couscous right here, in the hotel restaurant, but I'm committed, so I get underway and, as I transfer from train one to train two and train two to train three, the cars keep getting emptier and emptier and the clientele sketchier and sketchier. The last transfer puts me on the platform with a downright seedy looking crowd. A guy passed out on the bench here, some drug deal going on across the way there. But there's no turning back at this point, as I've already wasted the better part of an hour. I finally get to the right station. If I remember correctly, it's named for some colonel. Fabergé or something like that."

Danny took a swig of beer and leaned in toward Michael.

"You know, one of the things I love about the subway," he smiled, "sorry, the Metro, is that it's all the same underground, but when you come out of a new station, you never know what to expect. It's like coming out of a rabbit hole into a different world. I love that moment.

"But here there's nothing interesting to speak of. A typical but poor Parisian neighborhood. You can sense it's down at the mouth a bit, but the trees are pretty, their young leaves are a bright green in the glow of the streetlights. The rain is coming down in sheets, and I think to myself—what the hell am I doing out here, completely out of my element, all for a little couscous! I grew up in Philly, so I dig the whole 'hood thing—how straying one or two blocks in the wrong direction can throw you into a different world."

"Yeah, I grew up near New York," said Michael, nodding in agreement. "I know what you mean."

Danny nodded and returned to his story. "So picture this—no one about, not a soul. Nine o'clock at night by now. I fish out the napkin with the address on it and start wandering around trying to find the street the restaurant's on. I eventually get onto it, am runnin' down the numbers—1600, 1500, and so on. The address was 987. At this point, I'm soaked, my blood sugar is in the gutter, and I'll be damned if this area has any restaurants at all. Sure didn't look like it. I work my way down the numbers block by block and eventually get to 1000. 987 should be right there across the way, right? But all I see is a lot of dark doorways fronted by the damned plane trees! I make my way across the street and wander around till I find the right address. And guess what it is?"

Michael shrugged. He hadn't a clue.

Danny tapped the table with his forefinger for emphasis. "It's a Mosque! A doorway with a small brass sign next to it embossed with the crescent moon and the star. Definitely no couscous here. In fact, there isn't any kind of food to be had in the area. It's all residential, period."

"Weird," said Michael. He wrinkled his brow and took a swig of the beer when Danny held up a hand.

"Wait. That's not all, Tex. There's an epilogue—a postscript, if you will. Otherwise this would be a pretty boring story. Next morning, I'm shaving, keeping an eye on the little TV in the bathroom. It's the early news and a story on terrorism comes on—four men arrested in connection with some alleged plot, and what do I see but the front of the mosque I was at the night before! No doubt about it. These guys worshipped there, if you can call it that. It was one of those madrasas or whatever, spreading their hate."

"Right," said Michael, fishing for the right word. "Not madrasas—radical mosques or whatever."

Danny nodded. "Damn straight it was a radical mosque—affiliated with Al-Qaeda or ISIS and all that. But here's the good part. When they show the mug shots of the men, guess who's among them?"

Danny paused to let his question sink in. "You got it. Mr. Couscous himself! My guess is this guy had some kind of disconnect, and gave me the address of their mosque instead of the restaurant by mistake. Otherwise, it makes no sense." Danny frowned. "They were arrested for planning an attack on the Paris Metro of all things— coordinated explosions during rush hour. Unbelievable!"

"What about the woman?" asked Michael.

Danny shrugged. "Beats me. I did think about whether I should have gone to the police. But then what? No, I let it be, as they say."

He looked at Michael. "You know, I grew up in the fifties with the Russkies being the bad guys. They were there, we were here, the lines were clear. Who would have guessed that we would go from fighting the godless commies to this crazy religious war? I really thought we were beyond that."

Danny paused.

"I'm serious, man" he said finally. "Islam may be a fine religion for normal folk, but these days it seems to attract more than its share of wackos."

Danny glanced at his watch. "Shit!" he said. "Here I've been rattling on, and it's almost boarding time. I gotta go! Maybe we'll run into each other again somewhere. Take care, Mike." He swallowed the rest of the beer in one gulp and they shook hands before Danny strode away onto the concourse, satchel in one hand and sax case in the other.

Michael watched his lanky form recede with a pang of regret. Danny was a character and now that he was gone, his own world felt a little drab. Michael finished his beer and walked his way over to Gate 102, stopping to buy some water and a few magazines along the way.

Somewhere above, the airport muzak system was playing Chris Isaac's version of *Let It Snow*. A Christmas tree stood in the concourse. Not yet decorated, it looked rather lonely and out of place.

7. ANNETINE

Michael settled into his seat and watched the plane fill up. The window seat next to him was vacant and he found himself hoping it would remain so. He took out a *Time* magazine, put on his glasses, and started reading about the latest problems in the Middle East when a voice broke in on his thoughts.

"Excuse me, may I?"

The woman in the aisle nodded at the window seat.

Disappointed, Michael stood up to let her in. She was attractive in a simple sort of way. Nothing out of the ordinary, although he noticed that she was nicely dressed in a skirt and sweater and had a nice figure. He got up and let her in.

In his current state of mind, Michael was in no mood for company, especially that of a woman. It would be a long flight, and he was enjoying being alone. Please don't be a talker, he thought. A few years ago, on a fourteen-hour flight from L.A. to Tokyo, the woman next to him wouldn't stop chattering. Michael was obliging at first, sensing she was afraid of flying and nervous, but after two hours of non-stop chit-chat he grew terse and then went silent. The woman kept talking, and Michael finally put an end to it by leaning back, closing his eyes, and becoming unresponsive.

To his relief, this woman leafed through a magazine while the cabin doors were closed and the plane pulled away from the gate. After takeoff, she reclined her seat and napped. Later, she watched some movie on the small monitor on the seatback in front of her. From what he could see, it was a romantic comedy with Jennifer Aniston. Chick flick—same thing as Katherine would have chosen, thought Michael glumly.

He continued to read for a while, then pulled out a small laptop to work on some business. The desktop was a picture of him and Katherine sitting in two Adirondack chairs by Lake Winnipesaukee, holding hands. It was from their vacation in New Hampshire back in August. Their last?

Michael plugged his ear buds into his iPhone, and touch-screened his way to *Kind of Blue* by Miles Davis. The familiar opening notes of "So What" came on, and he leaned back in the seat, enjoying the prospect of rediscovering one of his favorite jazz albums.

Although he tried to ignore her, Michael was aware of the woman next to him, and occasionally stole a glance her way. Fine, light brown hair combed straight back off of the forehead gave her an impertinent air, and the soft hunter-green wool sweater set off the shape of her breasts well above a simple black skirt and stockings. Early- to mid-thirties, he guessed. Although her nails were well manicured, she wore no nail polish or jewelry. Feeling mildly annoyed at himself, Michael reclined his seat and closed his eyes. Triggered by the desktop image, his mind drifted back to the beginnings of his relationship with Katherine.

They'd dated for over a year in high school and had the usual adolescent run of kissing and making out in the back seat, or at home if the parents were out. First base, second base, third base, but no home run until the summer between high school and college when, fueled by a pint of Southern Comfort, they surrendered their virginity to each other one night in a squirrelly patch of woods behind the Catholic church.

It was all very intense and embarrassingly quick, and they lay together afterward, feeling peaceful and free in the summer night. The blue-white diamond of Vega, the brightest star in the summer sky, twinkled overhead. The old yellow muslin sheet he had brought covered them both and this, too, added to the sensuality of the moment, its organic smell cloaking them in its private veil.

Now, more than two decades later, here he was somewhere above the Atlantic, alone and uncertain about everything that mattered. Feeling like his sentimentality was being mocked by reality, by things beyond his control, Michael refocused on the music. It was something he knew, something he loved, something he chose. A sweet and certain shelter, a private pleasure. It was one of his mainstays and it had saved...

A tap on his arm broke into his thoughts.

"Sorry to bother you. May I?"

The woman had a nice smile, and her teeth—white and even but a little small—gave her mouth a delicate, feminine quality. Her lips were nicely formed and full, but not overly so. She was more attractive than he had originally thought—one of those girls where a closer look invites another.

Michael got up to let her by and noticed she had taken her shoes off. Five-six, he thought, maybe five-seven in her stocking feet. As she squeezed by him, he caught her scent—a mixture of caramel, raspberry, and something else he couldn't quite define. It came to him later—coffee, or at least coffee-like—an earthy, slightly musky undertone that made the whole richer and more complex. Subtle, not at all overwhelming. Just enough.

Damn her, thought Michael, but mostly damn me. Chris' 'predatory' came back to him, and while Michael still wasn't sure it was the right word (and maybe there wasn't a right word), there certainly was something terribly basic about the nature of attraction. The magnetism between two people is as powerful as any other force in nature. It is as inexorable as gravity and as intangible as sunlight.

8. NIGHT FLIGHT

She returned, and they did the reverse pirouette before sitting down. The woman pulled up the shade and gazed out the window. A flight attendant came by with the drink cart. Michael ordered bourbon on the rocks (hair of the dog, he reasoned), while she asked for white wine. Each lowered their trays in anticipation.

When Michael passed her the small bottle, she smiled and he noticed the neat white row of teeth again, and the dimples. Also, her lips seemed fuller, more inviting, and Michael realized that she had put on some lip gloss in the bathroom.

"Well," she said easily, as if they were old friends. "It's finally happy hour. Cheers!"

"Cheers," said Michael.

She nodded toward the window. "Pretty night out there."

Michael leaned over and, looking past her, saw the surface of the wing in the light of the three-quarter moon and, below, the silver sheen of the Atlantic Ocean. There was her scent again. Refreshed as well?

"Sure is," he said, as he unscrewed the Maker's Mark and poured it over the ice.

"Heading home or going away?".

"Away," he said. "I'll be in Paris for a month or so. You?"

"I suppose I'm going away" she said, "but also going back. I've been living in Paris for seven or eight months now. Gave up my apartment in New York back in March, so I'm not sure what home is anymore." She turned to face him more directly and doubled one leg underneath herself.

"Work or play?" she asked.

"Work." He let the silence hang to see if she would pursue it. She didn't.

"My name is Annetine Fournier," she said when he glanced at her again. She pronounced Annetine as 'Anneteen', and he thought he'd picked up just a bit of a drawl. She raised her wine in a toast. "To a smooth flight."

"Godspeed," said Michael as they touched glasses. "Annetine is a pretty name. Can't say I've ever heard it before. I'm Michael Boylen."

He swirled the cup to cool the bourbon and took a small sip. "What do you do in Paris, if I may ask?"

"I work for a company that makes medical stockings. They're setting up a European office, and I'm helping to get things going. They want me to manage the marketing."

He raised an eyebrow. "You mean those horrible things old ladies wear with their orthopedic shoes? The white ones?"

Annetine laughed and brushed the hair back off of her forehead. There were the dimples again. Damn her, thought Michael, yet he couldn't help but be drawn into the conversation. She was as easy to talk to as a stripper.

"Ha ha, very funny," said Annetine. "But no, not those. You'd be surprised at how big a business it is! Lots of people have swelling in their legs. After surgery, for example, or if their jobs require them to stand up all day. Pregnant women. Cancer patients. And no, they're not the old lady kind, although I know what you mean. Quite the opposite actually—they're very *chichi*."

Yes, there was just a touch of drawl.

Annetine continued. "A pair will cost you between seventy and a hundred dollars. Matter of fact, I'm wearing some right now. Want to see?"

She pulled up her skirt a bit and straightened one leg as best she could in the limited space. Michael saw a slim calf covered with a black stocking in a fine mesh. You flirt, he thought, although he had to admit that, despite his initial reluctance to engage, he was enjoying her company.

"They're excellent for long plane trips. You might want to try them if you fly a lot."

"I wouldn't look very good in them," he said, and pulled up his pants to show her his hairy calf.

She laughed. "Don't worry, we make them for men as well. They look like perfectly normal socks."

"I'm too young to worry about varicose veins," said Michael.

She didn't miss a beat. "How old are you, if I may ask?"

"Thirty-nine." Hell, he thought; since she had opened up that door, why not? "What about you?"

Annetine feigned surprise. "Men aren't supposed to ask women their age," she said.

"That's only for women over forty," said Michael reassuringly, "and you're certainly not there yet."

"How old do you think I am?" she asked coquettishly, cocking her head so that her hair hung down away from her face.

You are something else, my dear, thought Michael. Chris really did have it all backwards.

She looked to be in her early thirties. Should he go low or high? He decided to play along, and gave her an overtly appraising look. "Thirty-one?"

"Thanks," she said, "but you're off by six years."

"All right, twenty-five then," said Michael with a grin.

"Very funny, Michael," she said, using his name for the first time. "You're playing me. I just turned thirty-seven."

Their eyes lingered a moment, and Michael noticed that Annetine's hazel eyes were set off by dark lashes, which gave them a luminous quality. Interesting. She had struck him as being rather plain at first, but as she talked, her features came alive in their own right—the clear, sparkling eyes, the dimples, the finely drawn mouth with its neat row of teeth, the thrown back hair. Her overall gestalt was playful and a touch impudent. 'I've got life by the tail,' she seemed to say, 'care to come along?'

Michael decided to turn off the computer before he spilled the drink on it and, as he did so, the desktop picture reappeared for a few seconds before the screen went dark.

"Wife?" asked Annetine, nodding at the computer.

"Yes," said Michael.

"Hmm," she said, in a way that made him wonder what she was thinking. Seeing the photograph and hearing her comment brought back last night, and he felt a pang of irritation.

Annetine must have picked up on something, for she grew quiet.

Was she disappointed? wondered Michael, amused at his own narcissism. He decided to change the subject.

"Do you speak good French?"

Annetine smiled. "You mean do I speak French well? So-so," she said. "Had six years of it between high school and college but, honestly, I've learned more in the last few months than in all the time in the classroom. It's tough, though, as the French talk fast and mumble. There must be five ways to pronounce the letter 'O'! The people I work with are all bilingual so it isn't a problem. You?"

"Pretty weak," said Michael. "I took three years in college and tried to brush up with the Rosetta course these last few weeks but, as you say, it's one thing to know how to say something and entirely another to understand the lingo as it's being fired at you."

"Who will you be working with?" asked Annetine. "Will they speak English?"

"Most will, yes. It's only six or seven people in total. I'll have to say *excusez moi* a lot, or *répétez s'il vous plaît*. Ironically, my wife speaks better French than I do."

"Will she be joining you?" asked Annetine.

"I don't know," said Michael and, hearing the chill in his voice, added, "It's tough for her to get away, especially this time of year. She's a lawyer."

"Sorry to hear that," said Annetine. "How long have you been married?"

"It'll be nineteen years in May," said Michael, trying to put lightness into his voice even as he felt another swell of anger. Katherine had left him in this crazy limbo. What had he done to deserve it, after all?

Annetine continued to look at him, but didn't say anything more. The attendant came by, and they ordered another round of drinks.

"What about you?" asked Michael.

"What about me what?" asked Annetine.

"Are you married?"

"Nope," she said airily. "I've had a few serious relationships, but guess I haven't met the right guy yet. Or…" She hesitated. "Maybe I'm not quite ready for that. I enjoy my life these days. It's free and easy and I like it that way. It feels right, at least for now."

"So, here's a question for you," said Michael, holding her gaze. The drink was beginning to energize him. "Maybe you haven't married yet, but have you ever been in love? *Really* in love?"

Annetine looked at him thoughtfully, mulling over the question, and crossed her arms as she leaned back against the window.

"That's kind of personal, isn't it?"

Michael smiled. "Why? Love's a universal human condition and I hate small talk."

"OK," said Annetine, "I don't like small talk either and I suppose it *is* a fair question. But since you brought it up, why don't you go first, forever-married man? What about you?"

Touché, thought Michael. Deft. How many times *had* he been in love? How do you even know if you are truly *in* love? Isn't it relative? You love someone, but maybe later you meet someone else and realize that you weren't as in love as you'd thought.

For him, though, Katherine was pretty much it, simply a question of numbers. He'd had one or two girlfriends before her in high school, but those were crushes, teenage fluff. And he'd pretty much been with her ever since. With the spotlight turned back on him, Michael realized he ran the risk of appearing rather boring. One love in thirty-nine years was just so, so… dull.

"Two," he lied, adding, "maybe two and a half."

Annetine laughed. "OK. And which half would that be?"

"You know," he said, leaning into her conspiratorially. "There's an old routine along those lines. Want to hear it?"

She nodded. "Sure."

"It goes back to one of those old Rat Pack guys. I think it was Dean Martin. My dad was a big fan, and I heard it years ago, but it stuck. The shtick is that he's very unlucky—'when the lights go out in Macy's, I'm always in the piano department'—that sort of thing."

"So he gives another example or two to bait the audience, and then says 'I'm so unlucky that when I go to a magic show and they cut the woman in half, I get the half…'" Michael paused for emphasis and smiled, letting her mind consider the possibilities. "…that talks!"

Annetine laughed heartily. Full dimples this time.

"Definitely haven't heard that one before—I'd have remembered it! Pretty funny," she said. "But you're dodging the question Michael. Is your wife the only person you've ever fallen for?"

"Yeah," he said sheepishly. "My wife's pretty much it. We met in high school, way back." He shook his head. "It sounds rather pathetic, doesn't it!"

"Not at all," said Annetine soothingly. "Actually, it's kind of sweet. Why would you think it's pathetic?"

Michael shrugged. "I guess we males like to think we're very experienced in the art of love. Rather dull to have only been with one woman." He shrugged. "Anyway, enough about me. What about you?"

She thought for a second as she continued to look at him. "I, too, have only been in love once, if ever."

"Really?" he said, genuinely surprised. She was thirty-seven and surely received her fair share of male attention, for, while she wasn't strikingly beautiful, he found that the more they talked, the more attractive she became. She had a combination of vulnerability and panache, and it was a seductive contrast. And, he realized, there was an underlying gentleness about her manner, a femininity, which was appealing. At the same time, Michael sensed there was more to Miss Annetine Fournier than met the eye, and this only fascinated him more.

Annetine glanced down at her wine and ran a finger around the rim of the plastic cup.

"It was in college. He was almost twice my age and divorced, but we definitely had something special together. At least it seemed that way for a while."

"A professor?" he guessed.

"No," she said. "Not a professor. He was my boss. I worked as a waitress part-time and he managed the restaurant." A smile flickered across her face. "It's an intense business, you know—the late hours, the alcohol. It attracts the emotionally wayward. You've been on your feet all night dealing with people, and then it's past midnight, and you're all wound up. Things happen. He was…" She thought for a second. "…a good man."

Annetine paused and stretched before continuing. As she arched her back, Michael tried not to be obvious, but he noticed the lines of her bra under the green sweater and the generous swell of her breasts above the narrow waist. She certainly had some figure.

"Anyway," she said, returning to the original thought. "I'd like to think that the love of my life has yet to come along. Hey," she said off-handedly as she raised the glass of wine and held it between them. "One can always hope, right?"

"Always!" said Michael. "Here's to love." He raised his bourbon and bumped her cup before taking a sip. "Hope springs eternal and all that. But I'm curious," he added, "who ended the relationship?"

As soon as the words left his mouth, Michael regretted them, for a shadow passed across Annetine's face, and he felt her pull away. She swung her leg back to the floor and turned to face the seat in front of her. When she did answer, there was a touch of tedium in her voice.

"I suppose I ended it," she said, "but that's kind of hard to say, isn't it? I mean there is always one person that verbally ends it, but there's all the stuff that comes before, when things begin to unravel..." Her voice trailed off.

She looked like someone had splashed cold water on her. He should have known better. Or should he have? Annetine had an openness about her that invited informality, and her pullback wasn't consistent with what he perceived her personality to be, so it confused him. What nerve had he touched?

From there on out, she grew quiet and answered his questions politely but without adding any energy of her own to the conversation. Michael was disappointed and a little surprised, as his question wasn't *that* personal, after all. The dinner cart came, and they started in on the food.

At a loss for words, he settled back into his seat and refocused on the meal in front of him. The spell had been
broken.

9. ARRIVAL

As the swift night of the transoceanic flight progressed, the overhead lights dimmed and the interior of the plane grew quiet. Annetine slipped on an eyeshade and fell asleep with her head propped against the window on a small pillow.

Michael never could sleep sitting up, so he listened to music, drank another bourbon, and browsed the little touch-screen in front of him. It was midnight in New York—his normal bedtime—and 6 a.m. in Paris. Up here—God knows where—it was God knows what. Was it time for sleep or for that morning cup of coffee?

He reset his watch to European time, which made him feel more tired, and flicked on the in-flight GPS option. They were a few hundred miles northwest of Shannon, Ireland, traveling 647 mph SSE.

All this digital information quietly swirling around us, thought Michael. It was a little absurd in its detail. The electronic sensors regurgitating their streams of data on temperature, velocity, altitude, distance from, distance to, time from, time to; feet, meters, miles, kilometers mixing effortlessly. According to the latest readout, they were at 37,000 feet and 383 miles away from Paris, and would be landing in 53 minutes.

To uncoil the physical tension born of immobility, Michael got up, stretched, and wandered up and down the aisle. Many passengers were asleep in the semidarkness, half-covered by the airplane blankets and splayed in the awkward postures imposed upon them by economy class seats. Some sat in a semi-stupor, staring at the flickering rectangular screens directly in front of them. Others were awake, fingers tapping on their laptops or turning the pages of a book. He stood for a while in the galley at the back of the plane, washed his face in the little bathroom sink, and drank some seltzer water.

Walking back to his seat, Michael noticed a splinter of bright light under a window shade that wasn't completely lowered. He sat back down and had just closed his eyes when the cabin lights blinked on, along with announcements in French, then English, explaining that the breakfast service would be starting shortly.

Some passengers pulled up the window shades, brightening the cabin further. It was a rude transition— night to morning in a heartbeat. Michael stretched and rubbed his eyes, feeling thick and bleary-eyed from the abbreviated night. Next to him, Annetine stirred and slipped off the black eyeshade.

Half-awake, she stretched her arms over her head and looked over at Michael, eyes blinking and trying to regain focus. "Where are we?" she asked with a slight slur.

Michael smiled. Lucky lady, to be able to sleep. "Somewhere over Ireland," he said. "'An hour to go."

"*Mmm*," she said languidly. Eyes still heavy with sleep, Annetine leaned back on the pillow, but continued to look at Michael. Her expression was lidded, dreamy.

"Wow," she said. "Guess I was in la-la land. I was playing tennis of all things, near some beautiful stone mansion, and the air smelled like rain…"

Coffee came, then breakfast. Michael fortified himself with two cups of coffee but still felt as odd as he always did on overnight flights—here it was near one a.m. New York time, and yet morning light was streaming through the row of oval windows. It confused the biological clock, and he felt physically stiff and mentally dull.

It would be sweet to lie down once he got to the hotel. He would sleep for a few hours, shower, have a double espresso and a light breakfast somewhere. Then, he'd be good to go. At this thought, which would normally have been charged with anticipation, a little voice in his head whispered - *Go where? With whom? What for?* The nights this time of year would be long, and the evenings dark.

Michael felt a stab of loneliness. He didn't know a soul in Paris and would be working with strangers except for Alain Durst, the head of the Aerotel unit he was temporarily joining, a man he had met only once a few months ago.

The breakfast trays were cleared, and a change in air pressure signaled the beginning of descent. The interior of the plane was now suffused with light. He imagined Katherine fast asleep in their upstairs bedroom, as it was the middle of the night, the phantom hours back home.

A hand on his arm broke in on his thoughts.

"Michael, I hope you didn't think me rude."

"Huh?" he asked, caught off guard. "Rude about what?"

"About the way I reacted when you asked me the question about ending relationships. It brought back some bad memories, and I kind of shut down on you. I'm sorry, I just didn't want to go there."

For a woman who'd slept through the night in an airplane without makeup, she looked fresh and relaxed. Michael, on the other hand, felt worn out. He could feel the weight of his skin hanging on his face, and his eyes itched like they had been in a sandstorm.

"I did enjoy our conversation," said Annetine. "You seem like a very..." she smiled at him, "...a very decent man."

"Thanks," he said. "You were easy to talk to, and I guess I overstepped a bit. Can I blame it on the drink?"

She shook her head and smiled. "No need to blame it on anything. You stirred up some old memories I hadn't thought about in a long time, that's all. When are you returning back to the States?" she asked, changing the subject.

"Not sure. Sometime after the New Year."

"You mean you'll be in Paris through the holidays?"

"Most likely. Depends on how things go at work."

She wrinkled her nose. "What about your wife, your kids?"

"We don't have any kids." he said curtly. "As for my wife... well, I'm not sure. We're not in a great space right now."

"I'm sorry," said Annetine. "The holidays can be difficult alone, especially away from home."

Michael shrugged. "I expect it will work out, but you're right. The holidays or, more broadly, life, can be difficult sometimes. With people, one never knows, does one?"

"No," said Annetine thoughtfully. "One never does."

Michael looked at her. Although he barely knew her, he felt genuine warmth toward this woman, this stranger next to him. She stirred something in him that had been dormant for a long time.

"What are your plans for the holidays?" he asked, not wanting to end the conversation on a sour note.

"I'm going skiing with some friends in Switzerland," she said. "Our plans are still hazy. Train it there and back, drink lots of wine, sit in a Jacuzzi in the falling snow, and ski away the hangovers!"

Michael laughed. "Sounds wonderful! May I tag along? You certainly make it sound enticing. You should be in sales!"

"I am," said Annetine. "Remember? The stockings…"

"Ah yes" he said, nodding at her legs. "The stockings. How could I forget?"

"How are your feet feeling?" said Annetine. "I'll bet they're so swollen you couldn't take your shoes off if you tried. It's all downhill after forty, you know, and you're almost there," she said. "If you're interested, I can make you a good deal…"

"Nonsense," he said, "Forty's the new thirty, and my feets are just fine."

"OK," she said with a smile. "Have it your way. Can't blame a girl for trying." Her expression turned serious. "You know what I do, but I still don't quite get your line of work."

"That's 'cause you haven't asked," said Michael.

"OK," she said. "I'm asking…"

"I'm a penetration tester," said Michael.

Annetine's eyes narrowed a bit, trying to decide if he was serious. She raised an eyebrow and smiled. "Dare I ask what kind of penetrations you test?"

Michael grinned, as he knew that his professional title often gave people pause.

"Computer networks," he said. "Basically, I make sure hackers can't get into a network to pirate data or sabotage a system. 'Pentester' is the more common term. There's even a magazine by that name."

"Wow, way beyond me," said Annetine. "I barely manage my email. Who do you work for?"

"We're a small company that contracts with the government." Michael was intentionally vague, as Aerotel was a private firm that contracted with both NATO and the U.S. military. Their niche was the design of miniature drones for field surveillance, so there were security concerns.

Before Annetine had a chance to ask for more detail, he deflected her train of thought. "These days, hackers are pretty sophisticated and are often backed by governments, so having a secure network is what's called a 'front and center' priority. The Chinese and the Russians are always trying to steal something from us, and the Iranians. Even our so-called corporate friends can't resist a little snooping once in a while."

"What does your company make?" asked Annetine.

"Aviation parts," said Michael, intentionally vague.

Annetine nodded and said "*Hmm*," but didn't press him any further.

The pilot announced the beginning of descent into Charles de Gaulle. The plane shuddered as it passed through a layer of clouds, and the rural landscape of Normandy appeared below. The brown patchwork of fields was gradually replaced with a more urban terrain. Leaning over to get a better view, Michael caught a glimpse of the serpentine turns of the Seine and the unmistakable form of the Eiffel Tower in the distance.

They had arrived.

"Good flying with you, Annetine," said Michael as the plane taxied to the terminal. "You're nice to talk to. I enjoyed our time together."

"Me too," she said. "It was fun. In a way, it's a shame we'll probably never see each other again."

"It doesn't have to be that way." The words were out of Michael's mouth before he knew it.

Annetine gave him an apologetic look. "Look, happily or unhappily, you're a married man. Best if we have a nice memory of each other and leave it at that, don't you think?"

Michael wasn't sure what to think. He was happily married to a person who was not happily married. He would be alone in Paris for a month, maybe more. This woman was easy to talk to. She was fun. His marital situation was uncertain at best. It could be nice to have a female friend to provide some balance, with whom to have an occasional lunch or a dinner without the complications of sex, although he admitted to himself that he did feel an attraction to her. But still…

"I suppose," he said tentatively, adding, "I wasn't thinking of anything serious. A cup of coffee sometime. A walk? You're easy to…"

"*Uh-uh*, not a great idea," interrupted Annetine, with a shake of her head. "And that's a compliment. I enjoyed talking to you, too, but some doors are better left closed. Once they begin to open, they can be very hard to control."

Trying to regain the initiative, Michael said, "Look, we're both in business. Why not at least exchange business cards?"

Annetine smiled. "You're showing your age. Cards are *très passé*. I don't even carry one any more. It's all websites and emails these days."

"Fine, let's exchange emails then. Seriously, Annetine." said Michael, surprised at his own persistence. "It can't hurt. We're not teenagers after all."

"I know," she said, "and that's exactly what worries me." She gave him an appraising look. "But I suppose having each other's email would be OK."

They exchanged the information and continued to chat as the plane pulled up to the gate. The seat-belts-off chime rang, and the plane erupted in a commotion of passengers retrieving overhead luggage, making cell phone calls, and crowding into the aisle only to stand motionless waiting for those ahead of them to leave. Michael and Annetine stayed in their seats and continued to talk.

After deplaning, they rode the tunnel escalators unique to Charles de Gaulle, and eventually arrived at Passport Control.

It was time to say goodbye.

"Give me a hug," said Annetine unexpectedly, and Michael gladly obliged. Her body fit nicely into his, and he caught her now-familiar scent for the last time. Their embrace lingered a moment before ending.

"By the way," he said, as she turned to walk away. "What kind of perfume do you have on? I love the way you smell."

"If you must know," she said with a quick smile, "it's actually two perfumes mixed together—my own invention. One is *Shalimar*, by Guerlain. An old classic. The other one is called *Angel*, by Thierry Mugler." She laughed. "I mix them in my own secret proportion, something I discovered years ago. I'm glad you like it. You smell kind of nice yourself."

"Thanks," said Michael. "Especially since I don't wear any cologne."

Annetine smiled. "All the better then. Enjoy Paris, Michael. And take care."

10. POST-TRAVEL BLUES

Michael arrived at his hotel around nine a.m. but check-in wasn't until three, and none of the rooms were ready. Feeling tired yet wired from drinking too much coffee on top of a sleepless night, he left his bags with the concierge, a Tunisian named Ayman, and went for a walk down the narrow Marais streets to the Seine.

The chilly late autumn air revived him. He stopped and stood for some time, enjoying the faint warmth of the sun on his face. The bridges, the buildings, even the parapet he was leaning on—all made of natural, unpainted stone—were textured and sharp in the morning light. The Seine sparkled in front of him and the twin towers of the Notre Dame Cathedral towered above the horizon to his right, dwarfing everything in their vicinity. The one exception to zoning was always granted to the house of God.

Michael walked onto the Pont Marie and paused half way across. Large, half-bare poplar trees were evenly spaced on the quay next to the water well below street level. Their pale yellow leaves quivered in the late autumn breeze and, occasionally, one would break free and spiral down to the dark water. The scene was crisp, invigorating, and he stood for some time taking it in, watching some people on the stone benches down at the river level.

Closest was an old woman wearing jeans and a long black coat with an upturned collar so that only the top half of her face, crowned by a nest of wavy grey hair, was visible. She sat straight and still, gloved hands clenched between her knees, staring pensively across the water. Perhaps her husband just passed away, imagined Michael, and here she was a widow, unexpectedly alone in a suddenly-lonely world.

Two young lovers a hundred yards upriver offered a stark contrast. The girl was sitting on the boy's lap. Their foreheads were touching and they were holding hands. All eyes and smiles, thought Michael. Where was that expression from? They radiated the passion of youth just entering the mainstream of life. Everything important was still ahead. Theirs was a world within a world, all infatuation and flirtation. The guy said something to the girl and she jumped up and broke away, laughing, but he caught her sleeve and pulled her back into him. Hair flying, she tumbled into his lap and they locked in the stillness of a kiss.

Between the old woman and the two young lovers, reflected Michael, lay most of adult life. And where was he on that continuum?

He yawned and looked at his watch. Just short of ten a.m. and, by God, he was tired! Try as he might, he couldn't light that inner spark. How sweet it would be to darken the room and lie down.

He took a last glance around before walking over to a corner café for an omelet and some tea. After the food and drink were done, Michael sat, chin in hand, and gazed moodily at the Parisian landscape.

Melancholy enveloped him like a fog. Partly travel fatigue and the lack of sleep, but mostly, he decided, it was the juxtaposition of the situation with Katherine and the time with Annetine. Their interaction on the plane had had an organic effect on him—her company had changed his chemistry, and he now felt a sense of emptiness at the likelihood of never seeing her again. How odd. He remembered how she had sat on her ankle, leg doubled under her like a child; her bright smile with its dimples; how she had flirtatiously raised the hem of her skirt to show him the stockings; the sparkle in her eyes; her changeable, animated expressions. And then there was Katherine. Thinking about her created a different sense—a sense of loss seasoned with despair.

To hell with them both, he decided. *Enough. A few hours of sleep will restore my equilibrium. Time to move on.* He paid the bill and walked back to the hotel, listening to some early blues on his iPhone. "Nothing Stays the Same Forever" by Percy Mayfield came on, and the sweet old tune with its somber final lyric (*"For man was born to witness wonder, and man was also born to die..."*) paradoxically dispelled Michael's own blues, as music can.

Back at the hotel, Ayman held up the key and said the words Michael was longing to hear: "Monsieur Boylen, your room is ready. Number 30, third flight up those stairs."

Three hours later, Michael awoke, shaved, showered, and called room service for a pot of coffee. It was a few minutes after two. The coffee arrived and he drank the first cup black. It was strong and bitter, and he poured a second.

There was no balcony in his room, so he swung the large window fully open and stood, cup in hand, gazing at the building across the street. *Must be a bakery nearby,* thought Michael as he caught a waft of cinnamon in the air.

The street below was quite narrow, and he felt voyeuristic gazing into the apartment windows barely twenty feet across the way. Many were covered with white gauzy curtains, and many were dark. It was Sunday afternoon after all, a quiet time of the week.

Michael finished his coffee and shut the window. He entertained the thought of Skyping Katherine before heading out somewhere for the afternoon and evening but decided against it. It was still quite early at home and, truthfully, he wasn't ready to deal with her yet. Maybe tomorrow.

Instead, he decided to walk over to the Musée d'Orsay and kill a few hours taking in some art. It was one of his favorite places to visit in Paris and he had a small mission to accomplish that fit the bill. It would clear his mind, and it would be fun. And if he got sidetracked by something else, then so be it.

11. TALIA

Annetine met Talia—Natalia Amati—back in May, during her first few weeks in Paris. She'd rented a two bedroom apartment and decided to find a roommate for company and to share the cost. Initially, Talia said that her lease had run out and that she needed to sublet for a few months until school started again in the fall. As Annetine found out later, it turned out that the situation was far more complicated as, at that point, Talia was seeking shelter and anonymity, for she was avoiding the eye of the law.

The truth emerged weeks later, after they had become friends. Walking along the washed gravel paths of the Luxembourg Gardens together on a warm spring evening, Talia took Annetine into her confidence and confessed that the police had arrested Tameem, her boyfriend, for his alleged involvement in a terrorist plot a few weeks earlier.

He and his co-conspirators were in prison awaiting trial and the French authorities had no interest in speeding things along. Talia insisted that Tameem was innocent ("it's just anti-Muslim paranoia") but was afraid the authorities could come after her because of their romantic involvement. Luckily, she had been away in Lyon that week visiting a cousin and saw the news of the bust on television.

"You weren't involved, were you?" asked Annetine.

"Certainly not," said Talia.

What Talia didn't tell Annetine was that, a week earlier, Tameem must have sensed something, because he had given her a name and an address—a person to contact in case, as he put it, "things ever go wrong for me."

"Sadek will take care of you," he had said. "He is like a brother to me. If you need anything, go and see him. I've told him about you and he will treat you like a sister. Trust me."

After hearing about the arrest, Talia returned to her apartment, packed her things, and began searching for another place to live, preferably with someone who needed a roommate. That way, her name wouldn't be connected to any lease or address, and she would have effectively disappeared without doing anything illegal. She came across Annetine's ad on the Parisian Craigslist and moved in within a few days.

One evening, after a few weeks passed and all was quiet, Talia summoned up her courage and stopped in to see Sadek.

He offered her some sweet black tea and fresh figs. "I've been waiting for you Talia," he said warmly. "What took you so long, sister?" Sadek promised to take care of her because he loved Tameem and denied knowing anything about the alleged plot.

Over the next few weeks, she returned when she could, and they grew to be friends and then lovers. Talia moved out of Annetine's apartment in August, but the two women still kept in touch.

Born in Oman, Talia emigrated to France ten years earlier at the age of seventeen. She wanted to get away from her parents and their seventh century ways but, as she lived in France and began to understand the European culture, she found that her upbringing was difficult to shed. It wrapped her mind like a cloak, and Talia found herself noticing little things that annoyed her. As the random impressions added together, she became increasingly disillusioned with Western society. At the same time, she could never return home either—compared to the West, the traditionalism and misogynistic aspects of Oman society were too oppressive. But France was a godless, secular culture, and its individualism and selfishness grated on her as well. She constantly felt like an outsider—the immigrant's plight worldwide—suspended between two cultures yet grounded in neither.

Meeting Sadek made all the difference. After talking with him, she felt more in balance, for he was a like-minded spirit and a friend. He was gentle in his ways and, sexually, he was a nimble lover who, as an older man with more experience in life and love, understood the balance of tenderness and dominance that it took to please a woman, or at least please her.

As Talia confided to Annetine one evening, Sadek was amazing because—unlike the French men she had known—he understood the difference between what she wanted and what she needed. He gave, but he also took; and when he took, he took her in a way that made her feel like she had nothing left to give. In those passionate moments, she felt completely free of herself, part of something larger. It was the very essence of Islam—supplication, surrender, becoming one with Him. They would lay together for a long time afterward, until Sadek finally rose to prepare something to eat. They would partake but not speak, relishing the sense of union and common spirit.

As she got to know Sadek better, however, Talia realized that a deep sense of anger and injustice festered behind his tranquil façade.

He would often vent to her about the French. "They hate us Talia," he would say. "They hate all of us, and they want to get rid of us. They lie."

Sadek was bitter at the West in general and toward France in particular. Their prohibition of the hijab, involvement in the wars in Iraq and Afghanistan, in Libya, in Mali, and now against the new Islamic caliphate irked him. Their condescension toward the Muslim community—despite the fact that more Muslims lived in France than in any other country in Europe—triggered his indignation and sense of injustice. Moreover, this had been going on for half a century or more, dating back to the days of de Gaulle and the horrors of the *guerre d'Algérie*.

Talia and Sadek talked about this often in the evenings over tea and halvah, and they grew close in body and spirit. She began to see the world increasingly through his eyes. His vitriol troubled her at first, but it was contagious in its conviction. And so, Talia became complicit not only with Sadek's way of looking at things, but also with his will to vengefulness, with his desire to maim and hurt. Like the sweet odor of the incense he liked to burn (which she could still smell on her clothes days later, when she put them in the wash), Sadek's malice seeped into her spirit and began to corrode her very core.

12. THE DOPPLEGÄNGER

Rue Beautreillis ran toward the Seine from Rue St. Antoine, one of the busier streets in Paris. Without a key, Michael couldn't do much other than gaze at the façade of his soon-to-be apartment. Number 17/19 was like most of the other buildings on the narrow street, its classic limestone front faced with black iron flower boxes filled with geraniums. The entrance was through a large arched door: green and wooden and locked. He walked across the street and stood quietly for a few minutes.

The neighborhood had a nice feel to it, and it crossed his mind that one of old Paris' charms was how beautifully scaled it was to the human dimension. The buildings were a uniform five story height, very different from cities like New York, where the skyscrapers dwarfed and belittled. This street—in fact, the whole area—felt quiet and peaceful.

In preparation for his trip, Michael had read a book of essays on French culture by Julian Barnes, an English writer he liked. One piece was devoted to Gustave Courbet, a nineteenth-century painter known for his talent, but also for his flamboyance and arrogance. Barnes made a point of commenting on a particular painting that had, until recently, been privately owned. Titled *The Origin of the*

World (L'Origine du Monde), it depicted a female nude reclining on a bed, and was currently on display at the Musée d'Orsay, located on the left bank across from the Louvre.

According to Barnes, even in this age of ubiquitous digital imagery and pornography, the 150-year-old painting was shockingly explicit. The woman's naked belly and breasts occupied most of the canvas, and her most private part was front and center. Courbet had drawn it from a perspective focused on the torso, without showing the head or face. The combination of the in-your-face quality and anonymity was riveting and disturbing at one and the same time. The model, Barnes wrote, had been a lover of both Courbet and James Whistler, an American contemporary, and the painting attracted its share of attention over the years as it was so flagrant. John Updike had even written a poem about it! This intrigued Michael, and he made a mental note to see it firsthand, and consciously resisted the temptation to look it up online to preserve the element of surprise. Tracking it down would be the goal for this afternoon.

Michael stopped to have some coffee and a *Parisien*—a ham and cheese sandwich made with butter instead of mayonnaise, as is the French way, before walking the two miles to the museum along the quay that paralleled the river. The afternoon sun cast the city in a warm yellow light.

Inside the museum, he asked the woman at the information booth about the painting. She marked its location on the English version of the guide, and pushed it back his way.

"Is it popular?" asked Michael.

"Sometimes," she said inexplicably.

Rejuvenated by the nap and coffee, Michael felt his normal energy returning. He paused to admire the interior of the museum. The arched, translucent ceiling a hundred feet above him diffused the afternoon light and created a sense of space that was magnified by the silence.

He wandered unhurriedly into the main hall, savoring the hushed ambience, and lingered by a sculpture by Clésinger, remembering it from an earlier visit. Titled *Woman Bitten by a Serpent,* it was made from a mold of the artist's mistress. With the small snake wrapped around her wrist, it was life-sized, and the detailed eye of the sculptor even captured the cellulite on the back of her thighs. How odd, thought Michael, for one artist to be so realistic—almost photographic—in his rendition, while more modern artists like Picasso or Merello chose to depict the human form in an abstract, almost unrecognizable way. He glanced around to make sure no one was watching and, ignoring the sign that prohibited touching, ran his hand over the white polished marble—smooth and cool—before continuing on.

The Courbet was in a side gallery, and it was as brash and audacious as Barnes had described it. Michael stood in front of it for a few minutes before sitting down on a bench near the back of the room where he could see the entrance to the room. It would be fun to watch people have their first look at the painting, as it was certain to provoke. He remembered reading about a recent flurry of activity on Facebook in response to their disabling some French artist's page on which he had posted the Courbet painting as part of his profile.

Two teenage girls holding hands drifted in, saw the painting and—clearly taken aback—blushed and scurried away. Seconds later, he heard the squeal of giggles from the main hall.

In contrast, a thin, pedantic-looking young man with a shaved head, combat boots and dark clothes set off by a maroon scarf wrapped around his neck (*art student?* wondered Michael) came in and stood for the longest time perfectly still, head inclined to one side, examining the painting. After a few minutes, he pulled a small Moleskine notebook out of his pocket and scribbled something before slowly walking away. His mouth was pursed and his expression was serious, preoccupied.

That synergistic power of art and sex, thought Michael—Courbet's painting still goaded, embarrassed and surprised, just as it had a century ago.

He meandered around for another hour looking at the collection of Impressionists, then bought a book on Courbet in the museum store and went up to the restaurant for some coffee.

The gilded, high-ceilinged room was crowded with people of all ages and resonant with conversation. He ordered *Le café gourmand* and settled back to wait for the *"espresso served with delicacies,"* as it was enticingly described in the menu, to arrive.

Suddenly, he gave a start and sat straight up. It couldn't be! She had just come into the restaurant and was looking around for a place to sit down. It was Annetine, and she was alone. He jumped up and waved to her, trying to catch her eye. She looked directly at him, expressionless, and stood, waiting for the hostess who came and guided her in the other direction. Puzzled, Michael watched as she sat down with her back to him and began looking over the menu. Michael's heart was beating faster than it should have been as he walked over to her table.

"Annetine?"

The woman glanced up with a surprised expression. Surely it was her. A spitting image, and yet not quite. Something was different. It was the eyes—they were blue, not the hazel he remembered.

She picked up a pair of glasses from the table and put them on, peering at him more closely.

"*Pardon?*" she asked.

Thrown off by the uncanny resemblance, Michael said— "*Excuse-moi madame.* I thought I recognized you. I thought you were someone..."

His voice trailed off as his mind wrestled with conflicted impressions. She looked exactly like Annetine. Her hair was the same color and about the right length, although it was now pulled back into a ponytail. But the eyes were different, and the glasses weakened the resemblance further.

The woman gave him a weak smile, but it was too reserved to tell whether she also had dimples.

"*Pardon monsieur,*" she said, "I do not believe that we have meeted before."

Her voice was heavily accented.

Michael was still not convinced, although reason suggested otherwise—why would Annetine pretend to not know him? No—it wasn't, it couldn't be her. He ran his fingers through his hair, confused by the odd coincidence.

"I'm sorry too, pardon me" he mumbled. "You look exactly like a friend of mine."

The woman's eyebrows raised. She glanced past him toward the entrance, as if she was looking for someone.

"Je ne sais pas, monsieur," she said. Her face lit up. "Ah, here is arriving my friend," she said, and waved at a man who had just come into the restaurant.

There was nothing more to say, so Michael flashed his palms at her and backed away from the table. *Damn it,* he thought. *Except for the eyes, a dead ringer! What in the hell?*

Back at his table, he leafed absentmindedly through the art book, periodically glancing at the back of the woman's head and wondering how he could have been so mistaken.

13. MONDAY, MONDAY

The following evening, Michael walked over to Île St.-Louis. The air was chilly and it started to drizzle. He found a corner *brasserie* fronted with small tables and chairs neatly arranged under a red awning. After scanning the beer taps, he ordered a Leffe blonde.

"Small, medium or grande?" asked the barman, who was wearing a black vest over a white shirt with a black tie—the standard uniform of a Parisian bartender. The outfit was completed by the white apron beneath.

"Grande" answered Michael without hesitation. There was plenty to think about, as it had been an interesting first day on the job.

"May I sit outside?"

"*Oui monsieur,*" said the waiter. "I will bring to you. Sit anywhere you wish."

Michael made his way outside and sat down on one of the cane wooden chairs that are *de rigueur* outdoor furniture for Parisian *brasseries*. The street was empty and he zipped up his jacket to keep out the damp cold.

The beer came and, as the waiter carefully set it on the table, Michael's face took on an amused expression. He had forgotten that 'grande' in Paris means LARGE—a full liter, as evidenced by the thin black 1.0 L line near the top of the glass that contrasted with the creamy head of foam.

He picked the beer up carefully and took a sip. Cool but not cold, and sweet as Belgian beers tend to be, it was perfect. *Why is it that the beer always tastes better in Europe?* he wondered. Michael took another sip before setting the glass on the table. It was rickety and a little beer splashed out, so he made a wedge out of the coaster and slipped it under the base before straightening his legs and leaning back.

It was the time of day when evening tilts to night. The Pont St-Louis arched across the Seine to his right under a slate grey sky. Beyond was the Notre Dame Cathedral, towers shrouded in fog and flying buttresses gothic and sinister in the darkening air. The rain picked up and he became aware of its syncopated patter on the stone pavement below and the awning above. An ambulance or police siren hee-hawed in the distance. Everyday sounds of the city but, for Michael, it was all new. This was a pleasant pause in what had been a fast-paced day and exactly the kind of moment he longed for—private, anonymous and free.

The Aerotel office was four metro stops away from the hotel, not far from the George V metro station, but this morning he'd decided to walk to work to see more of the city, and to gauge how long it would take on foot. Forty minutes later, he arrived at the nondescript building that housed the company offices, and found his way to Alain Durst. Durst was a short, heavy man with a jovial pink face, close-cropped grey hair, and small blue eyes lined with the crow's feet of many smiles. His benevolent appearance was disarming, as he was considered to be one of the sharpest minds in the business and a tough taskmaster with little or no tolerance for incompetents.

Michael's assignment was to secure their network against data exfiltration, the subtle process that hacker malware was often programmed to do. The computers were already set up and linked, and it was his job to test and authorize the network. During the next few weeks, he would probe and re-probe its vulnerabilities by simulating various types of intrusions while reprogramming the software for better malware detection and tracking.

Durst showed Michael to his office—a small room with a double window overlooking the street. The two men went over their goals for the next few weeks and he was given a tour of the facility, which consisted of offices on the first floor and a cavernous laboratory space in the basement, where the mini-drone prototypes were assembled and tested. The overall impression was one of efficiency and professionalism, and Michael realized that it would be fun to be part of a new team for a few weeks, to get to know the personalities and backgrounds.

Only one person—a fellow named Adrian Khost—struck him as odd. Hairless and thin, with a pale, hawk-like face and large brown eyes, his appearance suggested a large, plucked bird. The physical impression was fortified by the quick, jerky movements of his head. *Creepy* was Michael's first impression. Khost initially averted his glance from Michael when Durst introduced him and mumbled something about it being a pleasure when it clearly was not. His handshake was bony and limp; it was like squeezing a bag of pencils.

It didn't help that Khost was blatantly unattractive, with several large black moles on his cheeks and forehead and a particularly unsightly one on the tip of his narrow nose. Michael consciously decided to reserve judging the man. The ugly duckling in childhood, he thought, teased mercilessly by other kids—there were surely some serious chips on that shoulder. Was the resentment he picked up on directed at him, or just the man's normal demeanor? He tried to engage Khost in a bit of small talk. After receiving curt, monosyllabic answers, however, he soon gave up and followed Alain Durst back upstairs.

"Don't worry about him," said Durst, picking up on Michael's vibe. "Khost is a little different, but he's okay. Not a bad guy once you get to know him. By the way," said Durst, changing the subject abruptly, "where'd you end up living?"

Michael told him. Durst leaned back and put his hands behind his head. "Beau-treil-lis," he said slowly, enunciating each syllable. "Beautreillis. Where do I know that name from?" He scratched his temple.

"Wait!" His eyes lit up. "I've got it," he said. "Isn't that the street that Jim Morrison lived on when he was in Paris? If fact, I think he died there. I'm not sure of the number, but you could surely find out. Is it a big street?"

"Not at all. Quite small," said Michael. "two blocks at most. That's interesting about Morrison," he said, intrigued by the coincidence. "I'll check it out."

"How long will this project take?" asked Durst, as their conversation returned to the business at hand.

They went over the objectives, and Durst took him to lunch at a small restaurant a few doors down from the office where they had some grilled fish with rice and a glass of white wine. It all felt very civilized to Michael, who usually had a sandwich in the office, or skipped lunch entirely in favor of a mid-day run.

He spent the rest of the afternoon setting up his workstation, updating files, and linking into the intra-office network.

Just before leaving, he remembered the conversation with Durst and Googled *Jim Morrison Beautreillis*. Durst was correct. Morrison had lived next door in Number 17 with Pamela Courson, his common-law wife. Michael wasn't a diehard Doors fan, although he did like the masculine energy of their music and had included a few of their songs in his playlists.

And now, here he was on the Île-St. Louis enjoying the beer on a moody, rainy evening. He would find a place to have dinner before going back to the hotel and packing. Tomorrow, he would check out, put in a full day at work and meet the landlord at six o'clock to pick up his key and move into the furnished apartment that would be his home away from home for the foreseeable future.

He thought about Skyping Katherine, but decided to hold off until tomorrow night, after he was in the apartment. Michael's sense of loneliness and isolation had crested last night and was now abating.

The rain eased, then picked up again. Realizing the weather wasn't about to cooperate, he swallowed the last of the beer, left some Euros on the table and, jacket pulled over his head, headed down Rue St.-Louis in search of a place to eat.

14. TROUBLE IN MIND

Apartment 3C was small but comfortably furnished, with high ceilings and wide double windows facing a small courtyard. During the next few evenings, Michael settled in and explored the neighborhood on foot.

Heading north, Beautreillis ran into Rue St. Antoine, a few blocks from the Bastille circle and Metro. With its fresh vegetable markets, banks, cafes, and stores, it had most everything he would need on a daily basis. To the south, the quiet neighborhood led to the river and, if one so wished, across to the Ile St. Louis and, beyond, to the myriad offerings of the Left Bank.

Michael also worked on developing a routine to anchor his new world. He woke at six and went for a five mile run in the pre-dawn darkness. This self-imposed discipline served as a springboard to the rest of the day.

To his surprise, Paris was a runner's delight. The path along the Seine and the many grand parks and gardens such as Tuileries and Luxembourg provided a fine combination of urban scenery and a firm, level surface to tread on. After, he would stretch and do fifty push-ups and a hundred sit-ups in the living room before showering and dressing. A pastry and a double espresso at one of the cafes on St.-Antoine and a walk to the Bastille Metro completed the morning pre-work ritual.

He returned to the apartment around six, walking home from work if the weather was pleasant. He took a cab one day and swore to never do it again, as it took close to an hour, mostly spent stalled in rush hour traffic, and it cost a bundle.

Once home, he would make a drink—vodka and soda with a twist of lemon—and unwind for an hour by listening to some music while catching up on the daily news via the *New York Times* and *Wall Street Journal* websites.

He would then prepare a simple dinner or, more often than not, go out for a bite followed by a walk, enjoying the storefronts and vitrines that twinkled with the holiday decorations. After, he would settle into the comfortable overstuffed chair in the corner of the living room with a cup of tea, read for an hour, and go to bed around midnight.

He and Katherine fell into a pattern of Skyping almost every day at first, as there was much to share. Every day still felt new and the impressions were fresh and varied. Michael did most of the talking and they avoided anything serious, focusing instead on establishing and maintaining a pleasant rapport.

Busy at work, and having created a daily routine, Michael found the time going by quickly. As the first week passed into the second, their Skyping sessions grew further apart, but they still talked every second or third day.

Sunday afternoon, exactly two weeks after arriving in Paris, Michael was in the apartment working on his laptop when he saw that Katherine was online. He video Skyped her and, after six or seven rings, was about to disconnect when she answered, sounding a little out of breath. Her hair was tousled and she had her bathrobe on. Had he awakened her, he wondered? After all, it was barely 9 a.m. back home. The *online* icon only meant the computer was on, not necessarily the person.

"I thought we were going to connect later," said Katherine, with a note of reproof.

"I know," he said, "but I saw you were online and figured I'd break the pattern and surprise you. A little spontaneity never hurts, you know..."

Katherine looked back at him absentmindedly, not saying anything in return, and Michael regretted the old dig as soon as he'd uttered it.

"I was sitting here by myself, thinking of you." He nodded toward the window. "It's cold and wet outside. Would be a nice afternoon to while away in bed," he said, adding "I miss you."

Katherine gave him a wan smile but continued to appear distracted. She was fussing with the belt of her robe beneath the table. Annoyed, Michael frowned and looked silently back at her image on the small screen.

"Don't take this the wrong way Michael," said Katherine, "but, to tell you the truth, I've been so busy I haven't had time to miss you. Work is killing me. How are things in Paris?"

"OK," he said. "Just catching up on some work here in the apartment. Nothing much doing."

"What are you working on?" she asked.

"Trying to write some new software," he said rather inanely, knowing Katherine didn't much care about his work. She was a low-tech person who used computers as tools to get the job done. As long as they worked, she had no interest in understanding how.

"How are the people you work with?" asked Katherine.

"They're okay," said Michael, "except for one guy who is a little odd."

"Oh?" Katherine's interest perked up.

"He's one of these people with no apparent social graces. Name is Adrian Khost. Even the name is kind of ugly—sounds like you're clearing your throat when you say it! Khost," said Michael, and again more throatily—"Khost." He made a face. "Looks like a plucked chicken with a face full of moles. Kind of creepy."

"What makes him creepy?" said Katherine.

Michael shrugged. "I don't know, he just is. At the office, he's the pebble in my shoe."

A wave of impatience swept over him. Katherine would likely never meet Khost, why did it matter?

"What about you?" he asked. "How are things at home?"

"Fine," she said, her voice flat. "Not much going on outside of work. It's gotten colder these last few days and they're predicting our first snow tonight. Four to six. How's the weather in Paris?"

"Cool and rainy," said Michael. Clearly, his earlier comment hadn't registered. "How cold is it back home?"

Their conversation was like a dance of two marionettes—predictable and wooden. *Shouldn't we be talking about something that means something?* thought Michael, as resentment built up inside him. Katherine's joyless initial response was still bugging him. Why were they talking about the weather instead of about *them?*

They continued to chat for another few minutes but without rhythm or energy. The conversation was adrift and the pauses began to grow longer and more awkward. Katherine yawned and looked at the clock again, and Michael grew sullen. Her heart isn't into this, he realized.

"I'm sorry, Michael," said Katherine. "I'm not much fun to talk to this morning, am I? My head hurts and I don't feel good today. I was in bed when you called."

"I'm sorry too, honey," he said, "but I understand. Are you coming over for the holidays? It would be great to see you."

"I hope so," she said, although the shake of her head suggested otherwise. "Work's been a grind lately, and Joanne is pressuring me on a case that's hitting the court next Friday. I worry it could carry into the holidays. I told her I had the flights booked and that they're not refundable, but she's not making it easy for me." Katherine gave him a weary look. "I don't know Michael. Also, I'm still…" Her voice trailed off, leaving the sentence unfinished.

Michael didn't notice, however, as he was blinded by a flash of irritation at her possibly cancelling the trip because of work. Work, of all things. Come on! Katherine was a tax lawyer and occasionally did have to testify in individual cases. He knew that. But this would be the week before Christmas and, considering their current predicament… More to the point, he wondered, where the hell was she at? Their relationship was not a subject of discussion, something they both avoided for whatever reason. In his mind, it would all be better addressed by being together again face-to-face, but this created a void of sorts here in the now.

"All right," he said with forced patience. "Let's see how things evolve. I certainly get the pressures of work, but it's not a reason to beg out. Especially now."

He saw Katherine's lips compress and she drew her head back an inch. She was looking at his image on her screen instead of the webcam, and the oblique perspective—eyes focused elsewhere, features sharpened by the angle—imparted an impersonal, yet telling quality to the exchange.

"I'm not happy about it either," said Katherine slowly, "and I'm not begging out of anything. I'm just sharing. Maybe I can re-book my flight, delay it by a few days and extend it at the other end. Let me see how things look tomorrow. Please don't lean on me Michael. I already feel like I'm under a lot of pressure. Try to understand for a change."

"I don't mean to lean on you," he said grudgingly, "but being together for the holidays would be wonderful. It's important, at least to me..."

"Look, I'll do my best," said Katherine in a controlled tone. Now *she* was annoyed. He knew her so well.

Katherine glanced away, then back at the cam.

Michael picked up on the signal.

"OK," he said, "enough for now. Why don't we Skype Tuesday night?"

"I can't," said Katherine, "we have our Christmas party at The Manor. How about tomorrow or Wednesday?"

"All right," said Michael. "I'll call you Wednesday around midnight—six p.m. your time. Will you be home?" He suddenly wanted to be done with the conversation, to be alone again. This was exasperating.

Katherine smiled. "I'll do my best," she said again. "I know it's pretty late for you."

"No, not a problem," he said.

His parting *love you* sounded like a throwaway, an afterthought.

"You too," said Katherine, and disappeared.

Michael let his breath out in a soft hiss.

He sat and stared at their vacation photo on the desktop screen for some time before keying off the computer.

With the soft whir of the laptop's cooling fan extinguished, the room went silent. Michael got to his feet and stood by the window, looking across the small courtyard. It was still overcast, but at least the rain had stopped.

His mind kept returning to their conversation—her distractedness, the carelessly-belted, half-open robe, the glances at the clock, the continued uncertainty about whether she would be able to come to France for the holidays—and felt a hollowness in his heart. Something was missing, which was not surprising given their situation and the distance, but it still dragged on him. It was subtle, but there was a change in Katherine's demeanor toward him, and it took him a minute to put his finger on it. Yes, he decided, that was it: she was a touch indifferent. Hadn't someone once said that the opposite of love wasn't hate, it was indifference?

Remembering his conversation with Durst, Michael got up and put on "Shaman's Blues", by the Doors. The carnivalesque organ riffs fit his mood perfectly. One of the surprises in this apartment was the Bose stereo, which had remarkable fidelity for its compact size, and bluetooth. He picked up his phone and turned up the volume to max before wandering back to the window.

Energized by the music, he decided to go out for a long walk and then get a little buzzed. There was bound to be live music somewhere in Paris, even on a Sunday night. Maybe some jazz in one of the clubs near Sébastopol?

15. GERVAISE

Michael pulled on his jacket and headed toward the river. There was a damp, coastal chill in the air, and he regretted not taking a scarf.

On his right was a small artist's studio. He peered in from the street and saw that it was full of copper sculptures, along with some paintings. Surprisingly, he had never noticed it before.

He pushed open the door and heard a buzzer sound somewhere out back. A woman came out through a bead-curtained door. She was tall and quite thin and wore a green paint-smeared sweatshirt over black jeans.

"*Bonjour, Monsieur,*" she said. "*Puis-je vous aider?*"

"*Oui, merci,*" said Michael. "*Parlez-vous anglais?*"

"Yes," she said, and held up her hand with a small space between thumb and forefinger. "A little. I spent a year in the States a few years ago at an artist's colony in Arizona."

She looked seventy, and one could see that she was once quite beautiful. In fact, she still was. Her large dark eyes were very alive, and her brown and grey hair was pulled back into a thick ponytail. Loose-limbed and upright, her carriage was that of a much younger woman. People often age themselves prematurely by adopting poor posture, thought Michael. Unlike all the diets, surgeries, and creams, not stooping was an easy fix for the most part, and this woman's youthful stance made her seem all the more attractive.

He smiled. "Arizona is a beautiful state. I'm from America as well, as you may have guessed. Renting an apartment up the street—number 19." He put out his hand. "Michael Boylen."

"Gervaise Geoffrion" she said, and gave his hand a gentle squeeze. "May I help you?"

"If you don't mind my asking, have you been here long?" said Michael.

"This was my mother's studio originally," she said. "I started working here after college. Must have been 1968 or 1969. I don't live here anymore though. My daughter runs the studio now. I live in Rouen."

"Ah yes," said Michael with a grin. "Joan of Arc country." Having just heard the Doors, an idea flashed in his mind.

"My boss tells me that Jim Morrison lived on this street. Is that so?"

"He did," said Gervaise. "He is our most famous resident. As you may know, he died here in '71," she said. "In number 17."

"I'm not a big Doors fan, but I do like history and I love music," said Michael. "I don't suppose you knew him, being here and all?" he asked.

"No," she said "I can't say I knew him. But I did meet him once, and I was here the day he died." Gervaise smiled. "Would you like a cup of tea?"

"Love it," said Michael with genuine enthusiasm. "I'm not pulling you away from anything, am I?"

"Not at all." She gestured at the curtained opening near the back wall. "There's a small kitchen back there and we can sit down. I just put on a pot of water before you came in."

Michael bent his head as he passed through the bead curtains and pulled a chair up to the small Formica table. Gervaise set two ceramic cups on the table and brought over an electric pot with water.

"Green or black?"

"Black," said Michael.

The tea was too hot to drink, so he stirred in some sugar and asked her to share whatever she remembered. The air was warm and smelled faintly of paint and old wood.

"Morrison and I were close in age," she said, "so I noticed him walking by, usually around lunchtime. He stopped in one day. That was the only time we met. Very soft spoken and polite. He introduced himself as Jim and asked me my name. I assumed he was an American graduate student here for a semester. That was very common those days—lots of students in the area." She took a sip of tea, remembering.

"He always carried this white plastic bag as he walked past my studio, which was odd, as most students carried musette bags over their shoulders. I asked him what was in the bag. 'Oh,' he said with a wink, 'every day's different. A notebook to scribble in. A book. Sometimes an apple or a pint of Irish whiskey.'

"I remember we laughed at that unlikely combination and I remember that wink. He was, as we say, *charmant*. When I asked him what he did, he said he was a musician and lived in California, but was taking a break and trying to do some writing here in Paris."

"So he seemed pretty ordinary then?" asked Michael, a little disappointed. He was hoping for something distinctive, unique.

"I suppose," she said. "I mean, we only talked for a few minutes and that was forty five years ago. But after that day, whenever he walked by my studio, he would knock on the window and wave in passing, though he never stopped in again."

"And you were here when he died?" asked Michael, probing.

"Yes," said Gervaise. "I remember that day well. Hot, humid, early July. Paris can get pretty unbearable that time of year. It was the kind of day when it seems like there's no air, just fumes. The police came down from St.-Antoine. Lots of disturbance. We didn't know what had happened, but I remember watching the body bag being loaded into a black station wagon, and a few young people standing around crying. It was all very sad, you know, especially on a midsummer morning."

Michael was enjoying watching the woman's face go through a range of expressions as she recalled the story.

"You know, Michael," said Gervaise as if they were old friends, "the thing was that I had no idea that it was him who had died. It was only later, when the news came out and I hadn't seen him walking by for a week or so, that I put two and two together. But I'll always remember the conversation we had here in the studio, and his 'apple and a pint' comment. It was so honest. Of course, in those days, rock stars didn't have the cache they now have. Time lends aura, if you know what I mean. Back then, there was no aura. No myth."

"Have you seen the Oliver Stone movie?" asked Michael.

She nodded. "Yes, I had to, didn't I? It seemed very..." she hesitated, not sure if she was overstepping.

Michael raised his eyebrows.

"Please don't be insulted, but very *Américain* if you know what I mean," said Gervaise. "So—how you say, *boom boom*? Too much."

Her face brightened. "You might find this interesting. I had a chance to go up to that apartment a few weeks after he died. A friend of mine lived in the building and he got the landlord to let us in. At that point, we were all starting to resent Morrison for all the..."—the corners of her mouth curled down in distaste—"...the degenerates he attracted. People sitting on the curb outside the building, drinking cheap beer. Wine. Hard liquor. Broken bottles. Sometimes a fight. My dog cut her paw on a piece of glass once. I was furious."

She paused. "I hear it's still much the same at his grave these days. Anyway, my friend and I went in and it was a nice enough apartment, mind you. High ceilings, hardwood floors, very typical of this area. But they showed this old, claw-footed tub in that movie, shafts of light streaming through the window. Remember? Looked like something from Napoleon's day! The bathroom in Morrison's apartment was actually small and modern. The tub was your average tub—white, porcelain, not very big. Absolutely nothing special about it. I guess the director had to use his artistic license, or the ending would have seemed pretty anticlimactic."

"I remember the scene well," said Michael—"The stand-alone tub, the long matted hair hanging over the edge, the shafts of light from some unseen window. It was all very melodramatic. And," he felt the laughter rising in his chest "what about that Indian prancing around in the background?" Michael slapped his forehead in sudden glee. "*Ayee!*" he exclaimed. "What the…"

"Ooh, yes, yes, the Indian," exclaimed Gervaise, infected with the humor as well. "*Merci!* I have forgot! The Indian! So serious, no! And naked no less!"

"I can imagine the actor now, at some pretentious cocktail party in New York. 'Oh yes', he says – 'I'm an actor. Was King Lear on Broadway. Been in several major films. Also, I played the Indian in the Stone Doors movie. A most demanding role!' " guffawed Michael, embarrassed at his sudden silliness but unable to stem the mirth.

But then Gervaise began to laugh as well and they both doubled over. Tears streamed from Michael's eyes and he clenched his ribs as they began to hurt, but there was no stopping the giggles. Their laughter renewed every time they made eye contact but eventually crested and subsided into gasps and then sighs.

"Wow," said Michael, "Haven't had a laugh like that in years. Forgive me."

"Me too," said Gervaise, wiping her eyes. "but it is good to laugh, no?"

Michael's thoughts returned to her words about the tub. "I hadn't realized that the reality was so very different, so ordinary," he said finally. "Somehow, I figured it was a pretty fancy place, but it sounds like my bathroom here in number 19."

Gervaise nodded. "Exactly. Fluorescent light over the sink, not an iota of charm. One of those cast plastic units. Although," she added, "the word around here is that Morrison overdosed in some club and was already dead when they brought him back to our little Beautreillis."

"Well, sad, but *c'est la vie*," said Michael.

"Yes, *c'est la vie*," seconded Gervaise. An amused expression appeared on her face and she took his arm. "Do you recognize this?" This time, she sang '*la* vie' in a downward, minor note. "The way you said it, it made me think of the song."

Seeing Michael's puzzled expression, she said – "Oh, you may not know. It's from "Orly" by Jacques Brel, one of our favorite *chanteurs*. He died a few years after Morrison. You ought to look him up, as I you bear a slight resemblance to him. Maybe it is your eyes."

"It sounds rather sad," said Michael, picking up on the minor note. "Is that it, the whole line, just 'life'?"

"No," said Gervaise. "It's"—and she sang it beautifully—'*la vie ne fait pas de cadeau*'."

Michael frowned, trying to translate the words. He didn't quite get it. "Life is not giving a gift?"

"Not quite," said Gervaise. "Literally, it's more like life does not make us gifts. In other words, life has no mercy."

16. BIT O 'TUDE

Their conversation began to meander as they continued talking about music and art, the neighborhood, and Paris in general. Gervaise asked Michael why he was here and he simply said "work." When the talk finally turned to the weather, he decided it was time to move on. Gervaise walked him to the door and, after he thanked her for the tea, she gave him a brief hug. It was his first human touch in two weeks, and Michael enjoyed its simple warmth.

He walked up past the Louvre through Tuileries, then crossed the river via the wide Pont de la Concorde, and doubled back onto the Boulevard Saint-Germain, stopping at a few street-side bars first for coffee, then beer.

An English couple sat down next to him in one of the bars and the woman reminded him of Katherine. The man and woman seemed very much in love, which put Michael into a funk as it reminded him of his own situation. He gulped down the beer and moved on.

Around nightfall, he wandered into the orange awning-fronted Brasserie Lipp. During the week, it was a bustling place where reporters and government workers congregated, but it was fairly quiet now with only a handful of customers scattered throughout the large dining room. The interior was classically French with mirrored walls, chandeliers, and orderly rows of white-clothed tables.

The waiter was a burly man with a shaved head and a heavy gold chain around his neck. He looked like a wrestler and his manner dripped with condescension.

Michael ordered and watched the waiter's round back and shaved head as he walked over to the bar. The bartender threw him a glance as he filled a glass with beer and set it on the bar. Michael sat gloomily, watching the waiter's reflection in the panel of mirrors that ran the length of the place. The man was taking his time, talking to the bartender.

Leaving the beer on the bar, he then sauntered off to serve some other customers. Five minutes passed, then ten. When he came back in, Michael caught his eye and nodded at the bar, annoyed. The man looked back at him with just the hint of a smile, then wandered outside to the heated patio where a couple had just been seated.

Michael got up, fetched his beer from the bar, and returned to his table.

The waiter came over with a menu and placed it on the table in front of Michael with exaggerated care. He then stood next to Michael's chair, hovering over him.

"I am happy to bring you the drinks *monsieur*," he said with a touch of sarcasm. "They pay me to do it. Do you wish for anything to eat?"

Ignoring him, Michael opened the menu and looked it over. The seconds ticked by and the waiter began shifting his weight from foot to foot. Michael took a perverse enjoyment in taking his time. Eventually, he ordered some duck pâté with sauerkraut, one of Lipp's staples.

"That is all?" asked the waiter disapprovingly. "Only two appetizers? Usually, we seat people here for dinner. If you just wanted a drink, you should sit out there," said the waiter, gesturing to the patio.

"*Oui, merci beaucoups*" said Michael, smiling up at the man as he handed the waiter the menu without looking at him. *Fuck you pal*, he thought, *and your attitude too*. He sure as hell wasn't moving and, if this jerk insisted on it, he would just continue walking right out to the street.

The waiter picked up the menu, tucked it under his arm, lingered for a moment, then shuffled off. Another American bunghole, he thought. Well, two could play this game. He would go take a piss, then have a smoke out back before putting in this guy's order.

Michael wouldn't have much cared, as he wasn't the least bit hungry. *Santé, Sláinte*, Cheers! Time to drink. He took a swig of the beer and pushed the chair away from the table so he could stretch his legs.

It was dark outside now and the surface of the boulevard glistened in the glare of the streetlights. The drizzle must have started up again. Perfect; he would ask the man to call him a cab just to irritate him a bit more. *Servez-moi garçon*!

The waiter eventually brought him a second beer and suddenly this petty roostering seemed very silly.

Michael's thoughts drifted back to Katherine.

They had stayed together through college, seeing each other as best they could, despite his being in Colgate in upstate New York while she was at Northeastern in Boston. Although they weren't exclusive, their sexual experiences were fairly limited, and they got married the summer after graduation.

His sexual inexperience was something that bothered Michael occasionally. He and Chris were similar in that regard, both having gotten married fresh out of college. When they went out for a few beers, inevitably one or the other would bring up the subject of women as a manifestation of some vague longing. Michael understood that that type of pensiveness was normal, and had accepted it in light of the benefits of a good marriage. But now, with things being as they were, it all came into question again as the thoughts swirled in his mind.

When it comes to a relationship, to a marriage, he wondered, how good is good enough? When it came to one's life, how did one know whether one is truly happy? Happiness was such a relative concept—salted with expectation, peppered with self-delusion.

Or was it?

Michael reverted to his computer training—the inputs, the outputs, the software, the hardware. OK, that didn't work. But what *were* the tangibles? Most people would put children at the top of the list, yet he and Katherine were childless.

Sitting alone in the cafe Lipp, far from home, Michael realized that, for him, this whole kid thing *was* a significant life regret. When he was younger, he wasn't interested in kids—they were too much work, a limitation on freedom, and all that other crap. But in the last decade, visiting friends with kids, he found himself wondering what it would have been like to have had a child of their own, to be a father. Being *daddy* could be very cool. Christmases would be very different. Would they have had a boy or a girl? And if they had a few kids, what would their personalities be like? Would he and Katherine have been more or less happy?

A few years ago, he'd brought up the subject after they'd had a few glasses of wine, looking to flesh out her thinking on the subject, but Katherine grew quiet and the conversation had withered. He remembered feeling frustrated and isolated in its wake. When the subject had come up before, she maintained that having a child would lead to a loss of independence, to drudgery. Katherine took her work seriously, and having a child wasn't a priority. They couldn't afford it. Maybe later. He could hear her voice saying these things in its dismissive way, and it now chilled him. Would their current dilemma even have even occurred, he wondered, if they'd had a child?

Katherine acquiesced eventually, as her biological clock ticked its way into the late thirties, and it certainly wasn't as if they hadn't tried, at least in the last few years. The doctor's advice had been to keep trying, and they had, but they had nothing to show for it. And then Katherine got pregnant and chose to have an abortion. He winced at the thought.

Katherine's personality, decided Michael, was typified by today's exchange. That undercurrent of coldness, of self-control. The willingness to shut him out and to not work together. Problems had come up for *her*. *She* would deal with it. *She* would see what she could do. And he would be a passive bystander, forced to the sidelines by what? *Kindness and optimism have gotten in my way before*, he thought in a wave of self-recrimination. *They have betrayed me more than once.*

The pâté came and Michael ordered a third beer as his mind ran its ruminative loop and circled back to the question that had plagued him earlier: how does one know whether good is good enough? Every relationship has its blemishes, but when does a blemish become a wart? And how many warts could one, should one, live with?

He remembered a system he and Chris came up with in high school for scoring potential girlfriends. It was based on three major categories—beauty, figure and personality. He smiled at the memory from a quarter of a century ago.

He'd scored Katherine this way: beauty, 7; figure, 8; personality, 6. He wrestled with the 21 out of 30 before deciding that 20 was an acceptable cut-off. Very puerile and very high school, but interesting that he had scored her lowest on personality.

It also occurred to him that, even as a teenager, he'd understood that happiness was a relative quality, and that a relationship (and one's perception of it) was one of the few entirely subjective things in life. The *we* was mutable by time and circumstance, by changes within and without. It was continually revisionist; it was Heisenberg's uncertainty principle applied to the human spirit.

Michael's mind continued to meander. Half way through the third beer, another memory came back to him, this one more recent. Chris, who had gotten divorced a few years ago, once told him that, when it came to him and his first wife, it wasn't the big stuff that mattered. It was the everyday, the mundane that unraveled their relationship: the underwear on the bathroom floor, the television turned on too loud, the need to always have the last word.

"Things one hardly notices or ignores in the beginning, when you're high on the infatuation," said

Chris. "But with time, the minor annoyances begin to take on a life of their own. In our case, the thing that drove me crazy was her bringing up something I'd said days or weeks before, something she had been stewing over without letting me know! Shit, man, I was always apologizing for something I couldn't remember saying. She'd go to the store intending to buy bread, milk, and eggs, and come home having forgotten the milk, but she could always remember my *exact* words from a month back. At least that's what she thought! I'd finally had my fill of it, and of her. Looking back, I wonder why I put up with it as long as I did. I should have left ten years earlier because, once I did, it all seemed so clear in the retrospectoscope. I instantly felt free and I haven't looked back since. Ever."

Michael had never forgotten that conversation, and found himself wondering whether this was true for him and Katherine as well. He oscillated between the suspicion that there was something fundamentally wrong with his marriage, his life, and the desire to turn a blind eye, to wish, to will it away. It was only a problem if he made it a problem, but tonight it loomed front and center and it wasn't letting him by. No, in his case, it wasn't the small things at all. At least not from his end.

He signaled the waiter, who was just coming in from the patio, carrying a tray with some empty glasses. Time to find some music to get lost in, he decided, followed by sleep. Sometimes a good night's rest would set everything straight and, if it didn't, then he would deal with it tomorrow.

The waiter brought him the check, put it down on the table without a word and stood patiently at his side. Michael pulled a bunch of Euros out of his pants pocket and, after giving them a quick glance, threw them, still crumpled, on the little tray.

"*Merci*," he said without malice. "*Le pâté était bon.*" He then smiled up at the man and said, without even a trace of sarcasm, *"Bon nuit mon ami."*

17. HUNG AND KHOSTED

Dizzy with hangover on an annoyingly bright Monday morning, Michael overslept. *Fine way to start the week*, he thought, glancing at the clock next to the bed. It was almost 9:30.

The dreamless sleep had been short on restorative power and Michael closed his eyes and lay in bed, connecting the dots from last night. Something was troubling him, but he couldn't quite put his finger on it. He remembered leaving the Lipp and having a hard time flagging a taxi, as it was a slow time of the week for cabbies, and rainy. He'd decided to skip the music in favor of a quiet dinner on Île-St. Louis.

Michael had found a restaurant and ordered a bottle of cabernet franc from Bordeaux, that night's wine special.

Uh oh, he thought, that was it, as pieces of the night drifted back into his mind. His disquiet had to do with the waitress—a stout, pale-faced girl with thin, wispy red hair pulled back into a chignon.

Her name was Chrystelle and she was half his age, but she had warm brown eyes and an engaging manner. When she told him she was majoring in music, Michael easily fell into a conversation with her about the merits of jazz vs. rock. There was no ulterior motive on his part. She was pleasantly self-assured, and he remembered thinking she was an old soul (although this old soul wasn't in the least bit old). And then it was wine and waitress, waitress and wine. Her red hair and fair skin must have tickled his Irish roots.

In the harsh reality of morning, a sobering thought entered Michael's mind. The best definition of middle age, he decided, was when youth becomes an attraction, an entity unto itself. It was that simple.

The memories from last night continued to percolate up as he shaved.

He'd invited her to have a drink with him after she got done and, of course, she refused. Old soul, old fool!

He remembered walking home bareheaded in the freezing rain. Crossing the Pont Marie, buzzed by the drink, he leaned over the rounded stone parapet of the bridge and watched the oil-black current of the Seine beneath. Its ever-changing ripples and eddies were dark and hypnotic. It would be so easy to tumble over into the icy water from this height, to be done with it all. He'd felt tired and empty and sad.

This morning, his face looked bloated in the bathroom mirror, and his blue eyes were watery and bloodshot. The mop of dark brown hair was matted with sleep, and the stubble on his chin was coarse and flecked with grey and white. Middle age indeed. When he turned his head, small brownish specks floated across his vision, and he felt weak and mildly nauseated.

Today will be an uphill trudge, thought Michael. It was all terribly predictable and pathetic. *Stupid bastard, what were you thinking? When are you going to grow up?*

Michael decided he needed some time to recover and called Alain to let him know he would be in around noon.

This would give him a few hours to rehydrate and have some coffee, to take the edge off of the hangover. He considered a run but decided against it and, instead, drank three glasses of tap water, showered, dressed, and headed down to the street.

Sitting on the sidewalk on St. Antoine in the brisk sunshine, sipping a third espresso, Michael's spirits began to revive. The headache had retreated to the back of his head, and the dizziness and nausea were subsiding.

He pulled out his phone to check his email. The Gmail came up and he scanned the messages. Lots of junk, but nothing from Katherine. Delete, delete, delete.

Suddenly, his eyes narrowed.

It was a message from *a.fournier@gmail.com* with 'Bonjour' as a subject. He touched the screen and up it came:

> *Hey Michael, comment ça va? Decided to write and say hello. Nothing much doing—working mostly, but I have thought of you a few times since our flight together. Hope you are well.*
>
> *Fondly,*
> *Annetine*

What the hell? Michael had learned to be careful with emails. From his experience, a quick, reflex reply to anything with an emotional angle was a prescription for regret, so he consciously decided to not reply immediately. Instead, he re-read the note more slowly, noting several things.

First, it was sent last night at 11:27 p.m. Sunday evening was a personal time of week and of day, so this wasn't fired off during the morning cup of coffee or in the midst of other things. No, Annetine must have been thinking of him on her day off, on the weekend. The "decided" and the "few times" further reinforced that this was not a momentary impulse.

He imagined Annetine sitting on her bed in pajamas, perhaps, or a t-shirt, hair hanging straight down, bathed in a pool of incandescent light from a lamp on the night table, those dark-lashed hazel eyes focused on the computer screen, choosing which words to use.

And the "fondly" was gracious, a touch of warmth. The communication itself was an opening, but muted; well nuanced, it didn't oblige a reply.

Michael paid his bill, and set off for the Metro, attaché case in hand and Annetine's message in mind. He got to work a few minutes before noon and went in to see Durst.

"Sorry, Alain, rough night last night," he confessed.

Durst looked at him and smiled. "One man party?"

"Right" said Michael ruefully. "Me, myself and I."

He and Alain were developing a friendship, a confidence, and Michael enjoyed being honest with him.

"We all need a release here and there," said Durst. "From the looks of you, you had a good one last night."

"That obvious?"

"Been there a few times myself." Durst gave him a serious look. "Everything okay?"

Michael nodded. "I suppose. Katherine and I have never been apart this long before and we're hitting some bumps. We mostly Skype, so there's a sense of closeness on the one hand since you can see each other, and detachment on the other because of the distance. I can't decide if I like it yet."

"Believe it or not, I've never tried it myself," said Durst. "Even though we're on the cutting edge of technology professionally, my personal communications are still mostly by phone and email. I've been divorced for a few years and my kids don't much care to Skype with the old man. They're tangled up in their own stuff."

"How old are they?" asked Michael. He realized he didn't know anything about Alain's personal life.

"Anita turned thirty last week, Alex is twenty six." Michael saw some kind of sadness pass across Alain's face. Some pain there, he realized, but it wasn't his business to probe, and this was neither the time nor the place.

"Want to grab a bite somewhere?" said Michael. "My turn to buy."

"Thanks," said Durst. "Actually, I'm up to my eyeballs today. Maybe later in the week?"

"Sure," said Michael. "Just say when."

Michael worked in his office for a while. Feeling stiff, he stretched and decided to take a walk down to the basement to see if Doug, one of the other employees he was getting friendly with, was around. It was almost one o'clock and the lab was empty except for Khost, who was sitting at a bench fiddling with some components.

"Hi Adrian," said Michael, infusing his voice with a cheeriness he didn't feel. "Is Doug around?"

Michael had hardly spoken with Khost since the first day. Since they were alone, this might be a good chance to break the ice.

"Lunch," muttered Khost without looking up.

"When will he be back?" asked Michael, leaning on the bench and peering down at Khost. He stood close to the man, invading his space on purpose.

Khost was holding one of the propulsion modules for the drone, adjusting the alignment of the internal fin unit through a binocular loupe strapped to his head. The tiny motor was a beautiful little thing. Stainless steel, the size of a thimble. Khost set the unit down so it was balanced vertically on the bench and flipped the magnifying glasses up on his forehead, but kept his head down.

"How would I know?" he said curtly. "I'm not his keeper. What do you need?"

"I wanted to ask him a question about the software" said Michael.

Khost swiveled sideways and looked directly at Michael for the first time.

"How are we feeling today?" he asked unexpectedly. The creases in his sallow face deepened, and the moles rearranged themselves into a new constellation. His expression was half-smirk, half-sneer. "Have we recovered from last night?"

"What?" said Michael, taken aback. How had Khost known? Surely, it wasn't something Durst would share. His jaw hardened in response to the directness of the question and to its sarcastic undertone. He stood fast and looked down at Khost, their faces barely a foot apart. Khost held Michael's eyes for a few seconds before lowering his gaze back to the table.

"I was at the restaurant last night," he said matter-of-factly. "You didn't see me because I was in the back, but you were hard to miss. Mister Personality."

"Why didn't you come over and say hello?" said Michael, annoyed and embarrassed at the same time.

"I was with a friend," answered Khost. "And you were working that poor girl pretty hard." He muttered something under his breath that Michael didn't quite catch. It sounded like 'coal.'

Caught off guard, Michael glared at the top of Khost's head. From this angle, the wart on his nose was especially prominent. The snub about the waitress stung. Damn the man! And for Khost, of all people, to see him last night!

"She was pleasant enough and I talked to her," said Michael, trying to keep the defensiveness out of his voice. He gave Khost a self-deprecating smile. "You should have come over and said hello Adrian. I'm alone here in Paris and it would have been nice to have had a drink together."

"You didn't need any more drinks," said Khost. "Look," he said as he gestured at the propulsion unit, "I need to get back to this. I'll let Doug know you were looking for him." He flipped down the loupe and bent down over the table. Conversation over.

Michael stood for a few moments, thinking. This guy was something else and, for whatever reason, he seemed to have it out for him.

"Thanks Adrian," he said. "A little personality isn't necessarily a bad thing. I highly recommend it. Sorry to disturb you."

Khost grunted and, not surprisingly, didn't look up.

Later in the afternoon, Michael went back down to the basement and met with Doug. Khost was bent over his bench, as before, and paid him no heed. When they were done, Michael walked back to his office and saw Durst at his desk, reading something. He knocked on the open door.

"Alain, can I ask you a question?"

"Sure, what's up?"

Michael stepped into the office and shut the door behind him.

"What's your take on Khost?" he asked.

Durst leaned back in his chair, looking at Michael for a second before replying. "Guess I think of him as a genius oddball. Why, d'you two have a run-in?"

"Not really," said Michael. "He just seems kind of weird. I get the sense he doesn't like me very much. Is he married?"

"Oh yeah," said Durst. "Four little kids and, though you'd never expect it, quite a beautiful wife!"

"Honest?" said Michael, genuinely surprised. It was hard to believe. Although he was embarrassed at Khost seeing him the night before, he decided to shrug it off. He hadn't done anything wrong, just expressed a surfeit of cheer that goes along with too much drink. Still, he knew Khost thought less of him as a result, and that did bother him. I need to be more careful, he thought. Let this be a warning and leave it at that. I am alone here after all.

Back in the apartment after dinner, he composed the following email:

Dear Annetine,

> *Good to hear from you! I'm doing well. It would be nice to have a drink after work sometime and reconnect. Or maybe a cup of coffee some weekend morning?*

> *Cheers,*

> *Michael*

Michael re-read it and was happy with his message. It was short and honest, and it put the ball in her court without being heavy-handed. He signaled that he wanted to see her again, but she could opt for a morning coffee, although that would have a hurried, businesslike edge, or a late afternoon drink. Or, she could drag her heels and not write back for a week.

Michael ran through his note one more time and amended it to: *"It would be nice to see you again—maybe a cup of coffee sometime?"* dropping the *"reconnect"* (too suggestive?) and the *"drink after work"*.

He honestly wasn't sure if he wanted to go there, at least not yet. Coffee was pretty neutral. If she responded, he would try to steer her onto the weekend to avoid the rush of a weekday morning. If they ended up enjoying each other's company, it was also more open-ended. He changed *"Cheers"* to *"Hope you're well"*, and pressed *'send'*.

18. TWIST OF FATE

Tuesday morning, Michael overslept by an hour because his phone had died. He didn't feel pressured to scurry off to work, as he was free personally, but also professionally. Durst certainly didn't care and there was no clock to punch. He had to get the job done, but it could be at his own pace. He decided to go for a run.

It was usually still dark when he ran, but this morning the city was bathed in the pastel hues of dawn. A white vapor veiled the river and there was no wind. He felt strong and clear, enjoying the crunch of gravel underfoot and the steady rhythm of his breath as he ran past the Louvre and through the gardens of the Tuileries.

Relishing the margin of freedom, Michael got back to the apartment, shaved and showered, then brewed up a pot of coffee and checked his email. Nothing yet from Annetine, but there was a message from Katherine. It was sent late last night, after he'd gone to bed:

Hi Michael,

I'm sorry our conversation didn't go well on Sunday. I was feeling out of sorts, and we weren't syncing, but no matter—this stuff can happen. I hope you're well.

Joanne is ok with my going to Paris! She didn't make it easy for me but I told her we needed the time together and that

Michael was pleased she would be coming to France for Christmas after all, and that she had signed off with "love." All of a sudden, there was something to focus on, to look forward to, and the holidays wouldn't be lonely. Terrific.

Katherine would be here in eight days. He wrote her back and, feeling rejuvenated, grabbed his bag and headed off to work down the wide stone stairway, through the wooden double doors and onto Rue Beautreillis. Having been in the apartment two full weeks, Michael was getting to know the morning rhythm of the neighborhood.

Usually, there was the burble of uniformed schoolchildren heading to school, grouping and regrouping, full of youthful morning energy. The girls wore plaid green skirts and white shirts, while the boys had dark pants and sport jackets with the school's emblem on the breast pocket. They were pre- or early teens for the most part, on their way to the Catholic middle school near the river.

Michael always noticed the two tall, skinny boys in their school jackets, clearly buddies, who seemed able to exclude everything but each other, although the girls had their eyes on them and teased them behind their backs. One walked with a characteristic swagger, and one of the girls would imitate it perfectly so that the others would laugh and launch into their own caricature when the boys weren't looking.

Then there was the aproned vendor on St. Antoine unfurling the awning and carefully arranging the trays of fruit beneath, prices handwritten on yellow squares of paper, pencil dutifully tucked behind his ear.

He also regularly noted the pair of workmen in their overalls sitting at the counter in one of the *brasseries*, each sipping a small glass of rosé. Side by side, they never seemed to talk.

And, closer to the metro, the whiskered old man wearing the same threadbare brown suit with the yellow artificial carnation pinned to the lapel. He sipped his *café au lait* while mumbling to himself, fully engaged in an animated conversation with whomever his imagination had conjured up that day. Joy, indignation, puzzlement, grief—one never knew what the mood of the day would be, but Michael made a point of checking in with a glance every morning just before descending into the Metro.

That was the beat of the eight thirty hour.

This morning was different, for he was heading to work later than normal, and all of the usuals were missing. No children on the street, fruit store awning already unfurled, empty stools in the bar. It was also much brighter, and the south side of the wide boulevard was bathed in sunlight.

As Michael approached the metro, he glanced at the café, looking for the old man, when his attention riveted to the two women sitting in his usual place. One had her back to him, so he couldn't see her face. But the other woman, the one facing him and chatting on a cell phone, *could it be?*

Michael slowed, watching, as she ended the conversation and put down her phone. She smiled at her companion and his heart skipped a beat. There were those dimples he remembered so well. The brushed-back hair. As if she sensed his gaze, Annetine looked up straight at him. Her face broke into a wide smile and she waved.

"Michael! Is that you?"

He smiled and walked over to their table.

Annetine was on her feet, beaming. "Wow, what a coincidence! I was just going to email you," she said. "How are you?" She looked genuinely happy to see him, and gave him a warm hug.

"Hi Annetine, nice to see you as well!" he said with genuine feeling. "What brings you here?"

"Just having some coffee with my friend Talia." She turned to Talia, who'd swiveled in her chair. "This is Michael," she said, "the man I was telling you about, the one I met on the plane."

Michael extended a hand. "My pleasure," he said, and Talia gave his hand a gentle squeeze and he saw some expression—was it recognition?—flicker across her face.

She looked to be in her mid-twenties, with thick and curly black hair that framed a squarish, pleasant face. He immediately noticed her large dark eyes—black as obsidian and flecked with gold. Striking.

"*Bonjour*," said Talia, squinting, as the sun was directly behind him.

Annetine took his arm and he turned her way. Energy radiated from her as tangibly as heat and, for him, the attraction was instantaneously reborn. Her familiar scent sealed the moment.

"What were you going to write?" he asked. "Are we going to get together?"

She didn't hesitate. "Sure, yes, I'd love to! Let's have coffee as you suggest. I can't tomorrow, but how about Thursday or Friday?"

Having thought this through earlier, Michael was prepared, and he shook his head apologetically. "Sorry, Annetine, I have early meetings both days, so that would be a cheat. Next Monday or Tuesday could work but, come to think of it, maybe the weekend would be better? I'm free both mornings, and it would avoid the weekday rush. We could have some brunch and catch up."

"Sounds good," said Annetine, "Saturday would work. Where and when?"

He had thought this through as well. "What about the McDonalds on Rue Du Renard?" he asked, with a straight face. "I love their sausage McMuffins."

Annetine shook her head. "Maybe not so good. I'm a vegetarian, remember?" (He hadn't).

"I was joking," he said, realizing that his attempt at humor fell flat. "What about the Café de Relais? Opposite City Hall, on the corner of Tivoli and de Ville by that big department store. Nice place to sit and people-watch. Ten o'clock?"

"Perfect!" she said gaily, "It will be nice to talk again!"

Michael took her hand and gave it a squeeze. "OK," he said, "sounds good. Till."

19. CONSTELLATIONS, PERTURBATIONS

The next evening, Michael started thinking about seeing Annetine again, as he had on and off throughout the day. What were the chances of running into each other in a city of four million people? If he hadn't headed off to work an hour late on that particular morning, they would surely have missed each other. Despite being raised Catholic, Michael was not religious, but he did believe there was more to life than what met the eye. Life's coincidences, while not preordained, were also not entirely random either, and now they would be seeing each other in three days.

After having dinner in a small Italian restaurant off of Boulevard Raspail, he took the long way home as it was a beautifully clear night. The lights of the city danced upon the river as he crossed the Pont Alexandre III, one of the most beautiful bridges in the world, with its gilt-bronze winged horses, cherubs, and art nouveau streetlights. The Eiffel Tower sprang to life with its nightly light show of flashing bulbs and sweeping searchlights, as it has every evening hour since the millennial New Year's Eve back in 1999.

Good to be here, he thought. *Life tastes sweet tonight.*

Back at the apartment, Michael was planning to Skype with Katherine, but now that it was a few minutes before midnight, he wasn't feeling up to it. Skyping with Katherine this late in the day required tapping into an energy reserve he couldn't quite muster tonight. There wasn't much news to relate, and he didn't want to end the day on another halting conversation. He plugged his iPhone into the small stereo and set it to shuffle to stall his sense of obligation. Although Michael was tired, he wasn't sleepy. A little music and a cup of tea would do him well.

He put a pot of water on the stove and parted the dining room window curtains, looking out at the dark wall of windows across the courtyard.

The room came alive with "River"—an old Joni Mitchell song. This version was a Madeleine Peyroux duet with K.D. Lang, and the plaintive "Jingle Bells" undertone perfectly fit the pre-holiday season.

"River" ended and, ironically, the next song to come on was "In My Secret Life" by Leonard Cohen. How appropriate and (again!) rather coincidental reflected Michael before catching himself; Cohen and Mitchell had been lovers back in the 60's.

He unfastened the latch, opened the window to let the night air in, and stuck his head outside. The temperature must have fallen below the freezing point, as there was frost on the stone windowsill.

The winter sky showed above the edge of the roof across the small courtyard. There was the sideways "V" of Taurus the Bull, fronted by the orange Aldebaran and the fine cluster of stars that was the Pleiades twinkling almost overhead. He could imagine Orion rising behind the building to the southeast, the great hunter eternally pursuing the Seven Sisters, the daughters of Pliny, while trailed by Canis Major, his faithful dog. That constellation was small and indistinct (*how imaginative, the ancients*, thought Michael), but one couldn't miss the beautiful blue-white jewel of Sirius, the brightest star in the northern hemisphere.

Astronomy was one of Michael's hobbies since he was barely a teenager, and he knew the night sky by heart. With its brilliant procession of constellations, the sky this time of year was his favorite.

As he gazed at the stars above the roofline, those earlier days came back to him in an unexpected wave of sentiment. He was fourteen again, walking home from school, taking the shortcut through the woods. The trunks were sharp in the afternoon light and the sky above was blue. Excited at the prospect of a clear and moonless night ahead, he would take out his telescope well ahead of time so the optics would not fog in the cold, and go outside after dinner, once it was dark. His father would often come out with a cup of tea to keep him company, and they would look at the stars and nebulae, the planets *du jour*—Jupiter, Mars, Saturn—each with their own distinct personality. How exciting to see the pinpoints of Jupiter's moons, their orbits perfectly aligned around the orange planet, or the rings of Saturn—tiny but distinct—in the small telescope.

Michael's expression became pensive. How long ago, how much time had passed since those innocent days with their simple sorrows and joys? Life with his parents and sister, the secure home of childhood where he occupied his own unique place, had his own vantage point—another world within a world. He thought about his current home three thousand miles to the west, and of Katherine. No putting it off further, he decided. I'm being selfish and I need to call.

He left the window open, enjoying the cold air, paused the music and turned on his laptop. In a few minutes, they were connected and the conversation was surprisingly light and friendly. With her coming to Paris, there was something to look forward to, a common focus, and they talked about some of the things they would do together. Katherine had just started telling him about her day at work and how bitchy Joanne was when Michael heard the familiar marimba ring of her cell phone in the background.

She said "Hang on a second Michael, let me see who that is," and walked off screen. Michael heard her say "Hello?" and then, more quietly—"I'm skyping with Michael. Let me call you back."

When she returned, he asked her who it was.

"Oh, it's just Kylie," she said.

"Kylie?" he asked, not remembering having heard the name before.

"She's new," said Katherine. "She joined us a month ago, and we've gotten pretty friendly." She smiled. "With you away, I'm socializing more," adding, "I *am* all alone, you know, and it's kind of boring without you here."

Michael wouldn't have thought anything more of it, except that Katherine sounded a little furtive, like she did when she was fibbing. He knew this from their days in school, when she occasionally lied to her mother about being at a girlfriend's house when she was actually with him, and he'd seen it a few times since when she had to make up a white lie for whatever reason. Her pitch raised just a tad and she talked more quickly.

Michael asked her about the Christmas party last night, and Katherine said it was "typical—a little dull." A pause crept in and they both stared at each other's images on their respective screens. The phone call had interrupted the momentum of their conversation. Katherine sensed it too—he could feel it.

She gave him a thin smile. "Listen, I'll let you go. Skype again tomorrow? I should be home by six."

"Actually, let's not," he countered. "You'll be here soon enough and we might as well save some stuff for face time. It's nice to Skype and all, but in some ways it only makes me feel lonelier. We hang up, it's midnight, and I'm here all alone in the apartment. Also," he added, "there really isn't a lot of new stuff to talk about. Sounds like we both have our noses to the grindstone these days. Why don't we Skype on Friday?"

"All right," she said. "I wish we could do it later in the evening, when I'm more relaxed, but that's not fair to you. As it is, I hurry home from work to be here on time, but it ends up feeling like it's another meeting. As you can see," she gestured at her outfit, "I haven't even had time to change. But wait..." She thought for a moment. "Some of the girls from the office are going out for a drink after work on Friday. What about Saturday? It'll be the weekend, more relaxed, and we could do it earlier if you'd like."

"Sure," said Michael. "Saturday sounds fine. I'll call you mid-afternoon your time."

They disconnected and he sat for a few minutes, thinking.

Still not feeling sleepy, Michael decided to surf the web for a while. He quickly grazed the day's news as his interest in politics had become watered down by being out-of-country; for whatever reason, it all mattered less here. Another saying he liked—*today's news wraps tomorrow's fish*—came to mind. He looked up Jacques Brel and listened to "Orly" on YouTube, remembering Gervaise's comment. It was an unusual song, but sounded quite dated.

On impulse, he googled *Adrian Khost* but came up empty and was about to turn in when an idea came to him. He went onto Facebook to check out the page of Hopkins and Lazzaro, the law firm Katherine worked for, to see if there was anything posted from their Christmas party last night. For some reason—probably because Katherine had been so dismissive—his curiosity was piqued.

Sure enough, there were already a few comments (great time, nice band, etc.), and a photo album titled 'Holiday party'. He clicked on it and saw that there were at least fifty thumbnails. How diligent of somebody to put them up so quickly, although he was not at all surprised. Digilife. Michael started clicking through the pictures, looking for Katherine.

Here we go—a photo of Katherine with her arm around Jenny. She looked happy and a bit tight, with Jenny's oversized glasses perched cockeyed on her nose. He recognized some of her co-workers from last year's party.

It was a dressed-up affair, and Katherine was wearing her favorite black dress—low-cut and tight in the right places—and the string of pearls he had given her for their 10th. All very familiar. He had unhooked those pearls and unzipped that dress on more than one occasion.

Michael felt a wave of desire for her, and continued clicking, although he was starting to feel sleepy. It would be nice to hit the sack. More photos of coworkers, but none of Katherine. Click. Click Click. Wait, back up—there was Jenny again, with her arms around Greg and another one of their partners, John. It must have been at the end of the party, as Jenny's head was on John's shoulder and her eyes looked watery and glazed. Katherine had often referred to her as "our party girl," apparently for good reason. Greg and John's ties were loose, and their grins were sloppy and angled.

What caught his eye, however, was in the background. It was dark because of the distance from the flash, but discernible. Over to the left, almost out of the picture was his wife sitting with a man he did not recognize. They were leaning into each other, faces inches apart at a table. He was dark-haired and European looking—Greek perhaps, or Italian.

The frigid night air was coming in through the open window, but Michael felt a wave of warmth pass up his neck into his head, and a slight sweat break out on his forehead. He zoomed up the picture, but there was no more to be gained as the resolution was low and the magnification only gave it a pixelated quality. He clicked through the remaining photos before returning to the image, then leaned back in the chair and ran his fingers through his hair. *Come on*, he thought, *this is silly. She had a few drinks, maybe they were just flirting with each other. Who are you to judge, after all?* But, try as he might to downplay and ignore his gut feeling, the picture unsettled him. What was it that she'd said: 'typical—a little dull?' Sure didn't look that way.

Michael continued staring at the photograph on his computer, thinking. The real issue, he decided, was trust. One could always read into things, envision conspiracies and deceits. But as one of his friends once said—you either see the world from a conspiratorial point of view or you don't. Michael tried not to because he saw how a conspiratorial mindset tricked one into making inferences that seemed perceptive and reasoned, but could well be completely off the mark. The mind pieced together its biases into a convincing house of cards. By creating a false sense of insight, of apparent logic, a conspiratorial mentality slyly reinforced its own version of reality. Could Katherine be having an affair? Sure. Was she? Maybe. But also maybe not. It was a Christmas party after all. If it was an affair, wouldn't she have been more circumspect, especially in the company of coworkers?

Objective by nature, his mind circled back to his earlier question...what about *him*? What about that morning coffee with Annetine in three days? Might that not make an interesting picture of its own? This kind of speculation was bullshit, he decided. Time for bed. In the end, wasn't it all *que sera, sera,* anyway? He powered off the laptop, washed up and, having successfully cleared his mind, fell into a deep sleep.

Riding the Metro to work on Thursday morning, he noticed a little girl sitting across from him. She must have been six or seven, and she held her mother's hand in one hand and a pink-rimmed *Little Mermaid* lunchbox in the other. Bright with images of fish and other sea creatures, it must have triggered Michael's memory, for the nightmare from his last night at home came back to him with new realization.

The dream wasn't about diving or lobsters—it was about loss, about separation, about *them*. Katherine's eerie smile, the wayward farewell wave. It was his mind dredging up that fear from the depths of its subconscious. Even his gazing back on the hills took on a new meaning—the landscape was symbolic of their past—of where they came from, of where they *had* been. His looking ahead to see Katherine swimming through the gauntlet and away from him into the open sea, through the present and into the future… it all made sense in this context. Not a believer in dream theory, it nevertheless gave him pause, for it reinforced the ever-present power of the subconscious.

20. INCIDENT IN THE METRO

As soon as he got to the office, Michael realized that he had forgotten his USB data stick at the apartment. It contained the latest version of a file he was working on, one he needed today. Damn it, he would have to go back to retrieve it.

He retraced his steps to the Metro, and then the apartment. Yep, there it was on the counter just where he had left it. Michael slipped the thumb drive into his pocket, locked the door and headed back to the Metro, this time choosing the Sully-Morland instead of the Bastille station to break the monotony. It was a few minutes before eleven, and the subway car was at most half-full—a far cry from the morning rush hour when it was standing room only.

He transferred at the Louvre and, after passing Champs-Élysée Clemenceau, stood up in anticipation of George V, his exit point. As the train slid into the station, he saw two young men scuffling with an older man on the platform. In their twenties or early thirties, both looked of Arabic or Middle Eastern descent, while the older man— thin, goateed, well-dressed—was vintage French. Hearing the train, one of the two youths pushed him away and bolted down the platform; the other one fished a small vial out of his pocket and smashed it against the wall as he, too, started sprinting for the exit.

The subway doors slid open and Michael stepped out onto the platform. Suddenly, he froze mid-breath. Something very wrong was in the air and his body told him not to inhale further. Knowing he may have already been poisoned, for he could taste the stuff—metallic, acrid—at the back of his throat, he began running toward the green *Sortie* sign at the end of the platform. He thought of stopping to help the old man, but it was pure survival at this point as he heard the steps of other passengers behind him. He needed air.

The Parisian metro can be deep and, after running up two sets of stairs, he looked up to see the long ribbon of escalator running up to the semicircular mouth of the tunnel hundreds of feet above him. His lungs were burning and he was getting dizzy. Christ, it was a long way! Could he make it? And where were the youths?

He had to breathe, otherwise he would faint. He took a cautious half-breath and was relieved that the air was fine—just the usual subterranean staleness. Michael sucked in great deep breaths as he continued striding up the escalator using his arms to help propel him two steps at a time. Up, up, up, through a turnstile and into another long corridor. He finally glimpsed daylight on the stone station entrance steps and felt the blessed fresh air as he vaulted up and onto the street where he stood doubled over, hands on knees, chest heaving.

As his breath returned, he explored his sensations with clinical precision. His eyes were stinging and there was a nasty burning sensation in his lungs. It was a good thing he hadn't put in his contacts today, as it would have been unbearable. He felt his pocket to make sure the USB stick was still there and it was. When he coughed, his chest ached and there was a sharp pain in his temples, but otherwise he felt okay. Trying to catch his breath, Michael became aware of a wretched wailing sound coming out of the mouth of the Metro station—it was a sound he had never heard before, the sound of pure human misery.

As he watched, other people began to spill out of the station, some with their arms around each other, others alone, all coughing and gasping. Their eyes were uniformly blood-red and watery. With passers-by stopping to watch, a crowd soon gathered. Many of the riders were moaning and rubbing their eyes. Some were crying. As the minutes passed and the fresh air took effect, the sounds quieted and the victims began talking to one another in French: *What happened? Did you see those men? What kind of gas was it? Does your chest hurt too?*

Michael wondered if it was some kind of nerve gas, but realized that if that were the case, he would now be feeling worse, not better. Comforted, he realized that it must have been some kind of a tear gas. The sharp taste in his mouth lingered and his throat burned. His eyes continued to water. Nerve gas, he reasoned, would probably be odorless, or possibly sweet—didn't cyanide smell like almonds, or was it new-mown hay? Michael continued to breathe deeply and to take stock of those around him.

His eyes met those of a tall, well-dressed man who was standing a few feet away. Michael spoke with him as best he could in his mediocre French, but there was no more information to be gleaned. The man was as puzzled as he was, and they both agreed it must have been a tear gas. The man had also seen the youths fighting and the vial shattering; he, too, had instinctively stopped breathing and started running. His eyes watered as he spoke and the whites of his eyes were so red that Michael fully expected blood to begin to ooze from them. But the man was otherwise composed and calm.

Slowly, as the symptoms began to dissipate, so too did the crowd. And, as is always the case in moments of need, there were no police in sight. Michael wondered how the old man who was being mugged fared. The toxic shock of the gas was such that no one in their right mind would have stopped to help him up. If one can't breathe, one can't help, and self-preservation triumphs by default. He could still have been lying on the platform, paroxysmal, possibly even trampled by the crowd.

Michael considered going back down into the station, but decided against it, and returned to work instead. He washed up in the bathroom and was glad to see that his eyes weren't nearly as red as those of some of the other passengers. He downed a few glasses of water and tried to work, but felt dulled and tired. The afternoon was a slog and, by evening, the pain in his temples had grown into a throbbing headache.

Except for the occasional self-infliction of a hangover, he rarely got headaches, and this one was worsening. Dispirited, he decided to avoid the Metro and walk home, but this only made him more tired. Back in the apartment, he cooked up some pasta and tried to read, but soon gave up. The pages were shimmering, his head hurt, and his mind wandered. He took a bath along with three ibuprofen and went to bed.

The next morning, Friday, Michael still had the headache, which had migrated to behind his eyes, and he felt physically weak and tired in spite of the long sleep. Shaving, he dropped his razor twice. What in the hell? His coordination was off and he felt slow of mind. Maybe it wasn't tear gas—could it have been some kind of poison after all?

There was nothing on the web about the incident, so he looked up the location of the police station closest to the George V station. It was in the 8th Arrondissement, and he wrote down the address, dressed, and made his way to the constabulary. The officer on duty was a heavy-set man with sallow skin and the puffy, watery eyes of a drunk. He sat behind a metal desk slumped in an old swivel chair, with *Le Parisien*, a French tabloid, spread out in front of him. He gave Michael a bland, bored glance.

"*Puis-je vous aider?*" he said, although his expression was less polite than his words. Michael described the incident in the Metro, and inquired about whether he knew any details.

"First I've heard of it," said the policeman as he continued to look down at his paper.

"Can't be!" exclaimed Michael. "At least a hundred people were affected, and it was only three blocks from here. Surely someone complained?"

The constable looked up at Michael and spoke slowly, as if to a child.

"Paris is a big city, monsieur," he said. "There are many things to worry about every day. I have not heard about this, and I was on duty all day yesterday. You might check with the metropolitan transit authority. Perhaps they can give you some explanation, but these things can happen. Nothing to worry about. What you describe sounds like tear gas or a pepper spray."

He returned to his paper with a dismissive "*À, bientôt.*"

Michael fidgeted, thinking about what else he could say. Could no one have reported such a thing to the police? It was hard to believe but, then again, he hadn't either, had he?

"*Merci,*" he said, barely resisting the temptation to slam the door behind him on the way out.

Later in the day, Michael did call the Paris Transit Authority, and the woman who answered the phone acknowledged that there was an *evenémént*—an event—in the Georges V station Wednesday morning. She hadn't heard about any gas; could Michael offer any details? He told her about the two youths and the old man. No, he wouldn't be able to identify them other than they seemed young.

She reassured him: It *was* the Metro after all. There are many petty crimes every day. The *Romas* no doubt—the gypsies. They were always up to something, and the Metro was their playground. The transit police would certainly be reviewing the videos in the days ahead, but there wasn't anything to do at this point. Could she help him with anything else?

21. BIRD MEN OF NOTRE DAME

Michael woke up on Saturday early enough to squeeze in a run before meeting up with Annetine. It was a clear, warm morning and, as he stepped onto Beautreillis, he felt energized and strong. But when he got to the river and started running, his legs started to feel rubbery and his breath began to rasp. After barely a half mile, he slowed to a walk. When he started to run again, he got a sharp pain in his side and, frustrated and a little troubled by this uncertain condition, reluctantly turned around and walked back along the quay.

The stone benches in the plaza outside the Notre Dame cathedral looked inviting and he decided to rest for a few minutes and gather his thoughts. The annual Christmas tree had recently been set up in the center of the square and he gazed moodily at its ornaments. Two men walked into the empty square and he recognized them instantly. They were the two 'bird men' of Notre Dame; Michael had seen them many times in passing, especially on weekends.

The two were of very different appearance and personality. One wore a hoodie and sweatpants and was plump and friendly. His round and freckled face was in a perpetual state of grin. The other was shorter, thinner, darker—Filipino? Older, he wore a black leather fedora with a matching jacket. His demeanor and body language were insular and he rarely met anyone's eye.

Later, when the plaza thronged with tourists, the bird men would return with their bags of feed and cloth-lined donation baskets, strike their individual poses and extend their arms, a handful of seeds in each. Used to the routine, the sparrows perched readily on their forearms and knuckles, and pecked away at the feed. The birds appreciated it, the children loved it, and the parents complied in turn by feeding the birdmen's baskets with coins.

Bird man #1 spoke with the children and encouraged their participation. He would allow a child to hold the feed and experience the delight of birds perching on his or her fingers. Bird man #2 spoke with no one and never smiled. He related only to the birds whirring around his fingertips while the children huddled close behind him taking in the birds' gyrations with their sharp young eyes.

Michael was surprised to see them come by this early in the morning—together no less, as they normally appeared to be completely independent of each other.

Sitting on the stone bench, he continued to watch them in the slanted morning light. This was a time, he realized, when they trained the birds, established a trust that would serve them gainfully later in the day.

Trust again, he thought—a recurring theme of late. But here, trust ultimately served both the calculus of profit and the fundamental instinct of survival in both bird and man.

After watching them for a few minutes, Michael lost interest and his mind began to meander. He started thinking about Katherine, then Khost, then the Metro incident and, as he tried to re-focus his mind on the present, he again wondered if he may have suffered some sort of brain damage from the gas. He was meeting Annetine in a few hours, yet he couldn't seem to focus, as his thoughts leapt around in a disjointed, questioning fashion: *which way is east... is this a leap year... what do evergreens have to do with Christ's birth... can madness lead to truth...can truth lead to madness?* Michael's mind felt like a tangled fishing line, snarled and knotted, and he had no control over its jumbled flow.

"Those whom the Gods wish to destroy" he thought, remembering a phrase from somewhere, *"they first...they first..."* The second half of the saying eluded him and, frustrated with this persistent mental dullness, he finally settled on *"...take away their minds."* Close, but not quite right. Ultimately, how fragile, how tenuous is our grip on reality, thought Michael. This morning, his consciousness felt tremulous and tentative.

He got to his feet and started walking back to Beautreillis, passing a large advertising column from which a red-lipped Madonna gazed back at him seductively. She would be at the Palais Omnisports arena on March 13th.

Michael felt as if he was observing himself from without instead of within. The world around him appeared oddly luminous. It was partly visual—the shimmering effect at the periphery of his vision was still there—and partly mental. Everything, including his own consciousness, felt foreign. It was a disturbing, disquieting state of mind. When he closed his eyes, jagged sparks of light flashed across his visual field for a split-second before subsiding.

Instead of the excitement and anticipation that he had felt earlier in the week at the prospect of being with Annetine again, Michael found himself wondering whether he should postpone their meeting. He glanced at his watch. Almost nine o'clock. Only an hour to go. No, too short notice, impolite. He couldn't do that. Plus, what would he do instead? Sleep? Sulk? And how would he contact her? No guarantees with email, and she hadn't given him a phone number.

No, he decided, succumbing to weakness is not my nature. I need to push through this and make the best of it. Maybe some food and Annetine's company will re-energize me. People affect other people through their bio-fields or pheromones or whatever. His time with Danny was a great example, and Michael perked up at the memory.

In a way, the same was true for Annetine: both times he had seen her, he felt her energy and a kinship of spirit. Maybe she was just what he needed to snap him out of this malaise, this madness. Madness... madness... the saying flashed into his mind, this time correct: *Those whom the gods wish to destroy, they first make mad.*

Back in the apartment, he shaved and showered before walking the five blocks over to the Hotel de Ville. In true Parisian style, the City Hall was massive and incredibly ornate for a government building. Michael remembered the little brick city hall back home in Montclair with the police station in the basement, and chuckled at the contrast.

Their reunion now imminent, he felt buoyed at the prospect of seeing Annetine again, and some of his normal energy returned, along with a growing sense of anticipation. There was the Café de Relais on the corner.

He walked over to one of the outdoor tables, ordered a double espresso and positioned himself so as to have a clear view of the intersection.

22. PROPINQUITY

Halfway through the demitasse, he spotted her, still two blocks away. Annetine was wearing a yellow sundress, and walking with an easy, carefree stride. Michael realized that this was the first time he had seen her walking by herself in an open space. One could easily mistake her for a college student in the ease and speed with which she walked—purse and jacket slung over one shoulder, and the sparkle of gold bangles on one wrist.

When she stopped at the corner, waiting for the light to change, she noticed him as well and waved before crossing the street at a half-run. Michael sprang up to greet her and she gave him a hug.

Annetine was wearing wire gold earrings of some abstract shape (fish perhaps?) that were set off by every movement of her head, and a single strand of gold chain around her neck. She looked fabulous, and he told her as much.

She laughed gaily and easily, and brushed a handful of hair back off her forehead.

"Thanks Michael, it took me a while. Did I get it right?"

"Spot on," he said approvingly.

"How've you been?" she asked. "You look a little tired—everything all right?"

He gave her an ironic smile. "I tell you that you look beautiful and you tell me I look beat. We're off to a good start. I'm fine," he lied, "tough week at work with some unusual twists—I'll tell you about them when we settle in. Coffee?"

"Absolutely." She looked back at him with a happy gleam in her eyes, which were a luminous sea green. This puzzled Michael, as he distinctly remembered their being darker, and hazel.

A waiter came over with two menus and smiled at Annetine.

"*Bonjour*, Annetine!" he said with evident affection. He was a handsome, Mediterranean-looking man of fifty with liquid brown eyes, curly black hair, and a five-o-clock shadow although it was only ten a.m. His most interesting feature was the delicate, feminine mouth that contrasted with an otherwise hyper-masculine appearance. *His head would look good on a Greek statue*, thought Michael.

"*Bonjour* Georges" she replied, giving him a warm smile in return. "*Comment ça va?*"

"*Très bien, merci. C'est un belle matinée*," he answered, and switched to lightly accented English as he turned to Michael—"*Monsieur*, another coffee?"

Michael nodded and they ordered some cheese omelets before turning their attention to each other, beginning with small talk about the weather and the city. Annetine told Michael she lived in the 20th Arrondissement, not far from the Pere Lachaise cemetery.

The food came as they continued to talk. Annetine brushed off the subject of work (boring) and told him instead about going to school at UCLA and getting into surfing; he told her about his job with Aerotel in more specific terms.

"Computers fascinate me," said Annetine. "They enslave us and yet I know nothing about them. It must be an exciting field to be in."

The conversation wound its way to childhood memories, and when Michael told her about his own childhood in and around New York City and asked about hers, she told him that she had been born in North Carolina.

"Whereabouts?" he asked, curious.

"On the Outer Banks, a town called Ocracoke" she answered.

Michael loved the way she said it with a slight southern drawl and it triggered a flashback, a phantasm from a college spring break bus trip to Daytona Beach. On the drive home, the bus had pulled into a roadside Dairy Queen somewhere in Georgia for an hour-long pit stop. He and Chris had chatted up two local girls on the serving line and, once they had their ice cream sodas, the girls invited them to come and sit in their car. He still remembered how they had said the word *Coke*. The simple vowel had become soft and rounded by their drawl. Here it was, almost 20 years later, and he still remembered the vignette vividly.

"What was your major in college?" he asked.

"Business," she said. "I started out as a psychology major but switched to business after the first week. Where'd you go to school again?"

Michael said that he went to Colgate in upstate New York, and had majored in computer science.

Annetine also told him she was an only child—she had a younger brother who died at the age of six from a childhood cancer. Her parents divorced shortly thereafter.

"It took its toll on them," she said, adding "and their divorce took its toll on me." Her eyes darkened with the memory. When Michael prodded her, she explained that her dad had moved to Texas, while her mother met another man, a military guy, and they moved to Whidbey Island, north of Seattle, where he was stationed at the Naval Air Station. This had happened in high school, the year before college.

Michael, in turn, told Annetine that his parents and sister were dead, that they had died in a car crash in the Catskills.

"Wow! How?" asked Annetine.

"My dad was driving and he tried to pass a tractor, but something went wrong and the car rolled into a ditch. No one knows exactly what happened. It was on my thirtieth birthday of all things. They think he might have broken a tie rod." Michael shrugged at the memory. "Stuff happens."

"Say," he said, wanting to get onto something more pleasant, "you look very fit," he said. "Do you work out?"

Annetine said she didn't run but liked to bike, and had taken part in some competitions in central Jersey, near where she lived. Michael thought she had once said something about living in New York City, but let it pass.

Their conversation meandered from topic to topic, as each filled in the gaps and put things together about the other's background.

"Annetine," said Michael, bemused, "you have to clear something up for me. When we met on the plane, I thought your eyes were hazel. Today they look blue-green. What's up?"

She laughed. "Come on Michael—every woman has her secrets! But no, you're right. I'm wearing green contacts today. The air on planes is dry and my eyes get itchy, so I took them out before the flight. What you saw was the real me—these are lightly tinted. They're good on bright days."

She paused and gave him a coy look. "We women have our bag of tricks, you know. But I can understand why you picked up on my eyes—the eyes are a person's most important feature, don't you think?"

"Definitely," replied Michael. "but the fact that they're the window to the soul, or whatever, implies a degree of honesty, unlike the other stuff. I'm surprised you would choose to mess with what most people would consider to be the most self-defining of traits."

"Oh, why not?" she said nonchalantly. "Anyway, that saying about the soul probably refers more to expression than color."

"I suppose so," said Michael, "But men and women see things differently. A woman once accused me of lying about some trivial thing, and I told her that women lie all the time! They lie about their age, they lie about their appearance, they color their hair, they wear heels." He gave her an ironic smile. "You meet a 25-year-old redhead who is tall and slim, and then you realize she has six-inch heels and is actually a brunette or whatever, and she's not a day under 30." Michael was on a roll. "Oh, and let's not forget the perfume. The eye make-up. The rouge. The jewelry. The falsies."

"The falsies?" laughed Annetine. "What are we, back in sixth grade? Anyway, it serves you right since we do it all for you! If men weren't so superficial and shallow, we wouldn't have to bother with the war paint."

"Touché," said Michael. He leaned toward her. "Between us, Annetine, I'm glad you're bothering. I love the earrings and your dress, and I presume that everything else is what it appears to be."

"When it comes to a woman, never presume, never assume!" said Annetine without missing a beat.

"I thought it was 'never complain, never explain'?" he shot back. "Now you've got me all mixed up again!"

"It's all very clear," she said with a playful smile. "I can already see you're an alpha male. I'm giving you the female counterpart—more gentle, more focused, as we women tend to be. As I already said, we're the subtler sex. And there *is* a slight difference between presuming and assuming, you know. Or maybe you don't know…"

Their flirtatious banter continued. At one point, Annetine excused herself to go to the ladies room and Michael sat there, thinking about how much he was enjoying her company.

Once Annetine returned, they started talking about music, and discovered much in common. Both loved old jazz and agreed that Coltrane's *Ballads* was perhaps the finest jazz album of all time, although Miles Davis's *Kind of Blue* was a close second. Both liked hip-hop, and occasionally listened to classical. Tchaikovsky was her favorite composer and *Easter Overture* her favorite piece, which would have also been his answer (here we go with the coincidences again, thought Michael). Not to be too agreeable and appear boring, he said that he loved Sibelius' *Finlandia* best.

They moved onto the subject of art, and he told her about seeing Courbet's *Origin of the World* at the d'Orsay a few weeks back.

"Never heard of it," said Annetine, "although I've been to the d'Orsay a number of times. I could spend all day in that place."

"Say!" she said excitedly, putting her hand on his arm. "Why don't we go there? It would be fun to look at some art! It's early enough so it won't be too crowded. The French are slow off the mark on weekends, you know."

Realizing she may have sounded overzealous, Annetine added, "But only if you want. Maybe you already have plans for this afternoon?"

"I want," he said. "No plans. Another coffee first?"

Annetine shook her head and Michael waved to the waiter. He was delighted at the prospect of spending more time with her and amazed that almost two hours had flown by so fast.

With Annetine, the turns of conversation were smooth and effortless. One minute they were talking about something in the news; the next, they were engaged in a discussion about art or music and then, just as quickly, they'd be onto a childhood experience or a dream.

Most of all, Michael realized he was feeling normal again, which thrilled him. There really was something to this interpersonal energy thing. As he stood up and looked across the square, he felt the warmth of the winter sun on his face, and the world seemed bright and magical.

23. REALITY CHECK

They crossed the Seine on the Pont des Arts, a pedestrian bridge. Nicknamed "the lover's bridge," it had thousands of locks chained to the railings. The ritual was for a couple to lock the lock, kiss, and throw the key into the river as a sign of eternal love. Michael took Annetine's arm in his and she didn't resist. Later, walking along the Quay d'Orsay, he told her about the incident in the Metro.

"One of the people in our office was on that train as well!" she said excitedly. "She's pregnant, and she was worried that whatever it was might harm her baby, so she went to the police. Naturally, they were of no use," adding, "they never are, you know. She went to a clinic and they ran some tests. They found a low level of something in her blood. The doctor said it was a, umm, a…"—Annetine hesitated, trying to remember the exact term—"a toxin of some sort. Not deadly, and the baby would be fine, but it was definitely something that acted on the brain. In fact, he told her she might not feel right for a week or so, but to not be concerned as she would eventually be fine."

Michael took Annetine's hand, and their fingers intertwined. He gave a gentle squeeze and she responded in like.

They walked unhurriedly past dark green *bouquinistes* —book kiosks that flank the riverbank—stopping here and there to rifle through some of the many posters and postcards.

He put his arm around Annetine's shoulders and pulled her closer to him, and she put her head on his shoulder. She smelled very fine, and he fought back the impulse to kiss her, although it was something his whole being yearned for. Willpower ebbing, Michael suggested they descend down to the river level.

Away from the traffic it was more quiet and private, with only a few pedestrians and the occasional jogger. They walked along the cobbled riverbank hand-in-hand, not saying anything, savoring the moment. They stopped at the entrance to the tunneled passage beneath the Pont Carousel and stood with their arms around each other. Michael put his hands on her waist and pulled her in towards him. Annetine didn't resist and put her hands on his shoulders, her face inches from his.

Michael wanted to kiss her, but resisted. He didn't want to hurry things. This had never happened to him before, at least not as an adult—with Katherine, they were kids when they met, and the teenage infatuation grew into love with time, but being here with Annetine was a whole different experience. As mature adults, with a longer perspective on life and on love, he hadn't expected this type of intense, irrational feeling. It bordered on obsession, a burning, an eclipse.

Over the last three hours, Michael was conscious of his bodily chemistry changing. It was peculiar. Everything was different. He was bowed by its power and felt impotent in its grip.

They stood in each other's arms for some time just before the semidarkness of the tunnel, eyes closed. Michael felt the rise and fall of each breath as their hips pressed against each other, and one of her legs slipped between his; it was a circle of sorts, a circle of energy and warmth. The seconds ticked by in silence. Suddenly, Annetine pushed back on his lapels and looked up at him.

"What *are* we doing, Michael?" she asked quietly.

"I don't know"

"You're married."

"I know."

"I don't want to be hurt."

"I won't hurt you."

"Yes you will," she said fiercely. "You *are* going to hurt me. Big time. You and I both know it. And," she added cryptically "I'll hurt you as well."

Caught off guard by the unexpected change in her demeanor, Michael took her hands and stepped back, looking into eyes. "I don't know what this means Annetine," he said. "I didn't expect it, but I do know that it's wonderful to be with you. We're together and it feels magical, and we're going to go to a museum and see some beautiful art. Why don't we let it be? Why get ahead of ourselves?"

Annetine looked at him with a curious expression. Wanton or remonstrative? He couldn't tell. Michael pulled her into him and they stood there melded together, folded unto themselves and utterly oblivious to the drone of the traffic on the street above them—man and woman, yin and yang.

24. TOSS OF THE COIN

Walking along the Quay Voltaire hand-in-hand, their conversation lightened. They spent the next few hours in the museum, and sought out the Courbet painting.

"Wow, right there, isn't it?" said Annetine. "Nothing subtle about that."

They walked over to the Boulevard Saint-Germain and had a small salad with cassoulet, followed by coffee. As the afternoon progressed, the tension of their unresolved desire became increasingly manifest. They stopped at a small *brasserie* and Michael ordered half a carafe of red wine. While they waited for it, his leg found her knees under the table. Kneecap to kneecap at first but then Annetine moved her other leg to cradle his between hers, and Michael's desire stirred as he felt the hollows of her bare skin above her knees.

They wound their way over to the old church at St. Germain-des-Prés and wandered around searching for Descarte's tomb. Only a few people were about. Alone in one of the alcoves, Michael put his arms around Annetine and gave her a kiss. Although it was brief, it lingered enough for him to take in the softness of her lips. He wanted it to unfold this way, gradually. He was content to feel, smell, be with her, at least for now. *The nearness of you…*

When they sat down on one of the wooden benches in the ancient church, admiring the ornate altar before them, he put his hand on her knee, feeling the warmth of her bare skin with his fingertips. It felt good in a rather naughty way, especially when Annetine leaned into him and pressed her leg along the length of his.

The afternoon light was growing weaker as they walked back across the Seine and over to the Place des Vosges, where they sat on one of the park benches under a plane tree. It was well after four. Michael kissed her again, this time on her neck and mouth, his lips tasting, exploring her skin. Annetine put her arms around him, and they sat face-to-face, looking at each other in silence.

They kissed again, more deeply. After a while, Michael pulled away and looked at her. His eyes had a mischievous twinkle. "Would you like to come over and see my place?" he said. "It's only three blocks from here."

Annetine laughed. "Aren't we subtle! This is only our first date. What kind of girl do you take me for anyway?" Her eyes were bright and flirtatious.

"You're reading more into this than I intended," said Michael. "I just thought you'd like…"

"You are *such* a liar," said Annetine, giving him a playful push.

Annetine left her hands on his shoulders, and the front of her dress fell away from her skin. He saw the curve of each breast and the edge of a white lacy bra. Her skin was olive and smooth and Michael felt his body getting out of control.

"OK," he said. "I'll tell you what. We'll leave it to fate."

"How's that?"

"We'll flip a coin. You can call it, and if it comes up your way, you can decide what to do next. But if it's my way you will agree…" He let the phrase hang in the air unfinished.

Annetine lips turned up in amusement. "Agree to what? You don't really think you can have your way with me based on some silly little coin?"

"Or you with me," he countered. "It's only fair. Afraid to take a chance?"

"All right," she said, "I like the idea of fate, and I like a challenge. Only *I* get to flip the coin."

"Fine," said Michael. He pulled a handful of change out of his coat pocket and plucked out a Euro. "I'll take heads."

"Wait," said Annetine. She took the coin and examined it. He looked at her quizzically.

"Just making sure it's legit." She laughed. "A girl has to be careful in the big city you know. Men take their advantage. And why do *you* get to call it? Not very gentlemanly."

He smiled. "I left my two-headed coin at home, so you're safe. Fine, go ahead and call it. I, on the other hand," Michael mock-gestured to the heavens "surrender my fate to the gods."

"The gods have nothing to do with this," said Annetine. "It's me you'll be surrendering to. Heads I win, tails you lose. Here we go…" She tumbled the coin in her palm. "Ready?"

"Nice try," said Michael. "But let's make it heads I win, tails I lose?" Michael held her eyes as he imitated a drum roll on the wooden slats of the bench. On cue, Annetine tossed the coin straight up in the air but, instead of following the coin with her eyes as he would have done, she turned back and looked at him. Michael glanced up at the tumbling Euro and watched it crest and begin to fall. It landed squarely in Annetine's open palm. He was surprised by the dexterity of the throw, and her confidence in catching it while still holding his gaze. *This girl might have some hidden talents*, he thought. *She could be dangerous.*

"OK, give me your arm," said Annetine. The coin was clenched in her hand. He put out his arm, still holding her gaze.

"There," she said, smacking the coin down on his forearm.

Tails.

Disappointed at his little gambit failing, Michael shrugged and smiled. "Guess the deities aren't with me today." He stitched an earnest expression on his face. "But fair is fair. So, what next?"

Annetine leaned in so her eyes were only a few inches from his.

"I'd love to see your apartment Michael, every inch of it," she said softly. Still holding his gaze, she flung the Euro carelessly over one shoulder.

"I don't mean to be presumptuous," she said, "but that might well have been the best spent Euro you've ever had."

25. TWILIGHT

Michael opened a bottle of champagne, blessing the impulse to buy one a few days ago on the walk home from work. He and Annetine sat side-by-side on the sofa together, talking and sipping the champagne, each well aware of what lay ahead. The *Veuve Clicquot* added its glow to the darkening afternoon. He found Ben Webster's "It's Easy to Remember" from *The Warm Moods* album and let the fluid notes of Webster's tenor saxophone, recorded more than fifty years ago, complement the intimate mood.

When they finally succumbed to each other, it felt natural and real as they made a passionate love. Annetine was a mélange of lips and teeth, eyelashes and tongue, the well-placed stroke of a fingertip and the scratch of a nail. *All girl in the best sense of the word*, thought Michael as the rhythm of sex became more animalistic and fierce. Their lips broke apart and their eyes locked on each other as they approached climax. Annetine closed her eyes and arched her head back and then forward, moaning, while he continued thrusting into her in sweet oblivion.

After, she rolled on top of him, chest to chest, belly to belly, her head lolling on his shoulder. With the sexual energy temporarily discharged, Michael drifted off into a daydream as the room grew dark. Later, when he opened his eyes, Annetine was still lying on top of him, head cradled in his shoulder, breathing quietly, eyes closed. She was asleep, peaceful in the aftermath of love. The music had ended and, except for an occasional street noise, it was perfectly quiet.

Michael savored the stillness of the apartment on one of the shortest days of the year as he watched the gentle rise and fall of Annetine's smooth bare back. Time slowed and he became lost in the warmth of her body on his, the softness of her breasts pressed against his chest, her now-familiar scent mixed with the animal smell of sex, and the slow and steady tide of their breath.

An hour later they awoke and made love again, this time less frenetically, more confident and comfortable with each other. *Nothing like the first time but, in some ways, the second was even better,* thought Michael. When it was over, they lay face to face for some time, arms around each other, and then took a long hot shower together, washing and nuzzling each other in the slippery warmth of soap and water.

With the windows closed, the apartment was heavy with the scent of love. Sex and candy; acrid and sweet.

While Annetine dried her hair in the bathroom, Michael turned on the green-shaded desk lamp and put on some music.

Annetine emerged, fully dressed, and stood in front of him. Her face was flushed from the warmth of the bathroom, aglow. Michael put his arms around her and gave her a kiss.

"Do you have any Nick Cave?" she asked suddenly.

When he said he didn't, she took his phone and found "Red Right Hand" on Spotify.

The music started on a minor chord with a strong rhythm and a haunting chime. Annetine closed her eyes and began dancing by herself a few feet in front of him. It was like she was a different person, a different spirit—her body moving in a sinewy rhythm, rippling the dark air with a swirl of her hands and fingers and hips, as she mouthed the words:

> *Take a little walk to the edge of town*
> *go across the tracks,*
> *where the viaduct looms*
> *like a bird of doom*
> *as it shifts and cracks...*

Michael liked the beat and Cave's voice, but it wasn't at all what he would have expected from Annetine. It was dark, sinister even, and Michael—head nodding in rhythm—stood quietly as she continued to dance around him in a circle, her arms weaving their own serpentine arc, dress rippling and adding its own measure of movement. For a second he felt like a new spirit had entered the room—a different presence—as Annetine continued to dance, wrists spinning in unison above her head with a hypnotic deliberation. *If she's Salome and I'm Herod,* thought Michael, *what is The Wish?*

During the organ solo in the middle of the song, she took Michael's hands in hers and pulled him into her. He joined in a dance that ended up with their grinding hip to hip, arms around each other's shoulders. She danced beautifully and he loved it. When the song ended, Annetine gave him a long, deep kiss. In the aftermath of love, Michael had been in a gentle mood, focused on her, on them, but he now felt energized and raw, aware of the energy coiled low in his spine.

Annetine walked back to the computer and found "Lovesong" by Adele. She took his hand and, as they began to slow dance, the earlier mood of intimacy returned.

Afterward, they went out to dinner on the Île-St. Louis, choosing a small restaurant on one of its narrow back streets. Its walls were dark red and draped with Persian tapestries, and the wall-mounted torch lights reinforced the medieval atmosphere.

Each had a Hendricks martini to start off, and then shared a bottle of Malbec with dinner as they sat across from each other in the warm glow of a small candelabrum centered between them. They were lovers now, and their conversation was infused with a new element of intimacy and comfort.

After capping the meal with coffee and a dessert of sliced pears topped by Roquefort cheese, Michael called for the bill. The night air was bracing and he and Annetine took a walk around Notre Dame and then past the white-lit Hotel De Ville for a nightcap at the Café Relais, where their day had begun, incredibly, only twelve hours ago. The café was crowded—noisy and a little punky—very different from the morning. In retrospect, the whole day had taken on an unreal, dream-like quality.

So much had happened between them so quickly that Michael found himself wondering if his life would ever be the same again. He was reeling with the impressions, the intimacy, and the ease of it all. Also, the conflict. Annetine was the first woman he had been with in decades other than Katherine, and the intensity of the passion combined with the unexpected closeness of spirit caught him off guard. She was very sensual, much more so than Katherine.

With a start, he remembered that he had promised to Skype Katherine today. Michael stole a glance at his watch—almost eleven. There was still time, but how could he do it with Annetine there? It would be too weird, too duplicitous. Unwilling to let guilt shatter his reverie, Michael convinced himself that it ultimately didn't matter—he would Skype with her tomorrow and tell her he was tired and fell asleep, or whatever. What was more consequential, and significantly so, was Katherine's arrival in four days. That, he decided, could prove to be a considerably more delicate situation.

26. PÈRE LACHAISE

Sunday morning dawned windy and wet, heavy drops of rain pelting the windows facing the street. Michael and Annetine lingered in bed, as there was no hurry. They made love and slept and made love again. Around noon, they showered and dressed and had a leisurely brunch at a nearby café. The rain stopped and the day brightened, but it was still unseasonably warm for late December.

"Ever been to Père Lachaise?" asked Annetine.

"Heard of it but no, haven't," said Michael. "Is it worth a look?"

"Absolutely," said Annetine. "Want to go?"

They emerged from the Metro and walked along the tall perimeter wall to an entrance. Inside, surrounded by stone, they stood for a while near the poster-sized map listing the 'residents' and showing the location of each individual plot. It was an impressive list that included Fredric Chopin, Edith Piaf, Oscar Wilde, Honoré de Balzac, and Jim Morrison.

They planned out a course that started with Michael's former neighbor on Beautreillis, as it was closest and, as they walked along the tree-flanked paths, the sun came out, dappling the trees and tombs with light and shadow.

A group of people stood around Morrison's simple, barricaded-off grave. Three swigged wine, passing around the bottle. A girl with a guitar kept her head down and strummed "People are Strange".

The trunk of the sycamore tree next to the grave was covered with graffiti—initials, Doors lyrics, quotes from Blake and Rimbaud, and excerpts of Morrison's poetry. One caught Michael's eye—*Now is blessed, the rest remembered.* He pointed it out to Annetine.

"I like it," said Annetine. "Short and sweet, with a nice internal rhyme. Alliteration, isn't that what it's called?"

Michael smiled and repeated the line in his head. *Now is blessed, the rest remembered.*

"I should dig up some of Morrison's poetry," he said, remembering the conversation with Gervaise. "I like the Doors' music but never took the guy seriously. Lizard King and all that, kind of pretentious. This is nice though—I wonder if it's a stand-alone?"

"Must be," said Annetine. "It seems complete unto itself."

Having a sharp eye for these things because of his profession, Michael also noticed the surveillance video camera discretely tucked away amongst the branches of the tree. Morrison would have been amused at the irony of having police protection post-mortem.

They moved on and eventually meandered off the main path into a secluded spot, and sat down under a large oak. Annetine pulled something black and cylindrical out of her purse and pressed one end. He heard a distinct click and noticed a small green light in the shape of a cross appear between her fingers. Annetine smiled as she brought it to her lips and took a draw.

"Vaporizer," she said. Her voice was distorted because she was still holding her breath. "Want some?"

Michael caught a faint whiff of marijuana as she let out her breath.

They passed the vaporizer back and forth a few times when Annetine said "Wait." She took in a breath and then kissed Michael, passing the smoke from her lungs to his. He held it for a few seconds before exhaling, feeling the tickle of the vapor in his chest.

After, she put the vaporizer away and they continued to sit under the tree holding hands and enjoying the faint warmth of the winter sun on their faces. The afternoon had turned bright and hazy and, as he looked at the landscape around him, Michael felt a new awareness of time creep into his mind. It was as if he could feel the earth turning beneath them. Unfettered by the pot, his mind began to roam.

The tomb in front of them was so weathered that the inscription was no longer legible. Partly covered with moss, it stood chipped and tilted by the forces of gravity and decay. This was a jagged landscape of tombs of various sizes and shapes interspersed with old trees. Angled by winds and time, some graves had heaved and trees had grown into the stones, the wood wrapping itself around and gripping the granite like flesh.

It all struck Michael as a testament to the absurdity of the funereal ritual. We live, we love, we laugh, we strive, we die. Our loved ones bury us with incantations to the eternal, to gods unseen as they crown our remains with expensive stones that deteriorate exactly as we do, but in a slower time frame.

Leaning back against the tree, shoulder-to-shoulder with Annetine, he closed his eyes, remembering his parents and his sister, buried on a different continent three thousand miles to the west. It had been years since he last visited their graves.

Michael's thoughts were interrupted by the sensation of Annetine's lips on the base of his neck. She worked her way up to his cheek ever so slowly with her lips and tongue. Eyes still closed, he felt the tip of her tongue circle his earlobe before her mouth slid over to meet his. Annetine slipped her hand under his shirt and he felt her fingers stoking his chest. He put his hand in her hair and they both slipped down onto the ground.

They lay at the base of the tree for some time, saying nothing—for there was nothing to say—fully immersed in the present. Slowly, as the high receded, their awareness returned to the world around them.

Annetine sat up, fumbled around in her purse and pulled out a small camera.

"Let's get a picture to remember this by," she said.

"You think that's a good idea?" asked Michael.

She poked him in the ribs. "Mr. Boylen, are you ashamed of me?"

Michael's instinct told him to avoid photos, but he capitulated. It was only a picture, and this *was* a moment to cherish. With him, it was always the paradox of caution and abandon.

"No," he said with a grin. "Quite the opposite. Hey, why not?"

He leaned into her and she held the camera at arm's length so it pointed towards them and put her other arm around his shoulder. "Smile baby."

The selfie was good but Michael thought they could do better, so they took a few more until they got one they both approved of.

"I'll email it to you," said Annetine.

Once they were back up on their feet, Annetine took his hand as they walked on the narrow path. She had grown quiet, as had he. The afternoon light was soft and diffuse and the air smelled of earth and fallen leaves.

They eventually got onto one of the paths that led to an exit, and—based on the map—passed by Oscar Wilde's grave. Annetine mentioned wanting to see it, as *The Portrait of Dorian Gray* was one of her favorite books. The day before, on the way to St. Germain-des-Prés, they'd passed L'Hotel, and she had pointed out the brass plaque over the entrance that commemorated Wilde's death in one of the rooms a century ago.

Unlike the many gothic tombs, Wilde's was of a modern design: a large block of red-mottled limestone fronted by a flying angel. A tall young man stood directly in front of it.

They slowed down and pretending to look elsewhere to give him a some privacy. He could have been a male model, with wavy brown hair and a stylish dark blue sport jacket over a white open-collared shirt.

The man kissed his fingers, touched the stone surface, and stood motionless, head bowed, mumbling something. They watched as he took out a small tube of lipstick and a vanity mirror, and carefully applied it to his lips, squeezing them together as a woman might. He then leaned in, kissed the monument, and stood for another long moment of homage before shuffling down the path.

As they came closer, Michael realized that the mottling he had noticed from a distance wasn't the stone at all, as he'd assumed. It was from hundreds of similar kisses in a variety of shades of pink and red—some faded, some fresh—that Wilde's admirers had left on the smooth surface.

"Sorry I don't wear lipstick" said Annetine, smiling at him. "I would have been glad to lend it to you."

"Thanks," said Michael, "but I'd rather kiss you any day." He glanced around, and pulled her closer to him.

To the older couple entering the cemetery, they looked like two people very much in love. The woman took her husband's elbow, urging him to slow down and give the lovers some space. There was no hurry as it was Sunday afternoon—the Sunday before Christmas.

27. NARCISSUS

Over dinner, an awareness that their idyll was coming
to an end crept into their consciousness via a minor
indiscretion on Annetine's part. The coffee came, and
Annetine put her hand on his and said "It's nice to be with
you Michael. What are you doing for the holidays? Is your
wife still planning to come?"

He'd been avoiding this topic, afraid that it would
break the spell, but there was no escaping it now, as
Annetine must have remembered his comment from the
plane.

"Yes," he said "Katherine is flying in on Wednesday,
and staying through New Year's. I believe she's going back
on the 2nd or 3rd."

"Oh," said Annetine quietly. She picked up the small
spoon and swirled her coffee, eyes lowered. The silence
grew between them.

"What about you?" asked Michael casually, hoping to
re-energize the conversation, "Are you heading home?"

"No," she answered, a bit gloomily. "I went home for
Thanksgiving instead, remember? I'll be around here for
Christmas, but I'm going to Switzerland for New Year's to
do some skiing. Some old college friends are meeting up
there, and they invited me to join them. It'll be nice to get
away. Now,"—she hesitated—"it definitely sounds like a

good thing…" Michael sensed that she was thinking about the loneliness of the holidays, and about when they might see each other again. In French parlance, it was a moment of *vin triste*.

Annetine glanced up and her expression was sharp. "Listen, Michael," she said, "this has never happened to me before and I'm not sure how to deal with it. I think you're setting me up for a fall. Honestly. Our time together has been incredible, but we need to think about how we handle all this, don't we? I mean, is this just a crazy little fling we walk away from? Aren't you heading home right after the holidays and, with Katherine here, how does that…?" Her voice trailed but she kept him fixed with her gaze.

"Talk to me," she said finally, as she gave his hand a squeeze.

"I do want to talk *with* you about this," he said, "but let me run to the bathroom first. I can't think straight with a full bladder."

Michael needed a few minutes alone to sort this out, to decide what to do—or not do—next. Certainly, he and Annetine were at a tipping point. He would soon be with Katherine and not see Annetine for almost two weeks. And then? He'd bought an open ticket on Air France that allowed him to leave at any time, and had considered going back with Katherine after the New Year, but now he found himself yearning for more time with this woman. He wanted to get to know her better, and he also had to sort some things out with Katherine. Their bottom line was far from clear. *If anything*, thought Michael, *there is no bottom line, except that I crossed a line, and that's bothersome. But there's no undoing it at this point.*

Sleeping with Annetine awakened feelings long forgotten, and the passion and intimacy, the discovery of a new human being, was overwhelming. Forbidden fruit or a gift from above? *Maybe both*, thought Michael. *I'm not at a point where I want to throw it all away.* That resolved, his thoughts returned to the situation with Katherine.

Someone once said that marriage is one long meal in which the dessert is served first and, while Michael understood where that came from, for him, the saying was much too cynical. Things changed with time in every relationship or, more accurately, time changed things. But until that last evening at home, he'd always subscribed to the one-life, one-wife model. The thousands of days and nights that he and Katherine had shared created a tapestry of time and experience. They had grown together from high school kids to middle-aged adults; she had known his parents before they died and he knew her family as well. Didn't that matter?

And yet, her actions of late—selfish and violate—had frayed the tapestry. While Katherine truly was *not* happy— he didn't doubt that—she had chosen to exclude him from the process of trying to understand the root of that unhappiness. Her having the abortion without involving him flew in the face of all the alleged fruits of a long-term relationship. In the time since, this was the one thought he kept returning to and couldn't let go of. Much as he tried, the seed of consequence had sprung and he couldn't will it away.

Michael wondered how this holiday stretch would go, and where he and Katherine would be at the end of it. Regardless, he reassured himself, the smart thing was to buy some time and not take any preemptive action. He would do his best with Katherine, but also stay in Paris for a few more weeks after the New Year to see how things evolved with Annetine.

Walking back to the table, he glanced at Annetine. Her face in the candlelight seemed strangely familiar, as if they had already known each other for years. The human dimension, he decided, was more perilous than the sexual. Lust alone would have been easier to compartmentalize and control. But Annetine drew him out of his comfort zone into a new kind of wilderness. She made him feel more alive and, right now, alive felt right. That sense of familiarity pleased but troubled him. So quick. What to do?

A phrase from Hesse's *Siddhartha* came back to him: *to think, to wait…*

There was no point in getting ahead of the arc of reality. Annetine's company was comfortable, yet exciting. Unique. Why force the pace, especially since the big unknown—the time with Katherine—was fast approaching? He would ride it out and see where it left them. After all, reasoned Michael, at this point he was holding a pretty decent hand of cards. The arrangement at work was flexible. He could easily conjure up a reason to stay another week or two, and spend some more time with Annetine. Durst wouldn't care. The apartment was under contract, rented through January. There were no sharp corners to worry about except for Katherine finding out about Annetine, but Paris was a big city and he trusted Annetine to be sensible, to not complicate things. It wasn't to her advantage to force the pace either. Who knows how the week with Katherine would go and how he would feel at its end? For all he knew, there could be surprises that he would have to deal with (the Christmas party photo flashed across his mind). It might be a telling holiday season.

No, this was not the time to change anything, he decided, and Annetine had given him a perspective he hadn't had earlier. Uncharacteristically, he would let go of the reins and let the horse take him wherever it wanted to go.

Michael sat back down and took both of her hands in his.

"Listen, Annetine," he said. "I don't know what to make of this either, but I do know that I don't want this to be a one night stand. Why don't I stay for a few weeks after the holidays so we can spend some more time together? I'm as confused as you and, quite honestly," he added, his eyes warming with affection, "I'm crazy about you. Thanks to you, my world's entered a new orbit that I don't pretend to understand. It's thrilling, and I don't just mean the sex. *You* thrill me—your mind, your energy. I can't get enough of you. I haven't said much about it, but there are some difficulties with my marriage that I'm trying to resolve. For me, getting to know you is healing in a way, and I promise to be honest with you. I'm not playing games. We still have a few days before Katherine arrives. You have any plans for the next few nights?"

"Only a company dinner tomorrow night," said Annetine. "It's a weekly thing, every Monday"—she shrugged and smiled—"but I should be free by ten."

"Great," he said. "Let's spend some time together. Then we'll take a break over the holiday, but it's only a week or so and, anyway," he said with feigned approbation *"you'll* be away skiing in Switzerland."

"Oh yes, and poor you!" Annetine wrinkled her nose. "Dear old Michael has to spend the holidays stuck in one of the most beautiful cities in the world. You poor, poor man!" Annetine's eyes became playful again. "But enough talk. You're not taking very good care of me. I'm still hungry and they have a fine dessert menu. How about something sweet to share?"

Back at the apartment, Michael took his laptop into the bathroom and emailed Katherine. Relieved that she hadn't written him first, he said he'd caught a bug and had slept most of the weekend, so he hadn't bothered to Skype her. Would tomorrow work?

In the morning, Annetine got dressed and gave him a kiss before slipping out of the apartment. "I need to go back to my place, but I'll see you tonight around ten." She poked him playfully in the ribs. "And don't be too tired."

Alone for the first time in almost two days, Michael lay in bed thinking about Annetine and replaying some of their most tender moments in his mind. Outside, church bells began to toll. Eight o'clock, top of the hour. He decided to skip the usual run, showered, and checked his email instead.

This time, Katherine had emailed him back and said that she hoped that he was feeling better, and that she would be working at home Monday afternoon. He could Skype her earlier if he wanted. *Sounds good*, he wrote, *I'll call 3 p.m. your time (9 p.m. here in Paris)*.

Walking to work on a grey and foggy Monday morning, it occurred to Michael that this was another minor but lucky turn of events, as he normally called

Katherine around midnight. Tonight, with Annetine coming over, that would have been difficult. Sometimes things resolve on their own, he reflected, especially if you don't force the pace. It was almost as if someone above was watching over him, helping things unfold in a benevolent way. Maybe everything would turn out well after all.

28. SADEK

Tunisian by birth, Sadek Murfati came to France in search of a better life. He settled in Seine-Saint-Lazare—one of the 'no-go' hoods northeast of Paris. Home to over half a million Muslims, Nine Three (as it's known locally because of the postal code) is a ghetto where Sharia law has displaced French civil law, and a place where few native citizens choose to venture.

Sadek had a talent for fine manual work and supported himself by making and selling silver jewelry—something he had learned from his parents, who ran a small store in one of the narrow side streets in Tunis. He didn't make much money, but it was enough to live on if one was willing to live modestly.

Eager for a sense of belonging, Sadek began frequenting a nearby mosque, but only attended on the holy day, and then not every week. He often skipped or, rather, feigned the daily prayers, going through the motions more out of custom than faith.

With time, he joined a group of young Muslims that lingered in a cafe across from the mosque after the Friday service. There, he befriended Tameem Muhammad. A decade younger in age and shy by nature, Tameem looked up to the more extroverted Sadek, and they would often walk together once the group broke up and banter about random topics. The conversation often related to some aspect of the sermon they'd just heard from Imam Fahad, a force in his own right and a sight to behold.

Short and pudgy, bright orange sneakers peeking out from beneath his black robes, Fahad was a Salafist—an ultra-conservative Sunni sect often associated with militancy. A bushy red beard streaked with black henna sprouted beneath a clean-shaven upper lip. Supported by the luxuriant beard, Fahad's round face with its wide mouth was hypnotic in its articulations. A loud, braying laugh and exaggerated swagger gave him a baseline charisma that was further magnified by his natural oratory skills.

Fahad's sermons were activist. The goal was to plant a seed that allowed his listeners to grow their own particular flavor of hatred in the fertile soil of imagination. A master of innuendo, Fahad avoided any overt expression of violence in his sermons, but his message was consistent and implacable: it was the duty of each Muslim to further the word of God and to counter the *kafirun*—the infidels—with action.

By spiking his talks with examples of the daily injustices Muslims are subjected to in Western society— the not-so-accidental elbow jab to the ribs in the crowded Metro, the rude manner of the store clerk, the occasional passing sneer or derisive remark – Fahad's sermons had the effect of sensitizing his listeners to subsequent dis-enfranchisements, and of re-priming their anger.

As Sadek listened to the imam's sermons, his inner fury coiled tighter and tighter into pre-strike mode. He began to see himself as a covert warrior planted in the heart of enemy territory. *Fuck the frogs and their "liberté egalité and fraternité"* he often thought, repulsed by the nationalism and smugness of the French. *Liberté* indeed! Apostate scum.

Walking behind a woman on the street in tight shorts, or a sheer skirt, Sadek felt a mixture of lust and guilt, of attraction and repulsion that tore at his soul.

And yet, he couldn't look away. Revenge fantasies began to prey on his mind. Troubled by their personal violence, he started thinking about taking broader jihadi actions that would eke out a larger toll on French society as a way of blocking these personal privations. When he confided to the imam, the older man's gentle and sympathetic words reinforced Sadek's sense of injustice but also made him feel like he was too passive.

"We can't all be warriors Sadek," the imam would say. "Only some have the spiritual integrity, the sense of duty that it takes to make real change. Most men are talkers. You have to look inside yourself to see what you are really made of." After they parted, the imam's words would linger in his mind and, alone in his apartment, Sadek found himself questioning whether he was indeed a coward.

One day, Fahad invited Sadek to join him for tea after the sermon. They walked downstairs to the basement room that Fahad used as an office and the two men sat down across from each other on oversized leather cushions. Sadek tried not to fidget as he listened to the softly wheezing breathing of the holy man and wondered what this was all about.

"I want to talk to you about something today, Sadek, something very important," said Fahad.

Sadek said nothing but bowed his head slightly in deference.

"Do you remember how we spoke a few weeks ago about the importance of taking action?"

Sadek nodded.

Fahad paused and looked at Sadek. "How would you feel about becoming a true soldier of Allah?"

Caught off guard, Sadek said, "I want to help, my Imam. I just don't know how."

Fahad smiled. His tone was friendly, casual. "Would you be willing to commit the ultimate sacrifice?"

Sadek flinched. The "ultimate sacrifice" was not at all what he was seeking! His father had told him that the Koran prohibited suicide. Action, yes, but not *shaheed.*

Seeing his hesitation, Fahad reached across and put a hand on his arm. "It's alright, Sadek," he said. "I had to ask, as martyrdom offers its own rewards. Perhaps it's not for you, at least not yet. Given your ability with people, I personally believe that you could be helpful to us in a very different way."

Relieved that the conversation turned away from the darkness of martyrdom, Sadek leaned in toward the imam, sensing something important but also more palatable coming his way.

"There's one particular plan I've been thinking about for some time," said Fahad. His hand continued to rest on Sadek's arm, and his expression was imploring. "The other day, your face came to me during prayers. I realized that this was a sign from Him, and this is why I wanted to meet with you today."

The imam continued to speak as Sadek listened, occasionally nodding in agreement. The plan involved his recruiting someone to carry out a terrorist act without their knowing. When Sadek asked how he could find such a person, Fahad said, "Pray and something will come your way. I know it, Sadek, for it is the will of Allah. You just need to keep your mind open to opportunity."

As he described the plan, Sadek's eyes widened, for it was indeed clever in its simplicity, and it made good use of both his human and manual skills. Fahad promised to provide all that was needed if Sadek was willing to do his part.

During his daily prayers—now grown more earnest and fervent—Sadek asked Allah for help, for clarity of vision.

Three weeks later, He sent him Talia.

29. SHUFFLING

Monday was uneventful, except that Michael met with Alain Durst and explained that he would need a few more weeks.

"Stay as long as you want," said Durst.

Michael got home around six and went for an evening run. He felt right, strong again and decided to impose an added measure of self-discipline on himself, so he ran a solid six miles, did some stretching and breathing exercises afterward, made a simple dinner of boiled red potatoes, asparagus and cheese, and avoided having anything alcoholic to drink. As he was washing the dishes, Michael's mind returned to the prospect of Skyping with Katherine at nine o'clock and then seeing Annetine an hour later.

Whew! This was life in its most errant and unpredictable form but, in an odd way, he was thankful for the privilege of being immersed in, and of surrendering to this unexpected maelstrom. He would to stay with his passive, acceptant approach as it seemed to be working. At least for now.

Chris had once told him that he had been talking to his father about his friends that weekend and, when the conversation turned to Michael, his dad had said that Michael was the most "psychologically courageous" of all his friends. The phrase was both original and flattering. He liked the idea that he pushed the envelope more than most. When it came to the triangle he was now a part of, he understood that he could easily be pulled under. Still, it was an adventure and he admitted to himself that he was intrigued by the wickedness of it all. To him, the formerly-faithful husband, this was uncharted emotional territory.

The clock on the stove said eight thirty five. Michael pulled out a book and settled into the corner chair to read, although his mind kept wandering away from the printed page. His thoughts ricocheted between Annetine and Katherine. Thinking about Annetine, he remembered their breakfast by the Hotel De Ville in the morning sunlight, the first kiss in the church at St. Germain-des-Prés, the coin toss at Place de Vosges, and their sweet twilight love in his apartment. Also, her sudden change of mood on the Lovers Bridge, and her odd dance in his apartment. Getting stoned in Pere Lachaise. It was odd that he felt so comfortable with her when, in reality he barely knew her.

When he thought about Katherine arriving in a few days, and what it would be like to be together again, Michael's emotions were decidedly more complicated. Restive from the mental conflict, he glanced at the clock: 8:55 p.m. Close enough.

This time, their conversation was pleasant but, again, there was a bothersome blandness to it. When he expressed his excitement at seeing her again, Katherine's response was that she was looking forward to it but that, "quite honestly" (he was coming to hate that word), she had so much to do before leaving that she hadn't given it much thought. "Work is killing me, Michael, and there's so much to do. I want to get the house cleaned up. I need to do laundry and pack. I want to get my hair cut but haven't been able to get an appointment with Dale..."

After that exchange, their conversation flagged and never regained its momentum. Both tried to put an extra measure of sincerity into their goodbyes and expressed an enthusiasm at the prospect of seeing each other again although, in light of the earlier conversation, Katherine's rang hollow.

Once they had disconnected, an aftertaste of disappointment lingered in Michael's mind. Katherine tended to get caught up in the small stuff while he was more apt to focus on the big picture. In some ways, it created a nice complementarity since she took care of the details while he kept the overall flow moving along. Still, it was annoying to him at times because his was the more sentimental nature and, frankly, he wanted her to be excited about seeing him again. Instead, she was obsessed with the details, the practicalities, to the point where she couldn't see beyond them to the broader view. Need this, want that.

9:35 p.m. Michael decided to refocus on the night ahead, and to cut his mind free from the drag of the conversation with Katherine. He put on some music, changed the sheets on the bed, and opened up a bottle of red wine to let it breathe. Then he undressed, wrapped a towel around his waist, and headed for the shower to wash away the dregs of the day and reinvigorate himself, for Annetine would be here any minute.

30. RUMINATIONS

Michael and Annetine spent two wonderful nights together and parted Wednesday morning on his promise to get back in touch right after the New Year.

After almost a month apart, Michael was apprehensive about seeing Katherine again. The familiar and the unfamiliar, the old and the new, the right and the wrong were all cartwheeling in his mind as he waited for her in the arrivals area of CDG Airport.

Could one man genuinely, truly, deeply love two women at the same time? It certainly was not the Judeo-Christian way although, here in Europe, monogamy with a mistress thrown in appeared to be tacitly accepted. It was almost *de rigueur* for artists, politicians, pretty much any man with power, and not only here and now, but across the oceans and the ages: Ann Boleyn and King Charles, Camille Claudel and Auguste Rodin, Lucy Mercer and FDR, Marilyn Monroe and Jack Kennedy. Pablo Picasso. Tommy Jefferson. Nelson Rockefeller (although that one didn't end well). Hadn't he read that Mussolini had over a hundred mistresses in his lifetime?

Visiting Paris years ago, Michael remembered coming upon a police guard at the end of a small narrow street. When he asked a store clerk about it, she had said "That's the street that President Mitterrand's mistress lives on."

She said it very matter-of-factly, as she might have said that the street was one way, or that it was going to rain later in the afternoon.

In some ways, thought Michael, it *was* the optimal situation for a man. You have the familiar, the secure, along with the fresh, the passionate—ideally, two parallel lines that never intersect. OK, a bit selfish and politically incorrect, but since the mistress was usually single and quite a bit younger, she might be appreciative of the older and more experienced (*and, yes, wealthier!* thought Michael) sugar daddy. It could work to mutual advantage. But what about the wife, the vow, the integrity of self? In his case, things were complicated by Katherine's actions and their currently rather grievous situation. He had been faithful all those years, and would have remained so, but now the rules had changed. Wasn't he allowed some moral slack?

If one separated himself from society's mores, from convention, it was difficult to argue against intimacy with another person being the ultimate life privilege, the most sublime human experience in terms of both body and soul. Michael's face turned wry at the thought. Maybe just a little self-serving, old boy? Ultimately, wasn't it mostly about pleasure? The soul thing got one into the question of meaning, hotter water. Souls belong to religions. Viewed as trust versus deceit, it was hard to argue against the former being a virtue and the latter a vice. But what about the individual who had been wronged? What about him?

Monogamy certainly ran against the natural tendencies of the male, whose biological lot was to spread the seed. In contrast, monogamy served both a woman's and society's interests well. OK, two to one it is, thought Michael. Of course, even the family unit was also subject to interpretation. What about polygamy? Wasn't it sanctioned by the world's most populous religion? How did Islamic women fare? Michael realized that he had no clue. It would be interesting to know. Maybe it worked in a certain way for them as well? And the children?

But these were all social values. Ultimately, in a spiritual and a physical sense, he reflected, every person *is* an island. The pains of infirmity and the joys of pleasure were equally private matters.

Half-lost in his rationalizations, Michael saw his one and only wife, Katherine, coming out of the arrivals gate. She looked lovelier than he had expected—high brown leather boots, a tan suede skirt and a white blouse under a long black coat and red scarf. Katherine had cut her hair shorter, which made her look younger, and had lightened it. She was more relaxed in her walk. She looked rather elegant.

Pleasantly surprised, he gave her a hug and they talked while waiting for a taxi. He was probably over-compensating in some way, but he showered her with compliments and affection. Katherine was also making an extra effort to the point where, for whatever reason, it felt a little forced, but Michael decided to not be cynical and to keep an open heart.

31. WITH KATHERINE

The holiday week flew by, every day filled with excursions to museums and historic sites (Katherine was a history buff and had come with a must-see list), interspersed with leisurely coffees at sidewalk cafes and, in the evenings, quiet dinners.

Their only problem was the nights. Katherine hadn't wanted to make love the first night, although they did sleep together. She was tired, she said, not having slept well on the plane.

The next night, they were in a small restaurant on the Île-St. Louis, the same one in which Michael had made a fool of himself in front of Khost several weeks before. The red haired waitress greeted him without letting on that she recognized him, and he appreciated her tact.

Their wine came.

"A toast," said Katherine, and held up her glass. "To the holidays!"

Michael was thinking more along the lines of "to being together," or simply "to us," but let the matter rest.

When the glasses were refilled, he said, "My turn to make a toast."

Katherine raised her glass and smiled, her cheeks flushed by the alcohol.

"First of all, Katherine, it's nice to be here with you, to see you again," he said, holding up the glass and looking her in the eyes. "So, to our years together—to all of it: the ups and the downs, but especially the ups. Thank you for being here. We may be in a bumpy stretch, but I hope that we can work through it and come out happy and well."

Her eyes lidded and her hand holding her glass dropped an inch. It was the most fleeting of expressions and the tiniest of gestures but, knowing her as well as he did, Michael noticed both and his heart sank. Secretly, naively, he was hoping that the problem had resolved itself, and that Katherine had at least committed to working together with him. Her mien spoke otherwise.

Katherine smiled and said, "Thanks Michael," as they clinked glasses. Normally, one appreciates a thank you, but this one bothered Michael as it fell short of simple reciprocity.

"You're welcome" he said and, hearing the bitterness in his voice, took a long sip of wine. They continued to sit at the small table, looking across it at each other in silence.

To hell with this, he thought. *Screw the tiptoeing.* "So Katherine," he said. "Are we going to sleep together again?" It was an intentionally forward remark, but after her neutral toast and irksome "thank you" in response to his heartfelt effort, he wanted to shake things up.

Katherine's swirled the red wine, watching its legs form on the glass before answering.

"I don't know," she said. "I haven't decided." She caught herself. "I'm sorry. I had some very mixed feelings about coming here, and I wasn't sure what it would be like to see you again. I wasn't sure if it would be connection or separation and, if you must know, right now it feels like a little of both."

Michael's eyes were watchful. "Not sure I understand what you mean," he said.

"I know you don't," said Katherine. "We know each other so well. We have such a long past—our friends, our families, our many, many nights together." Her words echoed his own thoughts a few days earlier.

"At the same time, it's almost like I know you *too* well, Michael, like there's nothing more to know, or"—she frowned—"I'm sorry, I don't mean that. That didn't come out right."

She put a hand on his forearm and slid it down so their fingers intertwined. "Look, I'm still wrestling with some things. I did contact a therapist and set up a standing weekly appointment for when I get back. I feel like I need some perspective. Yes, let's sleep together. We should. Otherwise, why did I come? But be gentle with me. Please don't force things. I'm not sure about the sex yet and, if it happens, it has to be because we both want it. Right now, I'm not sure I do. I feel detached somehow, isolated; I know you don't understand this and I don't blame you. I don't understand it myself." Katherine smiled. "That's kind of the problem."

Michael stared back at her with mixed emotions. Her tendency to overthink was working against him, against them. He saw that Katherine was being honest, and that she was trying not to hurt him. She did come to Paris after all, and that counted for something. At the same time, was it really that complicated?

"I'm sorry too," he said, squeezing her hand in return. "I still don't understand the root of it, of why you feel the way you do, but I'm willing to do whatever it takes to help us get through this, to help you. Some professional help wouldn't hurt."

"Thanks." said Katherine. This time, it was without connotation. "I appreciate that."

They slept together that night and cuddled, but didn't make love. *How strange*, thought Michael as he lay next to her wide awake and frustrated long after Katherine had fallen asleep. *After almost twenty years, how very strange.*

Christmas Eve, they went to midnight mass at the Notre Dame Cathedral and, once they passed through the now-customary metal detectors and security, the ceremony was joyous and majestic. Neither had ever experienced anything like it in terms of its grandeur—the forests of wax candles, great pools of yellow light flickering in the dark Gothic interior, the ancient Cathedral decorated in full regalia for the most festive Christian holiday of the year. Although neither Michael nor Katherine were particularly religious, the service made them feel serene and humbled, part of something larger than any individual.

The Parisian streets twinkled with holiday lights and, during the next few days, in addition to visiting the Louvre and other tourist attractions, they toured several Christmas markets sampling the local fare, rented skates at the open-air rink near the Eiffel Tower, browsed the famous Shakespeare & Company bookstore, and spent a fair amount of time wandering the shops and cafes on the Left Bank, near St. Michel. They were affectionate in public, but the nights were barren, and when he tried to start a conversation about their relationship, Katherine asked for patience, for time.

Once, after a few glasses of wine, when he pushed a little harder, Katherine retreated into monosyllables. Forcing the pace, he realized, would only backfire.

On New Year's Eve, they started walking the Champs-Elysees, but it was much too crowded, so they took a cab to Montmartre and sat on the steps of the Sacré-Coeur Cathedral, gazing at the twinkling panorama of Paris before going out to dinner.

That was when Michael decided to get Katherine drunk in an effort to break the sexual impasse. They were growing closer in bed—talking more as they lay face to face, holding hands, kissing. Last night Katherine didn't pull his hand away when he cupped her breast, as she had the nights before, but when Michael's hand wandered across her belly, she took it in hers and brought it back up to her hip. In the mornings, he pressed into her from behind and kissed the back of her neck, but she continued to sleep, or pretended to, and did not respond. After many years of conjugal nights, it was crazy, and it was driving him mad. Michael had kept his word and acquiesced to her gentle but firm deferrals, but tonight it was New Year's Eve and Katherine was leaving in two days. Short on patience and aware that their time was ebbing, he determined to resort to the most ancient aphrodisiac.

He thus diligently plied Katherine with wine at dinner, refilling her glass before she emptied it, making silly toasts, then suggested an Irish coffee (which she liked) with dessert. By the time they left the restaurant, she was visibly tipsy—giggling and holding on to his arm.

They wandered around the streets and bought some of the traditional hot holiday wine from a vendor before catching the midnight fireworks at Place de la Concorde, exchanging the traditional *bises* (cheek kisses) and *"Bonne année!"* afterward with fellow revelers.

Around one a.m., he pulled her into a small bar and ordered two shots of Powers.

"Trying to get me drunk?" said Katherine, slurring a bit.

"Damned straight," said Michael with a wink. He was feeling pretty inebriated himself. The whiskey came and, after clinking glasses, he downed the shot in one gulp and put the little glass on the shiny wooden bar a little harder than intended, catching the bartender's eye. Katherine's eyes were glassy but happy, and her cheeks rosy from the drink. *Time to head home*, he thought, and asked the bartender to ring for a taxi.

In the cab, Katherine slumped against him. All of a sudden, she was kissing his neck and he felt her tongue in his ear. Michael was surprised, as she had never done this before, but the warmth and wetness were arousing. After making sure that the driver couldn't see, he slipped his hand under her dress. Her head rolled back and onto his shoulder but she kept her legs together.

"No, not here," she said in a loud whisper, slurring. "Not here, not right. Later, when…" But her hand was on his thigh, and then it was touching him through his pants. Her sentence went unfinished and Michael pulled her in toward him.

Katherine was drunk.

32. TOUCH OF ROYALTY

"Happy New Year my dear!" said Michael, infusing false cheer into his voice.

Katherine groaned, but didn't open her eyes.

"I haven't felt this bad in years," she said after a few minutes. "*Ugh.*"

"Well, it *was* New Year's Eve," said Michael, adding, "and it *was* fun."

Last night, they had made sloppy, conventional love, reverting to the familiar patterns of the past. But this time, it was a *ménage-a-trois* with alcohol, and the drink took its toll. The momentum of lovemaking was mechanical, not tender. Each tried but neither was able to climax and, drenched in sweat from the effort, they finally gave up and fell back resignedly on the sheets.

At least she hadn't bothered to fake it. Katherine was honest that way. In fact, thought Michael, she was honest in most ways, and that was one of the things he most appreciated about her.

He snuggled up to her but, in the after-fog of excess, it was a half-hearted effort at best and he rolled onto his back. His eyes felt like they had sand in them, and he was nauseous.

Katherine rolled onto her back as well and covered her eyes with her hands.

"I feel like I'm going to have a stroke," she said.

"I know" said Michael. "Even my hair hurts."

"I need to get some water, I don't feel well," said Katherine. She walked unsteadily into the bathroom, leaning on the wall for balance and, seconds later, he heard her retch.

A fine snow was falling outside. Michael turned on CNN, went back to bed and lay there, staring at the screen, unseeing. He thought of the passion and intensity of his lovemaking with Annetine, and the present situation with Katherine only made him feel empty. She was leaving tomorrow and things were still emotionally out of kilter. *We didn't make love last night*, thought Michael, *we fucked*. And, to underscore it all, it had ended up being a cake without the icing.

Katherine decided to take a bath while Michael continued to lie in bed, eyes closed. His mouth felt rotten and dry. He decided that he needed to brush his teeth, so he got up and knocked on the bathroom door before going in.

The mirror was fogged and he left it that way. Katherine was lying back in the tub, the water still running. The air was steamy and smelled like pine from the bath salts. Her head was tilted back, eyes closed, and the outline of her pale body shimmered in the water.

Michael made some coffee. The sound of the hair dryer came on in the bathroom and, a few minutes later, Katherine emerged looking tired but presentable.

"Some toast and eggs?" he asked.

"I don't think I can eat," she said. "Do you have any tomato juice?"

They talked in subdued tones, sullied by hangover, while Michael ate. The conversation warmed somewhat, especially when their talk drifted back to their life together. Even though it was a new year, it was as if they could not go forward and instead sought comfort in the past.

Later, they walked arm-in-arm along the river in the grey winter light. The city was deserted, very different from yesterday, and the snow had picked up. It was cold. They stood for a while on Pont Marie, watching the large flakes dissolve in the dark green water. Michael had stood in the same spot on his first morning in Paris; the leaves spiraling down to the water, the solitary old woman, the animated young couple, and his own travel-weary cast of mind came back to him. Less pensive now, but it was tentative then and was tentative still. He put his arm around Katherine's waist, thinking she might turn toward him, but she seemed to be lost in thought and didn't respond.

This being their last night, Michael had made dinner reservations at Le Meurice, one of Paris' most ornate and luxurious restaurants. They sat at one of the smaller tables under the gilded chandeliers, enjoying the radiant heat from the great fireplace that is the centerpiece of the main dining room. Much to the disappointment of the waiter, neither wanted anything alcoholic to drink and they ordered a bottle of Perrier instead. The conversation was light and meandering as they waited for the escargot and ceviche.

Katherine leaned toward him. "Michael, there's a man over there that keeps looking at me. Kind of odd looking. Do you know him?" She nodded ever so slightly to her left.

"Wait," she said. "Don't look yet." A second later, she whispered, "OK. Now," and Michael looked up, scanning the tables. It only took him a second.

"Khost!" he said. "Remember? I mentioned him once. The guy I got a funny vibe from at work."

She nodded. "I do remember," she said, suppressing a smile. "You said he looked like a plucked bird. I see what you mean."

He glanced back toward Khost, who was sitting with a woman whose back was to him. Michael continued to chat with Katherine, periodically casting a glance in Khost's direction without making eye contact.

Katherine started telling him about almost killing a cat on the way to the airport when she stopped mid-sentence and glanced up just as Michael felt a hand on his shoulder.

"Evening Michael," said Khost. "Thought I'd come over and say hello this time. Happy New Year, man."

Surprised, Michael turned and half rose out of his chair.

"Hey Adrian," he said. His face twisted into an unnatural smile. "Happy New Year to you too."

Khost put out a hand to Katherine. "I'm Adrian Khost, also at Aerotel," he said, adding, "This is my wife Jenny. She came over from the States for the holidays."

Michael, now standing, found himself inches from Khost, who didn't step back even though there was plenty of room. It was awkward. The fine soap fragrance of the man was surprisingly pleasant, but too up close, too personal for him.

"Nice to meet you, Jenny," he said, turning to face her and shouldering Khost in the process to give himself a little space. He put out his hand. She took it and gave him a polite smile. Mrs. Khost was a pretty woman of fifty or so, with straight dark hair and a cheery round face. Her softness of skin, and the warmth of her blue eyes were a stark contrast to Khost's sallow, spotted complexion and bony visage. They looked like two different species.

"And this is Katherine, my wife," said Michael, gesturing toward his wife.

The women exchanged greetings and made small talk while the two men stood silently next to each other. Puzzled over this sudden and unexpected affability, Michael shifted his weight and glanced at Khost.

As if he'd read Michael's mind, Khost smiled.

"Hope I didn't surprise you too much," he said. There was a lively twinkle in his eye. "Nice to see you and, Katherine, nice to have met you. Enjoy the rest of your time in France."

Michael felt like he was in a movie, or in another universe.

After they left, Michael sat back down and shook his head.

"What?" asked Katherine.

"Wow," he said, his eyes still wide with surprise. "One never knows. Life can sure jangle one's perceptions sometimes. I haven't been able to have a decent conversation with him at the office, and now he comes over like he's my best buddy." He pointed to his temple and turned his hand while making a face. "Cra-zy," he said, realizing that he sounded just like Chris.

Katherine smiled but didn't say anything more.

After dessert, they waited outside for a taxi. It was sleeting now and the streets and sidewalks glistened with an icy sheen. Katherine shivered and took Michael's arm after they climbed into the warm taxi cab for the ride back to his apartment.

Tired from last night's excesses, they soon fell asleep, but he woke her in the morning and they made love. This time, they didn't hurry and it felt more familiar and gentle, although when he tried to kiss her afterward, she turned away and, after lying quietly for a minute, got up and went into the bathroom to take a shower. Michael got up and put his hand on the handle, wanting to join her, but this time the door was locked.

Katherine's flight home wasn't until 2:00 p.m., so they had a few hours to kill and went down the street for breakfast. Over coffee, Michael decided to dredge up the Christmas party. He had refrained from bringing it up all week but, with their time together waning, curiosity got the better of him

"By the way, how was the party at the Manor?" he said. His tone was casual.

Katherine leaned back in the chair and smiled. "If you must know, it turned out to be a little unusual. We're working on a case with Ohio, and their chief attorney flew in for a deposition that day. Joanne invited him to join us and asked me to babysit him since he was all alone and you were away. I might have mentioned it to you a while back. He turned out to be a nice man. Recently divorced after almost 30 years of marriage. Apparently, he had an affair with a co-worker, and his wife found out so she left him."

"Just like that?"

"Just like that."

On impulse, he said, "Did you dance with this guy?"

A small furrow appeared above her nose.

"I did," she said simply. "Why?"

He ignored the question. "Fast or slow?"

"I don't remember," she said. "Why does it matter?"

Michael smiled. "Liar," he said. "How can you dance with someone and not remember if it was fast or slow?"

Katherine looked at him for a moment, then laughed. "OK," she said, "We danced a fast song and then a slow one came on, so we danced that one too. Guess I wasn't sure how you'd feel about that."

"My wife dancing with a handsome philanderer while I'm thousands of miles away. *Tun-ta-run-tun...*" said Michael playfully, adding, "Should I be worried?"

"How do you know he was handsome?" said Katherine. She was still smiling, but her expression was quizzical. "I never said that."

Feeling mischievous, Michael pressed his point. "I'll bet he was. Dark and handsome no doubt."

"Well, he *was* attractive in a corporate kind of way," said Katherine. "But not my type. Anyway, who cares?" She glanced at her watch. "We ordered a cab for ten and it's only 9:30. A last walk around the neighborhood?"

"OK," said Michael. "But not before you tell me his name."

Katherine shook her head and smiled. "You are tenacious Michael, I'll give you that. You always have been. His name was Sergei. Sergei Romanov."

She said it the Russian way, with the emphasis on the "a". "Kind of a cool name, don't you think? Sounds like old Russian royalty." Katherine glanced at her wristwatch. "But enough already. Let's get some air."

33. AN UNCERTAIN FAREWELL

During the taxi ride to Charles de Gaulle, it occurred to Michael that their bottom line was still unclear. *How ironic*, he thought, *that uncertainty could be so tangible.*

Should he have had it out with Katherine—been more forceful, pushed it, to hell with the consequences? Katherine needed to own the problem, as it was all her doing, not his. Wasn't her behavior truant of *his* feelings? Michael stared moodily at the passing landscape.

After a few minutes, he felt her hand on his. "Are you okay?" said Katherine, puzzled by his sudden detachment.

"I'm fine," he said, not looking at her. Katherine glanced at him, and pulled her hand back onto her lap. In the silence, Michael regretted letting his self-pity bleed through. However unpalatable, he would just have to live with the uncertainty for now. *Suck it up*, he thought. *This is complicated. Don't be a jerk and do something you'll regret. You decided to take the patient approach, so stay with it.*

At the departures terminal, he helped the driver unload Katherine's bags and stood with her in the line to check luggage and pick up the boarding passes. It was crowded and the line was long, so by the time they were done she had to move on to security.

"When are you coming home?" asked Katherine as they were saying their farewells.

Michael was noncommittal. "I want to get back before the end of the month, maybe earlier. Depends on how things go at work. I'll let you know."

"OK," said Katherine. If she was disappointed, she didn't let on. "Listen," she said, giving him a quick hug. "I'd better go. Want to talk over the weekend?"

"Sure, sounds good" said Michael.

He gave Katherine a kiss and watched as she walked toward the screening area. When she didn't look back, he left the terminal and hailed a cab back to the city.

An hour later, he unlocked the door and stepped into his apartment. It had been a tough week in some respects, and he was happy to be alone again. At least for a little while.

He felt the tightness in the pit of his stomach. What now? He and Annetine had left it that he would email her 'after your wife is gone', as she had put it rather indelicately. Compared to the situation with Katherine with its long history and recent tumult, his relationship with Annetine was relatively simple. It will be nice to see her again, he thought, but not quite yet. Too abrupt. He could use a buffer, a little time to decompress.

Michael went for a run, showered, and looked at the calendar on his phone. Might as well lock things in. He needed to settle this in his own mind. Today was the second. There was a monthly exec meeting at the office on the last Monday of every month, and that would be the 25th. He would return home on Saturday the 23rd, which would give him Sunday to catch up and readjust.

He got online and booked the return ticket, which happened to be the same Air France flight Katherine had just taken. Michael then emailed Annetine, wishing her a happy New Year and saying he would love to have "dinner etc." tomorrow night if she was free, thinking how nice it would be to have a good night's sleep in his bed, alone.

34. ON TRACK

Waiting for Talia at the Café Mozart, Annetine felt happy about how things were progressing. Everything was going according to plan. Over the weekend, she had set up a bank account in Zurich and scoped out apartments. She had also skied for three days at Davos and met an Italian businessman from Milan. He befriended her on the chairlift and they skied the rest of the day together, had some drinks and an expensive dinner. He walked her back to her hotel and suggested a nightcap, but she had already decided to keep him at arm's length and politely declined, explaining that she was tired and had an early morning departure. The following day, she caught the TGV express back to Paris.

Most importantly, Annetine decided, she had Michael Boylen exactly where she wanted him: infatuated, maybe in love, and thinking that he was in control. That was the best part. With men, those elements were predictably intertwined and playable. They needed the illusion of control, but were also insecure and therefore vulnerable, particularly in the early stages of a relationship. From her experience, once you understood men, even the smart and successful ones were easy to figure out. In Michael, she sensed a weakness in spite of the tough masculine exterior. He was a beautiful man for sure—the wavy brown hair and soft blue eyes, the strong cleft chin and full, well-shaped mouth. Not that tall at six feet (she liked her men taller), but tall enough. He must have been a pretty boy when he was young, but age had taken away the softness of youth and replaced it with a solid masculinity. He was gentle and confident, but had a slightly harried air about him, a sense of the put-upon that she found amusing. He was prone to the furrowed brow and tended to self-pity. That, combined with what she perceived as genuine kindness, a generosity of spirit, was the Achilles heel that would assure her success. *How very odd*, she thought, *the way things work out in life. How something coincidental could, in retrospect, appear so preordained.*

Annetine glanced at the front of the restaurant just as Talia appeared on the sidewalk outside the ornate door. Tonight should be interesting, as Talia had promised to get things finalized over the holidays, and to at last tell her what it was that she was supposed to give Michael to take home as a gift when he returned to the States later in the month. They would use it to conceal the diamonds, and she would be fifteen thousand Euros richer as a result. Easy-peasy.

Annetine got up to greet Talia and the two women hugged and exchanged kisses. *We'll talk and have some dinner*, decided Annetine, *and then I'll get over to Michael's apartment with some of the evening to spare.* She realized that she didn't feel particularly excited at the prospect. It was always that way with men for her—fun at first, exciting, but then she got their number and the boredom started to creep in. *Well*, she thought, *life is short and that's just the way I am.*

35. REUNION

Michael opened a bottle of Sancerre, poured out two glasses, and carried them back to Annetine. She looked well-rested and radiant, her olive skin touched by the high altitude sun, hair pulled back into a short braid.

"The skiing was incredible!" said Annetine. "Best ever, and it snowed some every day."

"Where'd you go?" asked Michael.

"Davos."

Fishing around in her bag, she pulled out a small white box and put it in his lap. "Here," she said, "I bought you a present!"

It was a pair of brown leather gloves lined with cashmere. They were soft and fit perfectly. Michael said as much, and they clinked glasses and each took a sip of the cold white wine before kissing.

It was wonderful to see her again and they made love on the living room floor and then went out for a late night appetizer and a nightcap. Over cognac, Michael told Annetine about deciding to go back on the 23rd and she looked pleased to have a few more weeks together.

"I thought you might be heading back sooner than that," she said. Annetine's eyes brightened. "Listen, why don't we take a ski trip together?"

"Sure," said Michael, excited at the prospect. "That would be terrific!" He liked skiing, and it would make for a romantic and memorable ending to their time together.

After Annetine had fallen asleep, Michael lay on his back for some time—eyes closed but wide awake, contemplating his situation, their situation, wondering how it would all end. It was exciting, confusing, and oh-so-naughty.

Annetine was sleeping on her side facing him, one arm thrown carelessly over his chest. Her lips were slightly parted, and her breath was sweet with cognac. Her eyes were closed, but he took in the dark lashes and the sensuality of her slightly open lips. A line from an old song drifted into his head and he smiled grimly at the recollection, as it was so appropriate…

I got it bad and that ain't good.

36. GIFT OF TIME

Michael and Annetine arrived at the Hauptbahnhof station in Zurich, took a shuttle to Beckenried—a small town on Lake Lucerne—and checked into the splendid Vitznaurerhof Hotel, where they spent two hours in bed before going to the spa to relax in the Jacuzzi and swim in the heated outdoor pool.

A light snow was falling, and Michael felt relaxed and excited at the prospect of the three days of skiing, and of their being together. This was their last weekend, and his only goal in the days ahead was to enjoy it to the fullest.

He'd asked the concierge to make a dinner reservation for eight o'clock, which gave them an hour or two to wander around the shops of the charming lakeside town. They walked unhurriedly, holding hands, browsing the shop windows and pausing to watch the snow swirl around the old-fashioned gaslights.

"Michael, look!" said Annetine excitedly, pointing to a small store across the way. "It's a cuckoo clock store. Only in Switzerland! Let's take a look."

Michael didn't have any special affinity for cuckoo clocks, but he fondly remembered spending time at a friend's house when he was small. They had a cuckoo clock mounted on the dining room wall, and the boys were fascinated by its counterweights and chimes, and the painted wooden bird that popped in and out of its housing every hour. Actually, it would be a perfect thing to bring back home as a souvenir. Distinctive, unusual, and reminiscent of their last weekend together.

As if she'd read his mind, Annetine gave Michael's hand a squeeze. Her eyes were bright with excitement. "Listen," she said, "let me buy one for you as a take-home present! A timepiece makes a wonderful gift and you can think of me—of us—every time the silly little bird makes its coo-coo."

"You don't need to do that," he said, smiling at her. "I don't need a clock to remember you by, and I'm already coo-coo about you. But, sure, let's take a look."

Inside the store, they wandered around, entranced by the variety of clocks. Mantle- versus wall-mounted, one-day versus eight-day mechanisms, even battery-powered ones with fake counterweights for the forgetful or lazy. An endless variety of sizes and designs and ranged in price from fifty or sixty Swiss francs to several thousand depending on age, authenticity, and whether they were machined or hand-carved.

There were only one or two other customers in the store and the proprietor—an elderly, mustached man wearing a traditional Swiss black velvet jacket embroidered with red edelweiss flowers—took an instant liking to them as he explained some of the history and art behind the clockwork.

One clock in particular caught their fancy. Hand-made in Germany, it was an authentic Black Forest product. The woodwork was delicate and tasteful, and the eight-day mechanism with its large iron counterweights designed to look like pine cones would make the winding a weekend, rather than daily routine.

"You can remember me every Saturday morning when you wind it up as you have your first cup of coffee," commented Annetine gaily as she gave his hand a squeeze. "Beautiful, isn't it?"

Her enthusiasm was contagious, and the clock embodied both the aura of old Europe and the fairytale quality of their romance. Annetine was right—he would make it a Saturday morning routine, a private little ritual with a sentimental undertone.

The proprietor was delighted with their choice. He packaged it ceremoniously and wrapped the green box with a silver ribbon.

"It will bring you both luck," he said in parting, noticing the gold Claddagh wedding ring on Michael's hand. The woman wasn't wearing a wedding ring and he smiled to himself. He had assumed that they were man and wife, but these days, well, who was he to judge?

Michael and Annetine skied Klewenalp all day Friday and Saturday. He had to pull out every stop to keep up with her, although she would have never known it, as she mostly skied ahead of him and didn't see the few times that he lurched madly, on the edge of control.

"You're out of breath Michael," she said teasingly after a long downhill run. "I thought you said you were in shape!"

Michael's thighs were aching and his hockey stop was in embarrassingly poor form, as he'd almost crashed into her.

"Nonsense," he said, putting on his game face. "I'm taking in the beautiful mountain air. You're just showing off!"

Although he kidded her, Michael had to admit that Annetine was a much better skier than he. She was graceful and virtually effortless, while he had to carve and power through every turn. Although he was a runner, skiing demanded different muscles, and the thin mountain air was challenging.

Drenched with sweat underneath his parka, Michael would have liked to take a break and have some hot chocolate in the lodge, but decided to muster on. He poled ahead of her into the lift line. Childish? Maybe, but he was damned if Annetine was going to get the better of him.

"Come on," he said. "Let's do one more from the top and, this time, no stopping to rest. Then, to the hot tub!"

Ironically, the only time that Annetine showed any fatigue was in bed. Friday night, she said that she was too tired to make love (a first) but that she would make it up to him in the morning (which she did). On Saturday, she said her neck was stiff and acted a little distant. Michael attributed this to the emotional undercurrents playing out ahead of their separation. She must be working through some things, he reasoned. I'll return to my home, my wife, while she will be left in France all alone. It can't be easy.

That night, Annetine again said she was too tired to make love. Michael started teasing her about being out of shape but backed off after she showed signs of annoyance. After Annetine had fallen asleep, Michael—propped on one elbow—watched the graceful curve of her naked back rising and falling with each breath. This was a side of Annetine he hadn't seen before. Had he pricked a competitive nerve, or was Annetine more irascible than she appeared? The small crack in her affability was surprising, but women are complicated, he reasoned. There was Katherine, whom he knew so well and Annetine, whom he hardly knew. It was an odd triangle to reckon with, and an ever changing one at that.

Riding the train back to Paris on Sunday afternoon, they went into the restaurant car. Both were tired with that thorough fatigue born of fresh air exertion. The inside of Michael's thighs ached from skiing, which made him walk a little funny, but it was a pleasant kind of masochism.

They ordered some hot tea and sat staring out of the large windows as Luxeuil-les-Bains flashed by, then Chaumont and Troyes. The drama of the Alpine peaks dwindled to foothills and, eventually, into level winter fields dotted with white Charolais beef cattle. As darkness fell, Michael and Annetine stepped off of the sleek TGV train onto the long platform of Gare de l'Est and were soon snuggled together in a taxi, en route to his apartment.

37. FINAL DAYS

Wednesday morning, Michael awoke at dawn and started thinking about how he had only two days left in Paris. and of how much he would miss this apartment with its high ceilings, comfortable furnishings and white-curtained windows. He especially loved the morning sunlight that filtered into the bedroom from the courtyard, and the late afternoon mood when the apartment felt peaceful and subdued.

There was also the daily litany of the bells. It started at six a.m., when the bells of a nearby church would clang twice before a deeper-toned ring from another church joined them. The harmony of the reverberations—one clear and sharp, the other lower, less trebled—marked every hour. Because the timing was asynchronous, the peals would grow progressively out of phase until they were striking double-time. At night, their work would conclude at 10 p.m. with an affirmative final toll of the deeper bell.

It was a beautiful aural rhythm, and he and Annetine had often awakened to the six o'clock bells, made love, then cuddled and drifted in and out of sleep. Except for weekends, the seven o'clock bells became their unofficial alarm clock, when they would rise and Michael would shave while Annetine put on some coffee and slipped into the shower. The mirror would fog up just as he finished his last few strokes, and he would join her in the warmth of water and flesh. It was a fine way to start the day.

This week, a melancholy began to seep into Michael's consciousness. He flirted with the temptation to squeeze in an extra day and fly home on Sunday instead, but decided to stay with the original plan. It would be nice to have that buffer.

On this particular morning, listening to the tolling of the bells, he imagined being home again, and the bittersweet feelings that he would experience remembering Annetine's lively company and passionate lovemaking. At the same time, he admitted feeling a bit of relief at returning home to Katherine, and to his familiar routines, as he realized that the relationship with Annetine could not be sustained much longer without taking a real toll on his other life. 'Other life,' he thought—odd how we compartmentalize our existence, our feelings in the universe within our minds, where reality ultimately resides.

With Annetine, Michael was on the verge of passing from the first stage of mad infatuation to a second stage of comfort and habituation, and he already felt the extra weight in his heart as a result. This morning, he looked at Annetine sleeping quietly on her stomach, and leaned over and kissed her between the shoulder blades, wondering what she was dreaming about.

It was fortunate that Michael could not read Annetine's thoughts, for her mind was in a very different place—a place that he wasn't clued into in the least. She, too, had woken up a few minutes earlier and now lay with her eyes closed, thinking that, come noon on Saturday, she would once again be completely free. During this past week, Michael had become too familiar to her.

He'd opened up to her about his feelings on the train coming back from Switzerland when he told her that he loved her. This dropped him a degree of interest in her mind. From that conversation on the train, Annetine also understood that, given time and will, she could manipulate him into leaving Katherine, into abandoning the core relationship in his life. The children thing that he had confided to her after the second bottle of wine the other night was an all-too-easy card to play. A little vulnerability, a little neediness, and a little pressure on her part would surely pull him over to her side.

That would never happen, however, since she had no interest in conventional family life and took no pleasure from dominance or manipulation. The truth of the matter was that, unlike most people, Annetine simply didn't attach or habituate. Her therapist had said as much and even told her the scientific name for the condition: alexi-something.

She had always been that way. Unfortunately, it occasionally hurt others, but they got over it. Annetine thought of it more as a strength. She learned to compensate by developing behaviors that suggested affection and vulnerability: the slightly shy downward glance, the soft touch on the arm, the giving of gifts—in short, the affectations of sincerity.

Lying on her stomach with her eyes closed, Annetine felt Michael's hand slip between her thighs, but chose not to respond. She gave a slight moan and shifted her legs to be less accessible. Michael desisted. Would she ever find a man that would *not* comply, she wondered—one that would force his will upon her? It hadn't happened yet. On some level she wanted, needed to be swept away, and she fantasized about being forced to do things—naughty things—that she would never have initiated herself. Where were those men? She'd read books, but in life, every man she met, however forceful they first appeared, ended up wanting to please and take care of her.

While Annetine appreciated Michael's goodness, a restlessness had begun to stir inside of her these last few days. She would give him an affectionate hug at the airport, say a warm farewell, and get on with her life.

And she would be significantly richer.

After they returned from Switzerland Sunday evening, Annetine watched Michael tuck the clock into the back of the bedroom closet. It was in a large ornate paper bag and, while he was shaving on Tuesday morning, she removed the box with the clock and transferred it to a cloth shopping bag she had brought in her purse. She then fluffed up the soft tissue paper to make it appear intact and put the bag back in the closet. Annetine gambled that Michael wasn't likely to return to it until he began to pack later in the week. Unless he moved it for some reason, he wouldn't notice that the clock was gone. And if he did and asked her about it, she would make up some white lie about secretly having it engraved to surprise him, or whatever. Annetine understood that suspicion was binary in nature—a one or a zero, a yes or a no. Without a reason to suspect, he wouldn't give it a second thought. Here, too, she would have it her way.

Annetine had passed on the cuckoo clock to Talia and arranged to pick it up from her tomorrow at lunchtime. Talia was vague on the details, but intimated that her "friend" would somehow insert the diamonds into the counterweights. Once Talia returned it, Annetine would slip it back into the closet when Michael was sleeping or in the toilet. Come Saturday, he would pack it away and carry it to the States. Her job would be done.

Annetine didn't know what would happen afterward, and she didn't care, as it was none of her business. On the other hand, she did very much care about the fifteen thousand Euros that Talia promised to transfer to the bank in Zurich on Friday. Traveling around Italy, Greece, Spain... it would be a good year. Talia had already given her the new passport, which she kept in her apartment in case Michael rifled through her purse. Unbeknownst to her, it had come to Sadek via Imam Fahad. On Saturday, she would become Ms. Laura Greene from Bellingham, Washington. She would abandon her apartment and her identity, and stay at the Lutetia Saturday night. Every base was covered as well as it could be and it was now just a matter of slogging through these last few days.

Annetine rolled onto her side and looked over at Michael. He had fallen asleep on his back, and she saw the strong masculine profile and the tousled dark hair on the pillow. With the kindness of his eyes extinguished, the lines of his face took on a harder, tougher look. She thought of all of the love they had made in the last month. He was a good lover, she had to admit that. Somewhat conventional, but skilled. At this point, they had what— four, five more times left? She would enjoy it, fantasize if need be, as sex was mostly physical after all.

It's interesting, thought Annetine as she watched Michael's chest rise and fall with each breath, *how people inevitably drift apart*. She had felt the fade begin in earnest on the trip to Switzerland, although it had actually started earlier, on that Monday after New Year's—the lack of excitement walking to his apartment after having dinner with Talia. The separation over the holidays had taken its toll. For Annetine, absence always made the heart grow cooler instead of fonder and, while familiarity did not breed contempt—that was too strong—it didn't necessarily breed more familiarity either.

She would be true to herself and, if Michael picked up on her emotional malaise, she would throw in some encouraging words and a little extra affection to ease his mind. She would steer Michael to her sadness at their imminent farewell or, better yet, to the idea that she was putting up a wall to protect herself emotionally. He would understand, or at least think he understood. Michael was good-hearted and it wasn't his fault that she had grown tired of him. It was just life. It was just her.

38. SADEK'S DEVISE

Saturday—day of departure, day of farewell—was warm and overcast. A cold front was on its way and the prediction was for a turn to colder weather that evening, with rain predicted overnight. Michael and Annetine took a cab to Charles DeGaulle after having a last breakfast at the Café Relais. Michael liked the symmetry of having breakfast there at each end of their time together and Annetine was happy to comply because their cheese omelet, made with pungent Époisses de Bourgogne cheese, was her favorite. Afterward, they walked back to Beautreillis for the last time to retrieve Michael's belongings and called for a cab.

It was almost noon as the taxi pulled up to the CDG International Departures terminal. Annetine had slipped the cuckoo clock back into his closet on Thursday and watched Michael put it into the larger of his two bags last night as he packed. When Talia returned it to her, it was exactly as it had been before—still in its original green cardboard box, neatly tied with the silver ribbon. Looking at it, one would never guess that the poor little cuckoo clock had surrendered its Old World innocence to Sadek's crafty ways.

Talia had brought it to Sadek's apartment that same afternoon and, as soon as she left, he had set to work by putting on some latex gloves, untying the ribbon, lifting the clock out of its box and setting it on his desk.

He examined the iron counter weights, which were suspended on thin black chains fastened to the small loop of cast iron at the apex of each pine cone before disconnecting the chains and counterweights from the clock. He retrieved and carefully unwrapped two specially-prepared counterweights made of a lead alloy that Imam Fahad had given him. These were similar to, but a bit larger than the original ones that had come with the clock. Each contained five ounces of C4 plastic explosive and a blasting cap. The wire that would carry the current from the receiver/detonator was extruded through one end and held in place with a small plug of epoxy. To the eye (or an airport x-ray screener), each wire appeared to be a thin black braided chain, quite unremarkable.

Electron-opaque because of the thin lead shell, each faux pine cone would appear to be made of solid metal upon x-ray, as counterweights often were. After the units had been assembled, they had been sprayed with a thin film of glossy black epoxy. This secondary precaution created a non-porous, impermeable barrier that prevented any tell-tale molecules of the plastique from escaping if the epoxy plug had not completely sealed the small orifice through which the wires passed. If it were swiped for explosives, the clock would be given a clean bill of health by the otherwise-sophisticated molecular sniffer.

As with any plan, reflected Sadek, there were some uncertainties, for example, the random but thorough check by some overzealous official who knew and loved cuckoo clocks. He might want to take a closer look at the mechanism inside the clock and, if so, he might be puzzled by a small metal cube that was similar to the other components in its geometric simplicity, but appeared to be made of an entirely different material. To all but the most expert of cuckoo makers, however, the timer/detonator would look to be part of the complex mechanical mechanism that interconnected all of the moving parts of the clock. These included the automaton bird positioned on its telescoping wooden perch, the ornate wooden shutters that swung open to let it emerge, the music box with the small painted figures in traditional dress that circled beneath the bird, and the pistons of the air chime.

Sadek understood that the plan banked on the simple innocence of a cuckoo clock and the fact that everyone knew it was nonfunctional in a packaged state. In general, anything with an electronic timing mechanism was suspect by the authorities, which is why he warned Talia to tell Annetine to avoid buying a cheaper battery-driven version. This more traditional type of cuckoo clock only worked after it was hung on the wall, wound up beforehand by raising the counterweights. Most importantly, he reasoned, its traditional nature and childhood associations would avert suspicion, especially here in Europe.

A big part of screening was intelligence—the blip on the electronic record or the tip-off from an informant. Here, there would be none of that because only four people were involved and only he knew what the real plot was. The imam had called it 'vertical compartmentalization', and rendered it as being an essential part of the larger plot.

Although a cuckoo clock was an unusual component of luggage, that too would give it a cover of sorts. Unlike some more obscure gizmo, its identity was immediately apparent. There was nothing sneaky or subtle about it, and it was a mechanical rather than an electronic device. Simple. Low-tech. Universally recognizable. The chances that the average airport security official would be familiar with the inner workings of a cuckoo clock were miniscule. No, thought Sadek, it was brilliant.

He set the timer as per the instructions. Once the clock was safely stowed in the luggage compartment of the jet, it would detonate at exactly 4:30 p.m. on Saturday, hours after take-off, when the plane would be airborne at full cruising altitude.

Sadek carefully re-packaged the clock in its original wrap, re-tied the silver bow around the box, and returned it to Talia on Thursday morning to pass back to Annetine.

Later in the day, as she carried it back to Michael's, it occurred to Annetine that she could just take the diamonds and disappear. She didn't know their worth, but if they were paying *her* fifteen thousand Euros, well, it must be quite a bit more. But no, she decided, why be greedy? She would have to pawn them somewhere, which might prove difficult. Also, Talia's friends would surely come after her. As it was, she would end up fifteen thousand Euros richer, which was more than a generous reward for relatively little work on her part.

39. SWEET FAREWELL

Michael answered the security questions without missing a beat, checked his bags, and walked over to where Annetine was standing by the departure screens. The red digital clock above her head read 12:05 p.m. Boarding would start in just over an hour and he still had to navigate the substantial security line. He scanned the monitor and verified that the flight was on time, departing from Gate 73. Having anticipated this Saturday busyness, he was glad that they had woken up early enough to make love in the morning, take a walk around the Cathedral, and then have a leisurely breakfast. But now it was time to go.

Michael set down his carry-on and put his arms around Annetine. She looked like she might begin to cry, and he felt a heaviness in his heart as well.

He said "I have something for you to remember me by." He reached into his coat pocket and took out a small white jewelry box that contained a simple diamond necklace. It had cost him nearly three thousand Euros. He had drawn them out from the ATM in pieces over the last few weeks to cover his tracks, surprised at his own deviousness.

"Should I open it?" asked Annetine.

"No," he said. "It would be nicer if you opened it after I'm gone, when you're alone. I hope you like it. I think you will."

"Thanks," she said, and slipped it into her purse. "I may not open it until tomorrow. It would be nice to wake up and think of you first thing in the morning, when I'm still in bed."

"Michael," continued Annetine as she stepped into him and put her hands on his shoulders. "It has been an incredible time. I'll never forget you. Thank you for everything."

"No, thank *you* Annetine," he said, holding her gaze. "You'll always be in my heart. I love you."

"You're an incredible man and I love you too," she said, and pulled him into her for another long kiss. They stood for some time, arms around each other, perfectly still, surrounded by streams of travelers and a cacophony of terminal sounds—flight and gate announcements, laughter and excited chatter, and the nasal honk of airport carts ferrying the old or infirm.

There was no putting it off anymore. Michael gave Annetine one last kiss and, with a final wave, walked off to the security line under the large sign that said "All Gates." Just before entering the tunnel, he turned and scanned the terminal, hoping to catch one last glimpse of her, but Annetine was nowhere to be seen.

40. DEPARTURE

By the time Michael got to the gate, the passengers were already queued up for boarding. He strolled unhurriedly over to the big plate windows and gazed out over the tarmac. The blue and white Air France A330-300 airliner stood connected to the terminal by the long accordion of the jet bridge. A bank of dark grey clouds lay in the distance. Wh*at's the hurry?* he thought. *I'll soon be sitting for nine hours. Might as well eke out a little movement while I can.* His running routine had gone to hell this past week and he felt a little stiff and a little soft. And sad.

Michael walked over to a store and bought some sparkling water and an *International Tribune*. His mind drifted back to their time together that morning, and to the last kiss. *Would they ever see each other again?*

He and Annetine had agreed to try and meet again at some point, but it was all left vague and open-ended. From an emotional point of view, he felt like he had given her his all. Or had he? He had given her all he could in the moment—attention, affection, appreciation—but it was just that, in the moment. There was a curtain at the end of their one act play, and it was he who had chosen not to extend the play any further. Or was it? It was hard not to feel like he had ultimately benefitted more than she did.

For better or worse, he was returning to his wife, his home. And she…?

Michael wandered back to the gate, lost in his thoughts. Boarding was already underway and he was soon on the plane.

The pre-flight announcements began, followed by the notice about turning off all electronic equipment. His computer was still in its case under the seat. The lights dimmed and the plane pushed back from the gate onto the tarmac. Outside, it was dark and grey. The weather certainly fit his mood. He unfolded the *International Tribune* and began to read.

The plane taxied onto the runway and stopped. Michael looked outside, past his neighbor's profile. A young kid, maybe a college student. No Annetine this time, he thought with a grim smile.

The minutes ticked by, and he looked at his watch: 2:40 p.m. already. The plane's engines whined and it rolled slowly forward, then came to a halt. This intermittent pattern continued for another fifteen or twenty minutes, until the plane stopped and stood without rolling further. Ten minutes passed, twenty, thirty. Wishing to be underway, to detach, Michael gave it another few minutes before checking his watch. 3:25 p.m.

The PA system broke in on his thoughts, as the voice of the pilot came on. He spoke first in French, then English.

"Ladies and gentlemen," he said "there is a storm to our west and the airport authority has temporarily put take-offs on hold until the storm passes. They currently estimate a thirty minute delay. If you would like to use cell phones or other electronic devices, you may. I will let you know how things progress."

Michael looked around. The other passengers seemed unfazed; yet another delay in the annals of commercial aviation. He'd experienced worse. The minutes crawled by. He pulled out his laptop, turned it on, and started working a summary report for Aerotel, one he would be submitting on Monday along with the expense report. Drops of rain began to pelt the window. He looked outside and saw the sharklets on the wingtip quivering in a gusty wind and felt the entire plane begin to rock. It certainly didn't look good. Hopefully, the storm had some legs and would move on out.

Half an hour passed before the pilot's voice came back on the PA: "Folks, Flight control just issued a ground stop and, from my experience, we are unlikely to be given the go-ahead for two, maybe three hours. The good news is that the storm will pass, and we plan to take off later today and get you to New York. But for now, for your comfort, we will return to the gate. You may remain on the plane if you wish, but we have a long flight ahead of us, so if you want to stretch your legs and de-plane, go ahead and do so but stay near the gate area. Once we get the go-ahead, we will quickly re-board and get underway. If you had a tight connection in New York, speak to our agent and see if they can put you on a later flight. Thank you for your patience."

This time, a collective sigh of disappointment echoed from the passengers. Michael powered off his laptop and put it back in the case. He wasn't encouraged as his experience was that when a trip started off with problems, they only compounded with time.

"Damn," said the kid in the window seat, turning to Michael. "I'm flying to LA, so I have another long flight after this one. Now, bet I'll miss it and have to spend the night in New York! This sucks."

Michael nodded in sympathy and glanced at his watch. A minute before four.

41. A TERMINAL CONNECTION

The engines powered up and the plane returned to the terminal. Michael sat for a while and watched the other passengers de-plane. A handful of people chose to stay on board but, with a nine hour flight ahead, he chose to go back to the terminal to stretch his legs and have a drink.

Fifty feet to his right was a modern open-air bar where the server manned a rectangular glass counter flanked by high metal stools. Michael sidled up between two and caught the bartender's attention.

"Gin and tonic," he said. "Beefeater please, with a twist of lemon. May I take it over there?" he asked, pointing to the seats by the gate.

"*Oui, monsieur*," said the bartender, a middle-aged man with a sharp widow's peak beneath a bleached buzz cut. He looked ex-military, except that his earlobes were pierced and distended with oval jade gauges at least an inch in diameter. Each temple was tattooed with small red lightning bolts.

Michael put some Euros on the bar and, drink in hand, walked over to the tall windows that overlooked the tarmac. The rain had let up and there were a few bright streaks on the horizon.

The airliner stood twenty or thirty yards away off to the right, tethered to the terminal by the umbilical of the jetway. He glanced at his watch—4:28 p.m. Almost three hours wasted already. He took a sip of the drink, cold and strong.

Suddenly, there was a muffled boom and a flash as the baggage compartment door blew off and a cloud of debris shot out of the fuselage just below and behind the wing, followed by a billow of white smoke. Michael threw up his arms to protect himself as the window trembled from the shock wave but didn't shatter. Then, all was still as if nothing had happened, except that the tarmac was strewn with luggage. A clear stream of jet fuel dribbled out of the gash in the fuselage, splashing on the dark tarmac below.

To his horror, Michael saw the body of a large dog – a German Shepherd—body still inside the baggage compartment, head hanging out of the gaping hole at an unholy angle Blood was dripping out of its nose onto the wet asphalt, mixing with and forming red rivulets in the fuel. Plastic and metal shards of what was once its travel cage were scattered among the debris on the ground.

The animal had been killed instantly by the blast and Michael saw its eyes, already dull with death, and the long, pink tongue lolling out of its mouth limp and lifeless. Without the normal tone of the muscles to control it, it looked unnaturally long and straight, like a child's tie, extending at least six inches beyond the white hedge of teeth. It had been a beautiful animal.

Behind him, he heard screams and, turning around, saw that people had started to run down the terminal, away from the plane.

"Run!" screamed the bartender, waving his arms at the others as he jumped over the bar. "Get out of here before the gas tanks blow!"

Panic hit the crowd like a gust of wind. People began running down the terminal corridor pell-mell—mothers dragging their children, heels scraping on the linoleum, couples holding hands as they tried to put some distance between themselves and the plane. Some people used their hand luggage as cudgels, pushing those ahead of them out of the way without regard. The veneer of civilized behavior was preempted by the primitive survival instinct.

An elderly woman stumbled and fell. The crowd continued to surge on top of and around her as two young men wearing baseball caps stopped to help her up. Battered by the surging crowd, they started flailing with their elbows and linked arms, trying to redirect the crowd and protect the space around the old woman. It was all surreal, like a poorly-directed scene in a play.

With a glance back at the plane—nothing had changed—a chill passed through him as Michael realized that the explosion occurred directly under where he had been sitting. Had any passengers stayed on the plane? Struck by the memory of the Paris subway and determined to overcome that lingering sense of guilt, he ran to the gate and into the jet way.

The air smelled of burnt plastic and electricity and he saw a fog of grey smoke billowing out of the open door. A man stumbled out, moaning and clutching his head, yelling *"Je ne vois pas, je ne vois pas!"* (I can't see, I can't see!). Blood was streaming out of his nose.

Michael grabbed him by the elbows and kept repeating *"d'accord, d'accord"*—it's OK, it's OK—as he steered him toward the terminal although he truly had no idea if he would be okay. Somewhere outside, a siren began to hee-haw and he heard voices and the clatter of boots as a team of emergency responders came running into the jet way.

Orange flashlight in hand, the lead man yelled, "Is he okay?" and, reassured that Michael was in control, waved them on toward the terminal, shouting, "Go, go, go!"

Inside the terminal, Michael saw a large group of people teeming at the far end and that the exit had already been cordoned off by the authorities.

No need to hurry. The man was calmer now, hanging on to Michael and cooperating by walking next to him in a weaving, uneven gait. Michael steered him toward the end of the terminal and eventually sat him down in one of the empty chairs at its edge. A team of medics came through the still madding crowd and, seeing the man's bloodied head, ran over to help.

A team of police had appeared and were trying to quiet the frenzied crowd. At the same time, they were not allowing anyone to leave, and Michael realized that the gears of intelligence, forensics, and investigation had already begun to turn. This was *not* an accident and it would be a slow business from here on in. The captain's promise of departure was now utterly void. There would be no getting home today.

42. CAFÉ FRANÇAIS

Cushioned in the grey fabric of the Mercedes taxi, Annetine relished being alone again and was grateful that the driver took no interest in her. A Moroccan, the man was courteous but distant. Once they were underway, he started talking quietly, seemingly to himself, when Annetine noticed the bluetooth earpiece set off with a small blue LED that blinked rhythmically. At a quick glance, it looked like a high-tech, luminous earring.

Annetine reviewed what needed to be done in the hours ahead.

First, meet Talia at the Café Français near the Bastille station to update her on Michael's departure and make sure that the money had been transferred to the Swiss account.

Second, stop by her apartment to pick up her things. There wasn't a lot to take since the apartment came furnished and all of her belongings—mostly clothes and shoes—were already packed in two bags and a backpack.

Third, she would take a cab to the Lutetia, where she would check in using her new name and passport. Tomorrow morning, a Ms. Laura Greene would make her way to the station and take the express train southeast across the Swiss border. She would be there by midday, and safely ensconced in a new apartment by mid-afternoon. Then, she would ski a bit and decide what to do next.

Talia was sitting outdoors in front of the café under some heaters that glowed orange. The sky above was stormy and it was getting colder. She saw Annetine and jumped up to give her a hug.

"How'd everything go?" she asked anxiously.

Annetine gave her a reassuring smile and squeezed her arm. "Fine," she said, "no problems at all. I saw him off and the bag was on the conveyor. Were you able to transfer the money?"

"Yes," said Talia with a nod. "Here's the receipt."

A waiter came out and Annetine ordered a cup of coffee, stretched her hands above her head and let out a sigh.

"What's up?" asked Talia.

"Just glad this whole thing is over and done with. I was a little nervous, but it all went well on the whole. And now," she threw up her hands, "no more Michael. Nice man, but…" Her voice trailed off.

They drank their coffees and chatted about nothing in particular for another twenty minutes before Annetine glanced at her watch.

"Wow," she said, "almost four o'clock already! I should get going. Thanks for everything Talia," she said, "I'll be in touch. Come see me in Switzerland."

"I will," said Talia knowing full well that she would never see her again. It was nothing personal, it was just Annetine. "Don't worry," she said. "I'll get the bill…"

Annetine gave Talia a hug before hailing a cab and, with a last wave and a smile, she was gone.

Quite the girl, thought Talia as she picked up the check. *No moss will ever grow on that stone.*

Annetine asked the driver to wait and walked up the stairs to her apartment. Her bags were where she had left them and, a minute later, she was back in the cab.

"*Je voudrais aller à l'hôtel Lutetia.*"

"*Oui Madame,*" said the driver. At the Lutetia, he unloaded her bags from the trunk onto the carpeted brass baggage cart that had materialized along with a uniformed doorman, collected his fare, and watched Annetine's back as she walked up the stone steps and disappeared behind the revolving door.

43. INSPECTOR HENRION

"J'arrive!" called out Inspector Daniel Henrion, Deputy Chief of National Counterintelligence, as he began searching for his grandson. He clapped his hands twice to make sure the boy had heard, and imagined him snuggling into wherever he was hiding in anticipation of being discovered. The thrill of concealment.

They were playing a game of *cache-cache* although, these days, the seven year old boy much preferred the video game he got for Christmas to playing hide-and-seek with Grandpa. Henrion had heard the telltale creak of the steps when the boy tiptoed up the stairs to hide, and was about to follow suit when the cell phone in his pocket rang with the shrill, pre-programmed buzz of headquarters. *What now*, he thought, with mild annoyance. *Saturday afternoon, most unusual.*

He called out, *"Un moment André!"* before answering the call.

"Bonjour Henri, ça boume?"

Henrion's voice was soft, almost a whisper, and the expression in his pale blue eyes was a touch obsequious, a quality conferred by straight sandy lashes that gave him a sleepy, mildly apologetic expression. Of medium height with a thin cowlick of hair dangling from a receding hairline and fine oval gold rimmed glasses, Inspector

Henrion wouldn't draw a second look from anyone. One's overall impression was of a very average man who was a touch shy—a grade school teacher, perhaps, or a tailor. In fact, at 57, Daniel Henrion had spent almost forty years in police work and was considered among the sharpest minds in the business. The combination of being detail-oriented in perception and associative in mind served him well in a profession where quick impressions were often misleading, and sometimes dangerous.

To his way of thinking, detective work was like the written word—utterly defined by details. Clues were like letters, and Henrion approached his job by gathering observations, trying to understand the situation clue by clue, letter by letter, making sure that the order of the letters was correct so that the words, but more importantly, the sentence, the paragraph, could be deciphered. Context was also important, analogous to how missing a comma could impart an entirely different meaning; it was the old "eat, grandpa" vs. "eat grandpa" example. In his mind, the most difficult part of police business was staying on the track and not veering or blundering into the weeds.

Henrion's expression hardened as he listened to the voice on the phone, unconsciously nodding along with the speaker and occasionally saying *"Oui, j'ai compris."*

"D'accord Henri, merci," he said eventually and slipped the phone back into his pocket. He had heard enough. Time to get moving. He had instructed his deputy to have every passenger's passport scanned, and to have each person answer the following questions: First—were they holding a one way or round trip ticket? Second—for visitors, date of arrival in France and addresses they stayed

at and purpose of trip; for French passengers—home and work addresses and travel itinerary. Third—occupation and names of persons they had any association with in the three days preceding the flight. And, of course, detain anyone who fit a terrorist profile by religion and age for closer questioning and a background check.

"You know the drill", he had said, "we've been through this before." The files would be loaded onto the shared drive and grouped into folders according to nationality.

Each person was also to fill out a standardized lost luggage form that described their bags, and issued a cell phone that could be used to contact them. Unbeknownst to the recipient, each unit was coded and equipped with GPS software. By evening, Henrion and his team would have a digital map of greater Paris dotted with small red numbered circles that showed the real-time location of each passenger's phone. Moreover, a record of its movements from the moment of issue could be retrieved with another keystroke.

"Regarding the plane itself," Henrion had concluded, "follow the usual crime scene protocol and bring in some work lights. I'm on my way."

He gave his wife a kiss—no dinner together, but there was no need to say anything after 32 years of marriage—and reached for his jacket and scarf. The temperature had plummeted in the wake of the cold front, and he knew from experience that it always seemed colder at the airport, where the open spaces let the wind have its way.

44. NIGHT CHILL

Like every passenger before him, Michael was ushered into one of six small windowless rooms equipped with a ceiling-mounted video camera. The triage algorithm had been worked out and practiced many times, and the procedure only took five or ten minutes per person. Michael answered all the questions directly and filled out the lost baggage form. Two bags, canvas, hunter green—one medium, one large. He circled the drawings on the form that best matched his style of luggage. Asked about where he worked, he gave them the Aerotel headquarters address in New Jersey. When the official inquired about wives or girlfriends, he said that he was married and that his wife was back in the States.

"Any friends here in Paris?" asked the interviewer, without looking up.

"No," answered Michael.

Government-issue cell phone in pocket, Michael left the terminal an hour later. *What next?* He was told to stay in the Paris area and to plan to return to the airport tomorrow morning. The apartment on Beautreillis was rented on a monthly basis, and this was only the 23rd. He decided to call the landlord and explain that he had been delayed.

Heading back to Paris, Michael thought of seeing Annetine and realized that, other than her email, he had no way of contacting her. Their relationship was such that they never needed to call each other. Most often, she would simply come up to his apartment. The few times they planned to meet somewhere else, they just did. There was no need for contingency plans, as they were both punctual by nature. It now irritated him that he didn't even know her exact address.

She'd mentioned living near Père Lachaise once, and near the Parc de Belleville another time, but that was it. She said she lived with a roommate, which precluded privacy, so they had no reason to go there. He didn't know her cell phone number, although he had asked her for it at some point. But that had never materialized, had it? What was it that she had said? Something about not having service in Paris. He hadn't given it any thought at the time, but it now struck him as odd that a woman living in Paris and working for a business wouldn't have a functioning phone.

Come to think of it, he wondered, *what was the name of the stocking business? Where was their office located?* Again, he realized that he didn't have a clue. The truth of the matter was that they had been so focused on each other, on their intimacies, that everything else was a distraction, irrelevant. All he was left with was emailing her when he got back to the apartment.

Jangled by the events of the day, Michael asked the cabbie to stop at a liquor store on St.-Antoine. He picked up a bottle of Oban, his favorite single malt, along with a liter of Evian and some dry sausage. More than ever, he needed a strong drink to calm his nerves and ease his churning mind. He would call Katherine, email Annetine, listen to some music, and hit the sack. Today felt like a long day.

45. THE WINNOW

Inspector Henrion readjusted the scarf around his neck and peered ahead. The stricken airliner stood in the glare of the towering halogen work lights that illuminated the snow-white fuselage with "Air France" stenciled in large capital letters above the row of oval windows. The jet bridge had been retracted and the area was cordoned off with yellow police tape. Using shovels and some type of vacuum unit, several men in white hazmat suits were working on the removal of the spilled fuel, now contained within a large circle of absorbent material that looked like grey popcorn.

Henrion climbed out of the electric cart, ducked under the tape and walked over to the ruptured fuselage. Around him, several other investigators were photographing the scene and swabbing samples for chemical analysis. Henrion's expression hardened when he saw the dog. Pale and stiff with rigor mortis, the end of its tongue was bulbous and purple, grotesque. *Poor creature*, he thought, even as he noted that its skin and abdomen were intact. *Not a carrier.*

He ran his hand along the jagged aluminum edge and looked into the baggage compartment, then at the plane's puckered underbelly, trying to understand the nature of the explosion.

The baggage compartment hatch had been completely blown off its hinges and lay on the ground some twenty feet away. Three severed hydraulic pistons hung down from the hinge area above the compartment, and the tarmac was littered with bags and tatters of cloth and metal. The back part of the compartment was a tumble of bags, most singed and damaged by the explosion.

He signaled to one of the security men. "Pictures?"

The man nodded. "Yes, sir. We did a complete shoot before you got here. Inside and out."

"Good," said Henrion. "Let's get the flatbed in here and remove whatever is left inside." He pointed to a bag. "Start with that one here on the left and work your way clockwise around the compartment. Number and photograph each."

Minutes later, a truck pulled up, flatbed covered with a black canvas tarp, and Henrion watched as each bag was removed, marked, photographed, and placed on the truck. Most of the identification labels had been incinerated by the heat of the explosion, but many of the ripped, dented, or partly burned bags would might still be recognizable to the owner. All things considered, it was a modest explosion. If the bag had been tucked deeply into the center of the luggage compartment, it might not have ruptured the skin of the plane, although the blast wave would surely have damaged the hydraulics and electricals. And then there was that punctured fuel line. It didn't take much to bring down a plane if one knew what one was doing—a few ounces of plastic explosive could fit almost anywhere. *But why,* wondered Henrion, *hadn't the sniffers or x-rays picked it up during screening? Where had they failed?*

As the compartment was emptied, Henrion noticed that there were several shards impaled in the ceiling and walls. The largest was about the size of a pair of scissors—a crisscrossed piece of metal with some black charred cloth attached. Henrion borrowed a flashlight from one of the workers and, with the extra light, he could see that it was a piece of aluminum—the corner of a luggage frame.

Henrion put on a pair of latex gloves and climbed into the compartment. After some wiggling, he pried the piece free. Although the tatters of cloth were mostly charred, the fabric was originally dark green. He sniffed it and put the piece into a plastic bag before slipping it into his coat pocket. Most importantly, the open angles suggested that the explosion had come from within this particular piece of luggage. Also, it was lucky that the bag was green, not black, as this would help narrow down the search somewhat.

Later, back in his office, Henrion logged on and pulled up the master file that contained the list of passengers and the scanned-in luggage identification forms. His thoughts were interrupted by the buzz of his cell phone.

"*Oui, merci.*" he said. "I suspected as much, but now we know. Good work."

So it was C4. The lab crew had pegged it already. No surprise there. It could have been semtex or some other, newer plastic explosive, but C4 was the easiest to obtain on the black market. Malleable, powerful, it got the job done. The plane and its passengers would most certainly have been doomed had it already been airborne.

Henrion took out the plastic bag with the shard and examined it again before placing it on the desk. It was a fortunate discovery. He opened an Excel spreadsheet that contained all the files, and reviewed the summary sheet.

Of the 286 passengers, here were 137 French passengers, 74 Americans, 27 Asians, 16 English, 11 Russians, and 9 Germans. The remaining 12 were grouped into a 'Miscellaneous' category, coded as such because there were less than five with passports from any one country—4 Algerian, 2 Dutch, 2 Egyptian, and so on.

From here, it was a process of elimination. Based on the description of luggage provided by each passenger, he ran a search for all passengers who had described having green cloth luggage. The computer came up with the names of eighteen individuals—thirteen men and five women. All were either American or French.

The Inspector pulled up the files and read the information on each of the eighteen people who had checked 'green' on their luggage forms. Twelve of the passengers were either couples or families with children. Of the remaining six, he eliminated two more based on their hand written descriptions of the luggage: one described his bag as being lime green; another had a duffle bag, which was frameless. Henrion personally knew one individual (an ex-coworker) and categorized him as an 'unlikely.'

This left three people: two Americans—a Michael Boylen, 39, married but traveling alone; Roger Donegan, a 22-year-old University of Vermont student—and Chantel Feletou, a French widow, aged 78.

Henrion reviewed each file, watched the interview videos, and emailed his secretary with the three names and the numbers of their assigned cell phones, asking her to call them first thing in the morning and to have them come back to the airport for a second interview. He also asked her to issue a blanket call to all of the other passengers that had checked luggage to ask them to come in and identify their bags as soon as possible, preferably before noon.

He then put his computer in sleep mode and yawned. He was almost in sleep mode himself. Enough for today. Driving home, Henrion reviewed his line of reasoning. Not likely to be a suicide bomber, for he or she would not have detonated the explosion with the plane on the ground. No, the bomb was on a timer, which was most consistent with an unwitting carrier.

If he was lucky, he would identify the owner of the bag that contained the explosive by midday tomorrow and would begin the second, potentially more difficult part of the investigation—ferreting out the identity and motive of the actual perpetrators. After he had a chance to speak with the three individuals and get a better description of their bags, he would have the videotapes of the luggage x-rays reviewed to better understand why it got through undetected.

It also occurred to Inspector Henrion that it could have been an inside job. Despite the background checks and on-site security precautions, airport personnel were still the weakest link in the chain of precautions, and the bomb may well have been put into the bag after it had been x-rayed and before it was loaded on the plane. That was the most worrisome option, and if they couldn't find any confirmatory x-ray scanner image, that would be the tack to pursue.

46. LAST NIGHT IN PARIS

Annetine checked in to the Lutetia a few minutes after four as Ms. Laura Green. Holding the heavy brass-and-rope nubbin embossed with the number 615 in the palm of her hand along with its dangling key, she took the elevator up to the sixth floor. The room was high-ceilinged and light, with a king-sized bed and some generic impressionistic paintings on the wall showing typical Parisian street scenes. She parted the curtains and stood by the window, thinking about tomorrow, until she heard a knock. It was the bellman bringing up her bags. She tipped him with a five Euro note and, after he had thanked her and left, closed the door.

Annetine decided to run a few errands before walking over to the *epicerie* Le Bon Marché, one of her favorite places in Paris to pick up a few treats. The large specialty market was only two blocks away. Afterward, she would return to the hotel, transform and take a warm bath, and get a good night's sleep.

Back in the room an hour later, requisite purchases in hand, she undressed, went into the bathroom and, standing at the sink naked while the bath was running, cut her hair with a pair of scissors so it was quite short. She then dyed it black before spraying in three reddish-pink streaks with temporary dye. The haircut was far from professional, but her hair was straight and easy to work with, and the look she'd chosen wasn't known for its finesse. Rough around the edges was part of the punk style, part of the defiance after all. Tomorrow, after putting on the black hoodie, skinny jeans and red Converse sneakers that she'd bought, she would look a decade younger and close to the photo in her new passport for which she had worn a cheap black wig. Once in Switzerland, she would get a stylish haircut and become a brunette again. She was tired of the long hair and it would be just the right look for Spring.

After rinsing her hair in the sink, Annetine threw a handful of bath salts into the tub and luxuriated for half an hour in the warm scented water. Relaxed, content, she sat on the edge of the tub and shaved her legs, then dried and brushed her hair and put on the white terrycloth robe provided by the hotel. After cutting a baguette into thin slices and spreading some of the duck *foie gras* on a few pieces, she uncorked the bottle of Prosecco she had bought at the *epicerie*. Glass in hand, Annetine found the remote, tuned the TV to CNN, and lay back on the bed. It was almost six o'clock.

Momentarily, the news anchor came on with the lead story—a bomb detonation at CDG Airport! Annetine sat straight up and put the glass of wine on the night table. Her fears were confirmed by the "Flight 56" banner that appeared under the photograph of the Air France plane. A shudder ran through her, and she heard a rustling sound behind her head. It was the hairs standing up on the back of her neck—the prickle was unmistakable—and she could hear her heart pounding in her ears.

She turned up the volume as a reporter described the situation: *"afternoon Air France flight to New York... delayed by thunderstorms... a small bomb... baggage compartment... three people taken to the hospital... police trying to understand what happened... no one has claimed responsibility... authorities suspect Islamic militants in retaliation for earlier French government actions... "*

One of the passengers, an American college student, was being interviewed on screen. He was a blue eyed young man with a shaved head, and an eyebrow pierced with three concentric silver hoops.

"Can you tell me what happened?" asked the reporter. "We were on the tarmac for the longest time because of the storm," he said, "it must have been an hour, maybe more. They closed the runway and the pilot told us we had to return to the terminal. I got off and was buying a soda when *ka-boom!*"—his eyes widened and he gestured with his hands—"There was this explosion. People started screaming, running. We all tried to get as far away from the plane as possible."

"So you had no warning that something was wrong?"

"Not a thing. All I can say is God bless the bad weather!" exclaimed the student, shaking his head in disbelief. "If that thing had exploded when we were in the air..." His voice trailed off with implication.

Annetine half listened as the anchor exchanged a few more comments with the passenger. She instantly thought of the cuckoo clock and the alleged diamonds. Could it have been Michael? Could it have been a bomb? There was no way to tell, but her intuition told her that it had to be: fucking Talia must have lied to her, and she could have been responsible for the death of several hundred innocent people. Women, children! Shit! It sounded like several people might die still. Anger and fear welled up and mingled inside her.

Calm down girl, she told herself. *Calm down! It could have been worse. Nothing short of a miracle, in fact. The kid had that right. God bless the delay! But what now? What should I do?*

Annetine's first impulse was to flee. She started working her iPhone trying to find the train schedule. Damn! The last train to Zurich was 4:54 p.m., so she had missed it. Could she catch a slower train and get the hell out of Paris? Was that necessary? Annetine tried to quiet her mind and think logically. What would the police do?

They would first try to figure out what kind of bomb it was, what it was in, and who the responsible passenger was. The explosives must have been wired into the cuckoo clock. The pieces began falling into place. Of course— that's why Talia had taken it earlier in the week!

Annetine's thoughts raced on. The police would detain and interview all the passengers, as the student had said but, without knowing whose bag it was, what would they learn? How long would it take them to figure out who the carrier was? Were all the bags destroyed, in which case the carrier's identity might never be known?

No, she reasoned, unless there was a fire as well, some surely weren't. Still, it might take them a day or more to get to the person. What then? What would they do if they figured out it was Michael's bag that had contained the bomb? Ask a lot of questions, interrogate him closely about who he had seen and been with.

He wouldn't believe it was him, at least at first, but if the questions continued, he would soon realize that she was to blame. Would he tell them about her? How could he not? Why wouldn't he? He would be absolutely livid.

He wouldn't know that she hadn't known it was a bomb, that she was fed the tale about innocent diamonds. He would definitely assume that she had set him up. It was all so unfair, so wrong! Should she try to email him? Probably best let it be for now, she decided. The police would be keeping a close eye on his communications.

Her mind returned to earlier in the day, when they had parted. There was no doubt that the two of them had been caught on some video camera, the airport was full of them. Security would be scouring every minute of footage. How long would that take? They would come after her—Michael would come after her—with a vengeance! But how soon? Annetine began to pace the room, her mind feverish. So much for her peaceful, self-indulgent evening!

She sat down on the bed and tried to calm her mind by breathing deeply, as they had taught her in yoga class. Inhale, hold, exhale; inhale, hold, exhale.

After ten or fifteen minutes, her body began to respond and the frantic pace of her thoughts began to slow, although her mind kept fighting her with its questions and impressions. It took another ten minutes for her body to relax and her mind to calm. She could think more clearly now. How far had she gotten? Right—the fact that they would get down to a handful of passengers, probably in a matter of hours. But how would they know whose bag was whose? How many people were there on the plane—two hundred, three hundred? And how many bags? One or two per person on average, so there could have been five hundred or more pieces of luggage.

That could take hours, maybe even a day or two. This last thought comforted her.

Also, she realized, there was no Annetine Fournier anymore. She might as well stay with the plan and take an early train out of Paris. Once they identified Michael as the carrier, they would start looking for her. But with the new passport, her different appearance and a little bit of luck, she would be fine.

Annetine lay back down on the bed, propped her head up on a pile of pillows, and tightened the belt of the cotton robe around her waist. She lay there for another fifteen minutes reviewing the facts, remembering her conversations with Talia, considering the possibilities. Oddly enough, she never thought about what Michael had been through; she thought only about her own vulnerability and what actions she could take.

Tired of her jumbled thoughts, Annetine decided to have dinner in her room and get a good night's sleep. She poured herself another glass of Prosecco and rifled through the Guide for Guests, looking for the room service menu.

After dinner she took two tablets of melatonin to help her sleep, stared at some nonsense on television until eleven o'clock, and watched the late news. There was nothing new and she set the alarm for 6:30 a.m.

Before falling asleep, she thought things through one last time. Should she contact the police and give them Talia's name? No, no point. If they arrested Talia and whomever her friends were, they would get onto her, and onto the money transfer to the bank in Zurich. She would withdraw the money and close the account first thing on Monday, then decide if and when to move again. Reassured, Annetine closed her eyes and drifted off into a troubled sleep.

47. MORNING AFTER

Sunday dawned cold and clear—a cloudless sky with the extra measure of lucidity typical of a sunny Parisian winter day. The stone façades of the old buildings were bathed in a bright white morning light, the ornate curlicues of their cornices set off by sharp black shadows.

Michael woke to the sound of the bells after a fitful sleep, and lay in bed thinking about what the day would bring. He was on a short leash with the authorities and, although he wasn't involved in the incident, he would doubtless be scrutinized, as would every passenger on Flight 56. The prospect of going back to the airport, sitting through more interviews, waiting for the wheels of officialdom to turn, was tedious.

More than anything else, he wanted to see Annetine again. Once he was done with the police business, they could spend the day, the night, together. He'd emailed her last night, but it was late, so it was unlikely she'd responded. Maybe later this morning?

He shaved, showered, and brewed up a small pot of coffee before sitting down at the dining room table to check his email. His eyes ran over the bolded new messages. Nothing from Annetine.

Michael's mind returned to yesterday and began to meander: Was it a bomb and, if so, how was it planted? By whom? Was it one of the passengers? If so, did they know about it? Why was his flight targeted? Why did the explosion go off when the plane was still on the ground?

As if on cue, the shrill ring of the police-issued cell phone broke in on his thoughts. He picked it up, not sure what to expect.

The female voice at the other end spoke in English with a French accent. She sounded pleasant but official, and inquired whether he was doing all right.

"Yes," he said "I'm fine, thank you."

She asked him to come to the airport security offices as soon as possible to help with bag identification. The authorities might want to talk with him again and there were many passengers, so he should expect to be there for most of the afternoon.

"No problem," said Michael. "I'll be there by eleven at the latest."

"Perfect," she said. "We'll see you then. Please come to the same area you were interviewed in last night. Good day."

Good day, thought Michael. *You've got to be kidding me.* He put on the black jeans and light blue shirt from yesterday—his only clothes at this point—and walked up to St.-Antoine for some breakfast before catching a cab back to CDG.

48. FUGITIVE

Annetine overslept badly. The alarm didn't go off and she later figured out that she had set it for 6:30 p.m. by accident. Now, it was already 9:30 a.m.! The hotel room was still very dark, as she had drawn the thick curtains across the window. Annetine climbed out of the bed, ruffled her hair—momentarily surprised at how little was left—and went into the bathroom to wash up and shower.

Still dull with sleep, she didn't recognize herself for a moment, and the mental lapse gave her a fresh perspective on her new appearance. *Not bad*, she thought, *not bad at all!* Once she donned the punky clothes and glasses, it would take a close observer to identify this person as being the same woman that checked into the hotel the previous evening. The black, short hair altered the angles of her face and made her look very different.

She turned on the water in the shower and, as she waited for the stream to warm, it occurred to her that she would also walk slightly pigeon-toed and with a quicker than normal gait to introduce an element of social awkwardness into her appearance, and to reinforce the sense of youth. Annetine smiled. *I could have been an actress,* she thought. *Actually, I am an actress in a way, as I'm acting on the grandest stage of all—the stage of life. International no less!*

Annetine repacked her things, throwing out some clothes to eliminate one bag, and took a last look out of the window. Sunday morning traffic was light, and the scene was as she remembered it—the wide Boulevard Raspail below, with the Sèvres-Babylone Metro station and the small park across the way, only now it was bright and cheery in the morning light. She noticed a woman sitting on a bench, rocking a baby carriage with her foot as she talked on a cell phone. She was wearing a pink running suit and a matching cap. Somewhere in the distance, a bell began to toll—the Sunday morning call to Mass. *Maybe I should stop in and say a prayer?* mused Annetine half-seriously. *No*, she decided, *I need to get a move on; God helps those who help themselves.*

She went into the bathroom, wrapped her phone in a wet washcloth, and smashed it three or four times with the heavy base of the drinking glass. The face of the phone shattered. Just to make sure, she ran some water into the sink and threw it in for a minute. Then, she put its remains, along with the washcloth into the sanitary napkin bag and crumpled up the bag. Once it was in its final resting place in one of the trash bins in the Metro, not even a homeless person would venture a look. She checked out using the TV express service. *Au revoir* Lutetia. *Au revoir* Paris. *Au revoir* France.

Sitting in the first class carriage of the sleek TGV express hurtling towards the Swiss border at well over a hundred miles per hour, the girl with the red-streaked, short black hair watched the landscape of fields and towns flash by through a pair of oversized red-framed glasses. As Laura Greene bid France farewell, she thought one last time of Michael Boylen, wondering how he was doing today. Her thoughts quickly moved on to considering how she would spend the next few days, and what to do thereafter. She took out a travel guide to Switzerland, and began to leaf through it absentmindedly.

The businessman sitting opposite Annetine—crumpled, middle-aged and overweight—stole another glance at her over his paper and tried to imagine what this girl would look like if she was nicely dressed and made up. She was kind of pretty but very unfriendly, which made her less attractive. He had tried to engage her in conversation, but she had avoided his eyes and answered in flat monosyllables. No personality whatsoever. These days, young people could be so rude.

Several days later, when he saw Annetine Fournier's photograph on the evening news, he took notice. There was something very familiar about that face but, try as he might, he couldn't make the connection. Someone he saw in a restaurant in Paris? A store clerk? That stripper at *Chez Paree*? Tired of wrestling with his memory, he refocused his attention on the television, which was now onto some story about a fungal blight on coffee beans in South America. His wife called to him. Time for dinner.

49. WHEELS OF INQUIRY

Michael sat in Room 447 at the Charles de Gaulle International Airport, waiting to meet with an Inspector Henrion. He had been here for over an hour, and his mood had grown increasingly sullen. The air smelled of sweat and cigarettes, and he thought of Annetine again. She still hadn't answered his email.

The door opened and a short, balding man with glasses and a cowlick entered the small room. He was casually dressed in a white shirt and tan pants, and the only sign of officialdom was the photo identification tag clipped to his belt.

"*Bonjour* Monsieur Boylen," he said curtly. "I am Inspector Henrion. Please come with me."

Once they were in his office, he gestured to a chair before sitting down across the desk. He swiveled this way and that before tipping it back. His gaze wandered over to Michael and refocused into a benevolent but appraising look.

"Thank you for cooperating with us. I am looking into the circumstances of yesterday's unfortunate accident and I apologize for keeping you waiting. May we have a few words?"

He spoke quietly, in halting English with a thick French accent.

"Sure," said Michael, settling back in the molded plastic chair. "What happened, Inspector?"

Henrion smiled and held up a hand. "If you will indulge me, I will return to that question in a few minutes Mr. Boylen. The short answer is that we don't quite know yet. But first I have some questions for you. Would you describe your luggage?"

Michael leaned forward to hear better. At first he was surprised by Henrion's manner, which struck him as shy, almost apologetic. At the same time, Michael sensed that he was a professional who knew exactly how to play him. There was surely an agenda behind the slightly embarrassed tone, and he noticed that the pale eyes behind the gold-rimmed glasses were steady and watchful.

"I filled out a sheet for you yesterday, describing them in detail." said Michael.

The Inspector shrugged and continued to look at him without saying a word.

"Two bags," said Michael. "They were a set—dark green, cloth, zippered. Both with wheels. Pretty unremarkable. I bought them back in the States. One was larger than the other."

"And was it the larger one that contained a cuckoo clock?" asked Henrion.

"Yes," answered Michael reflexively, surprised at the directness of the question. The clock? How did they know? Why did they care?

"For your children?"

"I don't have any children," said Michael. "I bought it as a souvenir for my wife,"—the lie rolled off of his tongue effortlessly—"when I was in Switzerland a week ago."

"I see," said Henrion. His expression was pleasant but inscrutable. Henrion took off his glasses and held them up in front of his eyes before slipping them back onto the bridge of his nose. He adjusted them so that they were level and turned his attention back to Michael. The silence grew as he gazed across the desk without saying anything. h motion.

"Why?" said Henrion finally.

He uttered the word so quietly that Michael was not sure if he had heard it correctly.

"Why what?" said Michael.

"Why a cuckoo clock?"

"To hang on my wall at home," said Michael. Realizing he might have sounded flippant, he added, "A friend of mine had one when I was a child, so it brought back some fond memories. Seemed like a perfect souvenir to take back to America."

"Has it been in your possession since you bought it?" asked Henrion.

"Yes," said Michael. "I put it in my closet Sunday night. Then, when I was packing my bags Friday night, I transferred it into my suitcase. Why do you ask?"

Henrion ignored Michael's question and clicked the keyboard in front of him. The computer screen flickered and Michael saw a scanned-in image of the lost luggage form he had filled out yesterday.

While Henrion appeared to be reviewing the luggage report, he was in fact processing his impressions of this Mr. Michael Boylen. Neatly dressed. Fit. Direct in his communication. Clear blue eyes. Wavy brown hair with a few strands of grey at the temples. Good looking in an affable, man's man kind of way. Nothing sly about him, but there was something else, another quality he had picked up. The descriptor came to him quickly, as it was one of his favorite words—*"dépaysé"*. Boylen had this slightly naive, out-of-my-element quality about him—a sincerity combined with a vulnerability.

So he was married and bought the clock for his wife as a souvenir. It sounded very plausible but, having seen the surveillance footage of the terminal this morning, Henrion wondered who the woman he had arrived with was, the one that he was embracing and kissing in the terminal?

Henrion was a romantic at heart—he embarrassed himself by tearing up at movies, for example—but when it came to his job, he was objective, and an empiricist. For him, the '*Who?*', the '*Why?*' and the '*How?*' were the cornerstones of effective investigation, and this inconsistency warranted additional exploration. He would find his way to the truth and register any twists along the way. All in due time.

"Monsieur Boylen," said Henrion. His eyes held Michael's. "Were you alone when you bought this clock?"

Michael hesitated, as he was hoping to keep Annetine out of this situation.

As if he had read his mind, Henrion said, "As in your country, perjury is a very serious offence, especially in this type of situation. International law," he added, "is very unforgiving so, please, the truth."

Michael squared his shoulders and sat straight up in the chair.

"Inspector," he said politely but firmly, "these are very pointed questions. Exactly what are you..." His voice trailed off, as he saw a new coldness in Henrion's eyes and watched his expression harden. Mind awhirl with the direction this conversation was taking, Michael felt fear blooming inside him like an alien flower, and felt the sweat break out on his forehead. Lord, it was hot in here!

Inspector Henrion took off his glasses again. This time, he put them down on the desk and pressed his thumb and forefinger into the bridge of his nose, rubbing the corners of his eyes. Michael noticed the hollow above his nose crease and sensed, incorrectly, that the good Inspector might be struggling with a temper.

It was actually a moment of confirmation, for Henrion realized that Boylen was, in fact, an unwitting carrier, as he had suspected last night. He was thinking about whether to go hard or soft on Boylen. He decided that there was no point in stirring up his indignation. *Irish,* he thought, with the European inclination to nationalism. *Probably stubborn.* He would go soft, at least at first.

"We are dealing with a very serious situation here Mr. Boylen," he said evenly, "Whatever you say will stay between us. I am only interested in your private life as it relates to the investigation."

Henrion spoke slowly and authoritatively, without any hint of impatience or accusation. He wanted Michael to understand that they were both on the same side, and that he needed his cooperation.

At the same time, Michael decided to be honest with, to trust this man, although he was still disbelieving of any involvement on his part. They must have gotten onto the wrong track, he thought. He would set things right and, hopefully be out of here before too long.

Henrion swiveled to face him. "Let me answer your earlier question Monsieur Boylen. Your plane had a bomb on it, a bomb that was hidden in someone's luggage. Someone..."—he paused and looked at Michael, searching for the right words—"...someone intended this to be an act of terror, of mass murder. Including the captains and crew, almost three hundred people would have succumbed to a savage"—he pronounced it as *saváge*—"death if the plane had taken off on time. My job is to understand how this was planned and carried out, and this is what my questions are directed at. We suspect that the bomb was concealed in the clock in your bag. So please answer me directly and without prevarication. We..."—Henrion let the word linger for a second before continuing—"...need to figure out exactly what happened. For that, I need your full cooperation."

Michael swallowed. So he was not just another passenger. He was at the epicenter of a criminal investigation, of an act of international terrorism of all things. This was no game. This was bigger than him. Did he need a lawyer?

"I understand Inspector," said Michael, his voice cautious. "I just didn't..."

Henrion cut him off: "I understand too, Mr. Boylen. So to get back to my earlier question. Were you alone when you bought the clock and, if you were not alone, who were you with?"

"I was with a friend," said Michael, "a woman." Subconsciously drawn into Inspector Henrion's manner, he too spoke softly and deliberately.

Henrion's left eyebrow raised a fraction of an inch.

"The same woman you were at the airport with?"

Michael stiffened.

"Video surveillance," explained Henrion with a thin smile. "These days, this airport is one endless movie. In fact, so is most of Paris. Here, let me show you."

With this, Henrion swiveled the monitor on his desk so that Michael could see the screen. It was a remarkably clear color picture showing him standing by the taxi, holding the door open. One of Annetine's legs was on the pavement, the other still in the cab. It was odd to see her again in this official setting.

Henrion hit the space bar and another picture appeared. They were now standing behind the cab, suitcases on the curb, and Michael was paying the driver. Both faces were clearly visible. Henrion hit the key once more and a third picture appeared on the screen. Taken from somewhere above, it showed the crowded floor of the terminal near the Air France check-in. Over to the left, near the tall windows, Michael and Annetine stood locked in an embrace. Her head was on his shoulder and he saw her light hair, the dark coat, and black boots.

Henrion noticed a small muscle above the base of Michael's jaw begin to pulse rhythmically, along with a vein on his temple. *Good,* he thought. *He's getting the picture.* He leaned in across the desk and stitched an impatient expression on his face. Time to press his point, but not without a bit of reassurance. Give and take usually worked best with people.

"Monsieur Boylen. We French are not in the business of intruding into anyone's private affairs. We all have our secrets and I will be as discreet as the situation permits. But you are clearly"—he paused, searching for the right word—"as we say in French, you are clearly *intime* with this woman. Is she your *maîtresse*—your mistress? Here on the questionnaire," he pointed vaguely to it, "in answer to question 19—the one that asks you to list anyone that you had contact with in the last week—you listed some work associates, and your landlord. I don't see a woman's name. Again, I am here to understand what happened, not to judge your moral character. After all, we are both," added Henrion, pressing his point home with bonhomie—"Men. We understand each other, yes?"

Michael Boylen gazed across the desk at the Inspector. Henrion had certainly gotten to the heart of it quickly enough.

He smiled sheepishly. "Yes, Inspector, she is, as you say, my *maîtresse*. I didn't list her for," he paused, "for personal reasons. At the time, I did not think it was important."

"I understand," said Henrion. "Most men would do exactly the same. As I said earlier, my job is to figure out why and how this happened, not to make trouble for a man who"—his mouth pursed—"appreciates the feminine charm. That in itself is irrelevant, and something with which I am"—Henrion was pushing his English on this one—"I am of empathy with. *Compris?*"

Michael nodded.

"What does matter is that this woman was evidently close to you here in Paris. No one else was in a similar relation to you during your"—he glanced down at the paper in front of him—"your fifty seven days in France. Yes?"

"Yes," said Michael, "That's right." So it had been only eight weeks since he'd left home. It felt like a lifetime. Inspector Henrion had evidently reviewed his file most carefully. What else did he know?

Henrion gestured dismissively.

"Please, tell me the story of how you met, who she is, and how we can find her. I assume that you had an affair?"

Michael took a deep breath. "Yes," he said. "We did."

In spite of Henrion's reassurances, he felt morally diminished by the conversation. The realization that it was his bag that had contained the bomb was unsettling, and the little inconsistencies his mind had periodically raised but discarded regarding Annetine began adding up.

Her telling him that she didn't have a cell phone, for example. It didn't seem credible now, and wasn't she using a cell phone when he came upon her and Talia that morning in early December at the café? He hadn't thought about it, and had probably assumed that it was either Talia's phone, or…or what?

Was seeing them that morning coincidental or part of a plan? He was a creature of habit, and someone watching him would know that he walked to the Bastille station every morning. But why? Could she have been that cold and deliberate? It *was* an hour later than normal, and life has its coincidences.

The doppelganger at the Musée d'Orsay had also given him a momentary pause at the time, but he had put that out of his mind as well. Could it have been her? And what about that evening in Switzerland, when they were walking hand-in-hand down the street by Lake Lucerne? Wasn't Annetine the one who insisted on shopping in the clock store? Wasn't she the one who convinced him to buy the clock in the first place? Going back further, to the very beginning, was their sitting together on the flight to France a coincidence? She had sat down next to him, hadn't she?

Michael felt the sweat running down his armpits. Suddenly, everything was suspect, and yet, and yet...

She couldn't have known, he thought with conviction. *I know her and there's no way!*

Henrion broke in on his thoughts. "Mr. Boylen. What is this woman's name, how did you meet, and where does she live? Please. I need to know everything. Now."

50. TRAIL GONE COLD

An hour later, they were finished. Henrion had asked Michael all of the right questions, but there were few actionable details. Henrion contacted Europol and the FBI and put in for a criminal record check on one Annetine Fournier. Not surprisingly, it came back negative.

When the inspector asked about Annetine's apartment's location, the best Michael could do was to recall Annetine telling him that it was in the 20th Arrondissement near Père Lachaise and the Parc de Belleville. Henrion made some calls to put the wheels of inquiry in motion and escorted Michael to a waiting room where he sat for most of the afternoon. Finally, hours later, the door opened and the inspector came in. "We tracked down the rental and I'm going to take a look. Apparently, she rented it last September, four months ago." he said. "Want to come along?"

Henrion added that he doubted they would find anyone there, but he wanted to see her apartment and had ordered a forensic team to meet them there, so they drove the forty miles back into the city. Michael sat in the back of the unmarked car, separated from Henrion and the driver by a wire partition. The occasional inquisitive glance of a passing motorist made him feel like a criminal, but nothing could be done about that; more to the point, he felt like a complete fool.

It was almost dark by the time they arrived. The landlord met them and Michael waited in the deepening twilight, hands in pockets, while Henrion spoke with the woman. As he looked around, it struck him that he and Annetine had walked right down this street on the way to the Metro from Père Lachaise, and shared a bottle of wine in a corner cafe less than a block away. Yet, Annetine never let on that this was her street. Bitch.

The small apartment was furnished but devoid of personal things. Michael was getting the picture all too clearly. The forensic team arrived and began to comb through the premises systematically, bagging some items, such as a spoon left in the sink, photographing others. They were also able to lift some fingerprints. Henrion sat across from Michael at the kitchen table and worked on his laptop. He eventually came up with a cell phone number for an Annetine Fournier from Wayne, New Jersey; not surprisingly, there was no answer.

"She probably destroyed her phone by now," said Henrion. "We were too slow." His mood had grown quiet and Michael saw him fish some pills out of his pocket, walk over to the sink, and swallow them unceremoniously with a handful of tap water.

"Headache?" asked Michael, but only got a non-committal grunt in response.

Henrion ran some additional background checks and spoke with several colleagues. Michael watched and listened, amazed at the global web of data available to law enforcement. He was aware of computer capabilities, but the linkage and speed at which information could be accessed was impressive. Henrion had pulled up Annetine's address in the States, along with credit card information and a car registration. She had no state or federal criminal record. She did get a speeding ticket two years earlier in upstate New York, and a meter violation in Manhattan last July, but little else. Michael remembered her saying that she'd been in Paris last summer. Just another lie, he thought, and clearly no roommate either, unless they both slept in the one bedroom.

Henrion inquired about any places Annetine might have mentioned frequenting in Paris—restaurants, bars, cafes, hotels, neighborhoods, anything—but Michael had embarrassingly few specifics to offer. He told Henrion where they had dined and been, but this was of little use as Annetine would surely avoid anything having to do with him unless she was innocent, which no longer seemed credible. Michael began to accept that she was, in fact, the guilty party. It was that simple. Who had come up with the idea of the clock, he wondered? Had she known?

Henrion asked Michael if he had any photographs they could use to post an APB. He said that he had taken a few photos on their ski trip and they were on his computer back in the apartment.

"*D'accord*," said Henrion. "Let's go."

There was only one picture where her face was visible, and a poor one at that. Taken on a ski slope in bright sunlight, she had a pair of blue ski goggles pulled up onto her tuque.

"Nothing better?" asked Henrion.

Wait, thought Michael. *What about that picture of them together at Père Lachaise? The one she sent him via email?* And then he realized that she had never actually sent it to him, and that he had forgotten to ask.

Henrion jotted down her email address and, working on his own laptop, wrote up a physical description of Annetine based on Michael's recollections and requested that it be circulated to all police stations, regional airports, rental car agencies, and train and bus stations along with a ten thousand Euro reward. He requested a check of French, Swiss, English and American bank accounts in her name. The search would take a few days to run; this type of inquiry required a human hand on the tiller, and some person at the DST Center would be assigned to manage the process. The forensic team would see to it that her fingerprints were circulated as well. Henrion also requested surveillance on the apartment for a few days in case she returned, although both of them knew that was highly unlikely.

And that was pretty much it. They drove back to the airport and Henrion re-interviewed Michael, going over details again, looking for inconsistencies or additional information, asking different questions, or the same questions in a different way. He also questioned him about Talia, but Michael had only seen her once and had little to offer other than she was supposedly Annetine's roommate, which no longer made sense.

"Dark skinned, attractive, late twenties, unusual eyes," was all he could offer.

"I expect they've both left the country," said Henrion as he packed up his computer. "From what you've said, your Annetine likes Switzerland, and I wouldn't be surprised if she ended up there. The Swiss are obsessed with their secrecy and difficult to deal with in these things, but we'll give it a try."

"Do you think Annetine knew about the plot?" inquired Michael, as that was the question that plagued him most.

"I believe she knew she was doing something improper," said Henrion. "But I don't know if she knew it was a bomb. Terrorist cells tend to compartmentalize operations so that everyone knows only what they need to know. She may have thought that they were smuggling something into the States. It is difficult to say. With no criminal history and, from what you've told me, it's hard that to believe she was active in a terrorist cell. The profile doesn't fit, but I do wonder about her friend Talia."

The only other comment Henrion made was about the clock. "Clever bastards," he said, "with that cuckoo clock. Obvious, yet innocent. The counterweights provided plenty of room for the explosive, yet it wouldn't trigger any suspicion with the opacity. Who would have thought?"

"Also," he added, pointing a finger at Michael, "choosing you was smart. A middle-aged American citizen. An innocent."

"And a fool," added Michael.

"Don't be too hard on yourself," said Henrion. "You were duped, but that was through no fault of your own. Outside of your…"—he hesitated, then smiled—"…your dalliance, you didn't do anything wrong. Don't look back too much. You and the other passengers are still among the living, and that's what matters most."

"What now?" asked Michael, suddenly unsure about everything.

Henrion leaned back in his chair and smiled. "Now we have to find your Annetine," he said.

"But how?"

Henrion shrugged. "We'll be following every thread, however thin, and hope that it leads to something. In the meanwhile, I want you to remain in Paris for the next few days. Also," he added matter-of-factly, "we're going to fit you with an ankle monitor."

Michael said nothing as Henrion dialed and spoke briefly with someone. "*D'accord*," he said. "*Merci.*"

"Come with me," he said, and he and Michael walked to another nondescript door in a nondescript corridor. Minutes later, the electronic monitor was locked around his left ankle. The tech coded some information into a computer and nodded as she checked the readout on a desktop screen.

"*Merci, monsieur*," she said. "We have a signal."

"Can I shower with this thing?" asked Michael, trying to keep the annoyance out of his voice.

"Yes Michael," said Henrion. "They are quite waterproof. You can even take a bath."

Michael noted that this was the first time that Henrion had used his Christian name even as he mulled over the implication of the last statement.

"I'll be seeing the magistrate on Tuesday morning," he explained, "and will make a case for your returning home as long as you're willing to return on short notice. You'll need to sign some papers and we'll arrange for a local contact through the U.S. authorities."

"Am I under house arrest?" asked Michael, still bothered about the bracelet. He understood that just being released wasn't an option, but the lingering aura of suspicion and the plastic bracelet rubbing against his ankle were equally distasteful.

Henrion shook his head. "No, you are free to go anywhere in the Paris area, but don't leave the City."

There was nothing more to say. The two men shook hands and parted.

Back in a taxi, Michael found himself playing back their conversation in his mind, and remembered the inspector's use of the word "dalliance". Colored by Henrion's French accent, it sounded like a splendid thing. On the other hand, he found little comfort in Henrion's reassurance, for he realized that he was not simply a victim of circumstance. No, they had uncovered and exploited a weakness. With all that had happened with Katherine, he was emotionally off-kilter, and it all played right into the plan. Had Annetine sensed this? *Consciously or unconsciously, what did it matter,* thought Michael, *I was a dupe.* This word also sounded so much more benign in Henrion's accented English, but whenever his mind dredged it up, as it did repeatedly in the days and weeks ahead, it pained him more than any other.

Henrion called him on Tuesday afternoon and asked him to come back to the airport to sign some papers, and told him he was free to book a flight home.

Relieved, as his time in Paris now felt like penance, Michael secured a flight back to the States Thursday afternoon, and savored the prospect of returning to the everyday familiars that would come with being home again. Morning coffee at Starbucks, a few beers at Gleason's with Chris, and the familiar comforts of home.

The last night in the apartment, as Michael lay in bed, his thoughts kept circling back to what could have been—to the death he had so narrowly escaped, and to the terrible fate his trusting nature had almost inflicted upon hundreds of innocent people, including himself. The muffled explosion shattering the surreal airborne peace, the plane shuddering and beginning to tumble and plummet, the terrible knowledge that there was only a minute or two left to live, the chaos, the screams...

Haunted by his own imagination, the idea of revenge crept into Michael's consciousness. He didn't have a game plan yet, but he would come up with one. Damn it, he thought, this is *not* over.

51. HOMEWARD BOUND

As Flight 56 banked toward the coast, Michael took a deep breath and closed his eyes. Underway. Finally.

The light from the window was bright, and he readied to lower the shade when he saw the sprawl of Paris stretched out in all its glory below. There was the Eiffel Tower and the curved roof of the Musée d'Orsay; the dark ribbon of the Seine with its bridges, islands and embankments; the twin islands of Île de la Cité and Île Saint-Louis and, just beyond, the Marais district. Further still was the wooded expanse of the Père Lachaise cemetery with its tangled, modern-art pattern of paths.

His thoughts continued to return to Annetine frequently, but with less occasion and intensity. As much as he enjoyed her vivacity, her sensuality, Michael found that the memories of their time together now held no warmth, no life, for they were indelibly tainted by deceit. Much as he had after the incident in the Metro, he felt himself separating from and observing the workings of his own mind as if from without. He grew tired of its attempts at rationalization, of its piteous and repetitive chatter. He grew tired of himself.

Oddly enough, his relationship with Katherine and its queer little bestiary of related issues such as trust and intimacy also seemed less important now, occluded by the events of late.

It was an hour into the flight, while he was trying to draft up his summary report for Aerotel, that the idea came to him. He'd taken a break and started thinking about Annetine again, with the same question in mind. *Had she known?* Surely, she had seen the story about the explosion on Flight 56. It was in the papers and all over the news. If she had been used (and Michael decided that she probably had been), she too would be feeling some anger and guilt. Did these create an opportunity that could be exploited?

The only tool at his disposal was her email, unless she had already changed it. He'd thought of that last night, but decided that she might not open a message from him and, if she did, she certainly wouldn't write back. As he was writing the report on securing the network in the Aerotel office, cataloguing the potential threats and responses, his professional frame of mind generated an idea that put things in a different light. *It may not work*, he reasoned, *but it deserves a try, especially if I bait the hook.* After all, it was pretty much his only chance.

52. PENTESTER

Katherine was waiting for him in the arrivals area. Michael again noticed that her appearance was hipper somehow, with a new black coat set off by a red silk scarf and dangling ruby earrings. She gave him a brief hug and, with no bags to pick up, held his arm as they walked to the car.

Their rapport was superficially warm but still held an undercurrent of distancing on her part. Over dinner, he started to think that he may be imagining it, but when Katherine informed him matter-of-factly that she moved his things into the guest bedroom, "at least for now," he knew that he was right. "It's better that way," she said, as they came out of the Lincoln Tunnel into the shadowy darkness of a late January afternoon. "Trust me."

Michael lapsed into silence and stared out of the window at the flat landscape of the Secaucus wetlands. *Trust you?* he thought, *trust you to do what?* Surprisingly, he felt no anger. The reality of being stateside again hadn't sunk in, and he felt placid and detached, as if in a dream.

When they arrived at home, when he saw his clothes laid out in the guest bedroom, the situation rankled him anew. He changed into some clean clothes, told Katherine he had a few hours of work to do, and closed the door to the den. If she felt snubbed, then that was just the way it was.

Encoding the GPS malware was the first—the easy—task. He programmed it to send spatial coordinates in burst mode. Whenever Annetine's computer was turned on and connected to the web, the information would be transmitted and updated every 10 minutes if (and this was still a major if) he could get her to open his message.

The second step—infecting her computer—was also simple, as malware was his profession. The pentester world broke neatly into two halves: protection and tracking. Ideally, one tried to protect a network by blocking malware infiltration. Often, however, despite best efforts, a network became compromised and, if the protection failed and data exfiltration was detected, the objective was to figure out where, and from whom, it originated. Although Michael worked on the edges of corporate rather than government legitimacy, this type of activity was precisely his expertise, and he set to work.

Once he had the GPS malware programmed, Michael logged onto his Gmail and examined the inbox format. One line per message, with the subject heading bolded, followed by the first few words of text. He might have a total of some 200 characters to play with, maybe less on a small screen, depending how her Gmail was set up. This had to be the sell, as it was what Annetine would see without opening the message.

He took some time composing it until he was satisfied that he had it right. When the job was done, the message sent, he entertained the fantasy of finding her himself—of tracking her down wherever she was, but decided that was silly. No, he would lay the trap and the authorities could spring it. He'd talk to Henrion. As he imagined her squirming like a fly on a pin, Michael's face twisted into a cruel smile. The wide-eyed glance, the innocent, pleading look—he could picture it all. It wouldn't fool anyone, but only if she took the bait.

There was nothing more to do tonight. He was now in a waiting game with no certainty of closure, and Michael steeled himself to fate. Oddly enough, he thought, once again it was in the digital realm. Or maybe it was not so odd. The analog world seemed so much more natural when he was growing up but, in fact—whether it was the genetic code, the marriage proposition, even suicide—many of the things that mattered most in life were actually binary in nature.

Michael turned off the computer, satisfied that he'd done the best he could. It was only 8 p.m., but his body was still on European time and he was tired. He'd slept poorly the last two nights, as the Beautreillis apartment had no longer felt like it was his. He hardly noticed the syncopation of the bells this morning and, when he did, it was just meaningless background noise.

53. EVENING IN ZURICH

Annetine stepped off the tram and walked the five blocks to her new apartment. She'd spent the last four days snowboarding in Zweisimmen, a ski resort less than two hours from Zurich by rail.

Tired but happy, she sniffed her sleeve and scrunched up her nose. Hard to believe how many people smoked here in Switzerland, especially on public transit. Once home, she would air out her jacket, throw the clothes in the wash, and take a nice long bath before having dinner. Good to have an "in" night since she'd stayed out until dawn last night clubbing with some of the instructors at the resort.

It was a fun crowd, and they all bought her being 25 and from the great American Northwest. Jonas in particular had taken to her, and she liked his naïveté and six-foot-six frame. A giant Swiss boy and, although she'd played it coy, Annetine fully intended to go back next weekend and take him up on his promise of off-piste skiing.

Talia and her friend had come through, and she had withdrawn and re-deposited the Euros in a safe deposit box at a different bank after putting two thousand aside as play money. A slice of the high life was in order after everything she had been through. She deserved it. *Have to hand it to the Swiss*, thought Annetine, *they are so wonderfully discreet when it comes to money.* There was almost an air of reverence around the banking profession, and customers were treated like royalty. They'd even offered her a complimentary three-day ski pass for her business, and she had taken it. Why not?

She unlocked the front door and hung up her parka, knit cap and gloves on the peg in the entrance hallway before going into the bedroom and undressing. After a long, physical day, getting naked was always a wonderful moment. Simple, childlike, free.

Annetine ran the bath and poured in two cups of Epsom salts. Her bones could use it. In one quick gesture, she swept up the pile of clothes on the floor, threw them in the hamper, and padded over to the kitchen, humming to herself. A minute later, she returned with a glass of white wine and the vaporizer. A bath with some candles, wine and a toke. What could be better?

She lit the candles at each corner of the tub and took a sip of the wine before leaning back and closing her eyes, reveling in the warmth of the water.

Half an hour later, Annetine dried herself, pulled on a t-shirt and a pair of shorts and, after re-filling her glass, sat down on the living room couch. *I'm getting high,* she thought. *I should be careful. Go easy, girl.*

With her phone gone, she'd purchased a new Samsung tablet last week and was planning on becoming familiar with it tonight. No real need for a phone in her current situation, and this would serve her well.

Annetine took another sip while the tablet powered up. She browsed the web, downloaded an album by Neko

Case and played "Local Girl", a song she'd heard at the ski area.

Goddamn the time, goddamn the miles that take me away from you, and change your face, and change the way I love you...

For whatever reason, those particular lyrics had made her think of Michael, as she had a few times during the last week. They'd had that "bond of song," as he'd referred to it, and she wondered how he was doing back home in New Jersey. They had presumably cleared him of any wrongdoing, although she didn't know that for certain. After the first day, the news had gone mum and, frankly, she hadn't thought much more about it.

Looking through the inbox on her Gmail, she scanned the usual Google alerts and commercial messages, checking the little box to the left as she went along so she could delete them *en masse.*

And then she froze.

It was a message from an Inspector Henrion at the *Renseignements Géneraux: "Mme. Fournier: Vous êtes priés de vous contact ...,"* was all she could see on the one line, but it looked official. Annetine googled *Renseignements Géneraux* only to find out that this was the intelligence unit of the French internal security service, the *Direction de la Surveillance du Territoire (DST).*

Unnerved, she checked the box next to it so it, too, would be deleted.

Annetine continued scanning down the list of messages, as she hadn't been on her email in almost a week. Click, click, click. Suddenly, her eyes widened: *Boylenmi@gmail.* It was a message from Michael! It came in at 1:47 a.m. on Thursday, four days ago.

Although she was tempted to open it, especially after that other message from the Inspector, Annetine hesitated. Was she being paranoid? The damned Gmail only showed one line that included the subject—*'My near miss'*—and the first few words: *'My dear Annetine, How are you? I made it home safe and sound (eventually!), and find myself still thinking of you. I fondly remember our time together and was wondering if...'*

Annetine leaned back in the cushions, thinking. Her index finger bobbed up and down nervously as it hovered over the message link. Should she, shouldn't she? Should she, shouldn't she?

She would later blame it on the wine. Or the pot. Or the empty stomach. Or being dog tired. Or an involuntary twitch. Whatever the reason, Annetine should have known better, for her fingertip brushed the pressure-sensitive surface of the touchscreen ever so lightly, and it sealed her fate.

The knock on her door came some thirty hours later, around 3 a.m. on Tuesday morning. The uniformed policewoman deferred to the man in civilian clothes with the French accent.

"Bonjour, Madame Fournier. I am Inspector Henrion and I apologize about the late hour, but we will need to speak with you down at the station."

Annetine's face went white as she clutched her robe. Her voice trembling, she said, *"Je comprends Inspecteur.* May I get dressed first?"

"D'accord," said Henrion, with a nod to the policewoman. "Sargent Hebert will accompany you."

54. THE UNSAID

It was February 11th, a Sunday evening, and Michael was at home in his den. The incandescent light of the desk lamp was bright enough to illuminate the snow swirling outside the window. He could hear the drone of the wind in the trees, but here in the den it was cozy and warm. A fragment of poem came to him:

…the tumultuous privacy of storm.

Emerson? How fitting a phrase for the night outside, but also for the internal storm that he had been through. As his Paris experience receded and he reconnected with his familiar routines, he welcomed the stability and warmth of home. After the last conversation with Inspector Henrion, he was satisfied. Annetine was back in Paris, accused of complicity, with a court date set for May 1st. Until then, she would have free room and board in the A Block of the *Santé* prison in the heart of Paris.

Au revoir my love.

Michael also came to see that the incident with the plane changed his perspective on everyday life. Consumed at first by the actual events and then by the process of the investigation, his mind had since become beset with the realization of what could have been. As it was, the bloodied and disoriented passenger he'd helped out of the smoke-filled cabin was the only real manifestation of the horror that luck and circumstance had spared him.

The reality hit Michael in earnest on the flight home. He had gone into the bathroom in the back of the plane and, just as he closed the folding door, the plane hit an air pocket and shuddered violently enough to knock him sideways against the sink. His heart began to race and pound as a tightness gripped his chest. It became difficult to breathe. He started to tremble and sat down heavily on the toilet, struggling to regain composure. Afterward, his imagination kept returning to the terror of an airplane death, dwelling on that eternal minute when one knew with cold certainty that all was lost. The instant of turbulence unblocked his mind and let the emotions he had been suppressing pour into his consciousness.

Since then, he'd experienced the equivalent of a panic attack several times, although with diminishing intensity. He also had developed a new attitude, and found himself appreciating the daily pleasures of life that he'd never paid much attention to earlier—the clarity of the winter air, the lilt of a birdsong, the pleasure of a fine cup of coffee.

Life can certainly deal out some strange hands, he thought, and occasionally in a most ironic way. As trite as it sounded, that expression about not letting the perfect stand in the way of the good summed up his new (or at least revised) approach to Katherine. Wait and see, and what will be, will be...

Michael yawned. It was almost 1 a.m. and he was sleepy, but he needed to finish up this report for Aerotel. Almost there—another half hour would do it.

He typed for ten or fifteen minutes but his eyes began to strain and he realized he didn't have his glasses on.

Where in the hell are my glasses? he thought. The small glass of Woodford Reserve that he'd poured out an hour ago was almost empty and he took the last sip of bourbon along with an ice cube remnant into his mouth. That must be it—he had gone downstairs to make a drink earlier and must have left them on the kitchen counter. If he could just find those glasses, he'd finish things up and hit the sack.

He checked upstairs first, just in case. Nothing.

They also weren't in the living room, and the kitchen counter was bare.

Michael walked back upstairs and searched the den again without any success. Bathroom? Likewise. Perplexed, he went back down to the kitchen and stood by the sink staring out of the window, thinking. The late-night silence was interrupted by the sound of sleet pinging against the windowpane, and a glance at the thermometer confirmed his suspicion. Thirty-three degrees. Typical New Jersey— first snow, then ice, and eventually rain. It would be a nasty morning commute.

He searched the rooms of the house one more time, feeling between the cushions of the sofa where he had briefly sat, looking under his desk and through the drawers. Did one *ever* find something the second time around? Frustrated he rifled through the waste can under his desk. Nothing.

And then it came to him. He'd broken a glass earlier and must have swept his glasses into the garbage by mistake while cleaning up. This had happened once before.

Great, he thought—*nothing like poring through your own garbage at the end of a long day, especially when it contains broken glass!*

The garbage can was almost full, topped by a tangle of wet paper towels, cucumber peelings, and bones from the lamb chops they'd had for dinner. But no glasses. *Damn it,* he thought, *I'd better get some gloves and do this right.*

Michael went down to the basement and found the pair of rubber gloves that he kept for messy jobs. He also grabbed a few sections of newspaper on which to lay out the garbage.

Excavating the trash a handful at a time, taking extra care with the sharp-edged pieces of glass, he slowly worked his way down into the depths of the garbage can, and was beginning to lose hope when he spotted them. There they were, lying on their side near the bottom amidst some wet, stained shreds of paper and a few jagged shards of glass.

Michael reached in and carefully picked up the glasses. One of the pieces of paper, lodged between the earpieces, came out with them and he was about to throw it out when he noticed that it was bright pink. He looked at it more closely. What in the hell?

It looked like a piece of a Valentine's Day card and the neat, slanted scrawl was unmistakably Katherine's. Surprised, he reached in and retrieved the other torn pieces, taking care to avoid the glass shards. Discolored and flecked with coffee grounds, the card must have been ripped up and thrown out early that morning. Was it meant for him?

Piece by piece, he arranged them out on the counter like a sloppy jigsaw puzzle, then rinsed off and put on his glasses. Michael's eyes narrowed as he read the message below:

Dear Sergei,

Please accept this card as a token of our friendship. You are a wonderful man and I have enjoyed every minute of our time together. I apologize for making it as difficult for you as I have. You have been caring and patient while I wrestled with my conscience.

Dancing with you at the Christmas party was incredible, and whenever I remember that last slow dance, I melt inside. I have honestly never felt so good being in another man's arms. You are a very, very sexy man, so please don't feel like my hesitations have had anything to do with you. In the end, I had to step away because I couldn't bear the thought of hurting Michael. I just can't burn both ends of the candle. I will always cherish and remember our times together. I will never forget.

Love,

Katherine

Michael let out his pent-up breath in a hiss and re-read the card—this time more slowly, absorbing every word, every nuance: *wonderful man... melt inside... very sexy... will always cherish... I will never forget.*

He glanced down at the ugly pile of garbage on the floor. The pile of refuse had the fetid smell of overripe vegetables along with a less identifiable, earthy odor that may have been the wet paper towels or the coffee grounds. It was the detritus of their life together, the material outflow of their habits and appetites. Among all that was the one thing that was *not* theirs, but hers and hers alone.

Michael took the pieces of the card, wrapped them in a clean paper towel, and slipped them into his back pocket before stuffing the garbage back into the plastic bag and closing the lid.

Adult reality, he thought, is more intense and frightening than any childhood game could ever be. Who needs vampires and goblins when the forces of everyday life cut so much deeper into our very core than any fairy tale, any fantasy ever could?

Gripped by a maelstrom of feelings, he went upstairs and sat in his den. He saw life as it is—unbounded and fragile, a network with the heart of one tied to the web of all. The house was hushed and the only sound was the tinkle of sleet against the window above his desk.

On the whole, reflected Michael, a lot of disparate things had tumbled into place tonight. Apparently, Katherine had been a woman seriously courted these last few months, which explained the business about questioning her love for him, the photograph from the party, their uneven communications, her indecisiveness in Paris, even her new look. She had flirted with and possibly succumbed to temptation, but if one believed her words (and there is no reason not to, thought Michael), she was ultimately still with him in heart, still committed.

He felt happy, even a little giddy at the affirmation, and thought about when—whether?—to tell Katherine about tonight's discovery. This private knowledge conferred a power of its own. It might be interesting to give it a day or two and observe things, observe her, from his new perspective. Or was he just being childish?

This wasn't a game after all.

Teeth brushed, face washed, Michael slipped quietly into bed.

A few minutes later, on the edge of sleep, he remembered that she had signed the card "Love, Katherine". This bothered him momentarily, although he reasoned it away as a gesture of kindness meant to temper the rebuke.

But then another thought crept into Michael's weary mind like an uninvited guest, and this one gave him serious pause.

Why, he wondered, *didn't I think of it before?* His focusing on the meaning of Katherine's message to Sergei completely missed the point! The important thing was not the message at all. It was the card itself or, more precisely, its final disposition. Michael imagined Katherine sitting there, quietly plumbing her feelings, carefully choosing her words as she penned the card. But then, in the end, she had decided to rip it up and throw it away.

And that changed everything.

*****

ABOUT THE AUTHOR

George Osol a Professor of Obstetrics and Gynecology at the University of Vermont College of Medicine specializing in vascular physiology, particularly hypertensive diseases of pregnancy. He lives in Williston, Vermont.

Although many of the places in this novel are real, the characters and events are entirely fictional and bear no resemblance to persons living or dead.

For additional writings, photos and music links, visit:

www.georgeosol.com